The Order of the Owl

E.G. Stone

Tarney Brae Creative Endeavours

For the Queen of the Universe:
The Queen is dead, long live the Queen
You will be missed

Contents

1. In Which I Steal Some Diamonds   7

2. In Which I Get A Job   21

3. In Which I Eat Some Fish   39

4. In Which I Outsmart Some People   55

5. In Which I Flee the Country   73

6. In Which I Meet Some Old Friends   89

7. In Which I Scream, A Lot   105

8. In Which I Am Too Tall for History   123

9. In Which I Meet Different Old Friends   139

10. In Which I Resort to Snark   157

11. In Which I Travel In Time   173

12. In Which I Meet Fred, the Younger   191

13. In Which I Open a Bank Account   209

14. In Which I Attempt to Steal a Book   225

15. In Which I Stage an Escape   243

16. In Which I Hire Professional Goons   261

17. In Which I Fix the Reality that I Broke   279

18. In Which I Go Back to Work   295

Afterword   305

Acknowledgments   307

About the Author   309

Also by E.G. Stone   311

Chapter 1
In Which I Steal Some
Diamonds

Crack. A bit of concrete by my left foot splintered. I didn't waste time looking over my shoulder, instead just shouting, "Did you seriously try to shoot me?"

Crack ding. This time, the shot ricocheted into a metal light post. They must have been small calibre bullets or the post would have been toast, not just pleasantly musical.

"Someone is going to call the police if you keep that up!" I shouted.

"Give us back the diamonds!" was the response.

"No can do!" I called and kept running down the street.

I decided that I was having a fairly good day. Apart from the whole running for my life sort of thing, I mean. But then, I figure any day in which it rains first thing and I get my requisite cup of tea in the morning *plus* breakfast is a good day, regardless of any gun-waving thugs that happen to be chasing me with the intent to kill.

See, my name is Bailey Duane, and despite what you may think, I am not a detective. I have this thing about detectives; they don't like me and I don't like them. At all. I am of the profession of "Gofer and Girl Friday" (Actually, my full business card reads "Gofer for hire; services rendered. I take care of what needs doing, so life doesn't get in the way"), which, unfortunately, gets me occasionally mixed up in the line of work of detectives. Technically, I do have a private investigator's license, but I try not to mention it to clients. On days like the one I was having—good, despite appearances—I wanted nothing more than to keep out of the way of detectives. And police officers. Really, I was avoiding any law enforcement of any kind. So far, I was doing fairly well.

In one hand, I held a pair of heeled boots—terribly hard to run in—and in the other, a box with a set of uncut diamonds my client had stolen from him by some fairly unsavoury people. My client, however, was a rather unsavoury person himself and so I got settled with retrieval instead of the police. Too bad the police never approved my concealed weapon permit. It would have been extremely useful in a situation such as the one I was currently in.

Behind me, running loudly, were two thugs hired by the thief. I had named the taller, stockier one with the receding hairline and permanent scowl on his very wide mouth Brutus, and the other, slightly shorter but much skinnier and quite intelligent-looking one, Octavius. They seemed to be quite determined to get the diamonds back.

"Come on, guys, give a girl a chance," I called back to them, dancing into an alley and leaping for a fence. I scrambled over it—years of being chased on the playground as a kid will give you that skill—and continued running. Octavius was the first one over and Brutus didn't even try to go over, instead just ripping an even larger hole where before there had only been a small one.

"Give back the diamonds," Octavius replied. I put on an extra burst of speed as I turned back onto a main street. Unfortunately, given that it was past midnight, the sidewalk was pretty much empty and didn't present many obstacles with which to distract my companions. At least there were no sirens.

"Sorry, no can do. I'm on commission, here," I said and ducked into the first place that was open that I could see. It was a low-ceilinged, dimly lit bar and was surprisingly busy for this time of night. As was typical of my luck, it was full of characters more or less like the ones following me and that didn't give my chances much hope. I pushed my way past a few people as politely as I could and ducked into the ladies' room just as Octavius and Brutus burst into the bar.

I pressed against a stall and locked it behind me, fumbling hopefully with the catch on the locked box. It would be easier to stuff the diamonds in my pockets rather than toting this box around. It was, stupid client, a fairly fancy lock which would be hard to open in a pinch without the key. I didn't have the key and I was in a pinch. I took the heel of one of my boots and slammed it into the lock. Hopeless. I huffed and blew my hair out of my face, listening intensely for the noises that would indicate my two pursuers were nearby.

The bathroom door opened and the familiar clumping steps came in, along with their heavy breathing. I literally held my breath so they wouldn't hear me and stood on the toilet, ducking down so as not to be seen over the top of the stall. "Come out, come out, wherever you are," Octavius sang in a nasally tone. I ignored him, instead listening while Brutus slammed open bathroom door stalls. He was only two away from me when the bathroom door opened again.

"This is the girls' bathroom," someone said, obviously female. She didn't sound too very pleased by the two thugs in there, wreaking havoc on the musty bathroom. Brutus, true to himself, grunted noncommittally and Octavius took over speaking.

"We're looking for a friend of ours. She came in here a while ago and we became worried. So we decided to come look for her," he explained, and I tried not to snort at his lie. It wasn't very convincing. So much for being intelligent.

"Yeah, sure," the woman said. I could imagine her crossing her arms or putting her hands on her hips or something of the sort. "Look, get out before I get Ol' Jones to kick you out of here."

"I don't think so," Brutus said thickly. I rolled my eyes. Really, could these two possibly be more stubborn? Or cliche?

"Alright, fine," the woman said. I heard the door open and she called out to "Ol' Jones." A moment later, I heard more heavy footfalls and a fourth voice joined the debate.

"Get out of my bar," he said, voice cracked and worn with age and weariness. There was silence from the two thugs apart from some shuffling. I heard someone crack his knuckles and there was quiet grumbling. The door opened and shut again, and I let out a quiet sigh of relief.

"Alright," the woman said. "They're gone. You can come out now."

I climbed down off the toilet, shifting my boots in my hand and readjusting my grip on the box. My heart was still pumping as I opened the stall door and came face to face with a fairly pretty woman. She was dressed in a very tight pair of jeans and had a t-shirt that barely covered her midriff. Her golden skin and slight accent told me she was of Spanish descent, though the sass in her look was pure New Yorker. She had one hand on her hip and a half sleeve of tattoos around her right arm.

"Hmph," she said, as if unimpressed with me. I wasn't surprised. I was tall and sort of gawky with long limbs and not much else. I had been chastised by my mother and her numerous friends for being too skinny and knobbly. My hair, after running and hiding, was a brown rats' nest and I was certain my face was flushed. I never looked good when my face was flushed. I wore jeans that fit well enough, despite being short on me, and a baggy t-shirt. "They'll be watching the entrance," she said, and I nodded. I had been expecting that.

"Right. Thanks. Um.. back way out?" I said. That's me, Bailey, ever the articulate one.

"Go behind the bar and there's a door. They'll be watching that, too," she replied, moving to the mirror to touch up her make-up, which was overdone to begin with. I shifted my weight uncomfortably. "I suggest climbing out the window."

"Uh, what?" I asked. That hadn't been in my plan. Then again, being chased by Octavius and Brutus hadn't been in my plan either. The woman looked at me with a disbelieving look on her face, then shook her head and turned back to the mirror. I shrugged, then moved towards the window. It was small and square and was set barely above ground. Goody.

I set down the box and shoes and fumbled with the catch on the window, opening the frosted glass with a grunt and some effort. Then I reclaimed my items and clambered onto the sill, shoving myself out of the slight hole in the wall. There are benefits to being skinny and knobbly; this was one of them. I was out on the street after some wriggling and muttered complaints. I looked around for any sight of the two thugs and was greeted by the image of Brutus standing dumbly at the entrance to the bar, leaning against the brick and looking bored. Octavius, I presumed, was guarding the back entrance.

I snuck around another building and then started running again, just in case. After a few minutes of that, I hit a more busy street with actual taxis on it and called one, only to be ignored. I gritted my teeth and reminded myself that I was having a good day. I tried again and was ignored again. So instead of waiting to be ignored three times, I started walking. And walking. And walking.

It took me an hour of wandering through the city to get to my destination. I looked up at a rather impressive hotel made with fine stone and with a uniformed doorman standing outside, looking bored, his grey moustache twitching every now and again, as if itchy. I walked up to the hotel and the doorman opened the door for me without question, yawning. I tried my hardest not to yawn as well and failed.

I walked over to the elevator and swiped my card, given to me by my current client, just for this purpose. The elevator dinged and started moving up to the top floor at a relatively slow pace. I had sagged against the wall and was feeling like falling asleep when the doors opened onto a plush, carpeted hallway. The hallway was fairly short, leading only to the penthouse, but it was enough to make me wish, not for the first time, that I wasn't living in a studio apartment on the west side of town.

I knocked loudly on the door of the suite and heard shuffling from behind it. A thug, much like Octavius and Brutus, opened the door, black suit crinkled as if it had been poorly washed. I looked at the man in the eye, being of a height, and he looked back at me. This had been a ritual of ours since meeting and finally, he stepped aside. "Thanks, Steve," I grumbled, and he glared at me.

"Jon," he said simply and I waved my hands with my shoes in them, realising belatedly that I had forgotten to put them back on. That might explain why my feet were cold. Bother.

"Right, Steve," I said and moved into the suite. The entrance was finely furnished in typical posh hotel furniture, but the main living area was done up in Queen Anne décor. There were thick rugs and wooden furniture and the lighting was from an honest-to-goodness wood-burning fireplace.

"Why do you insist on giving my people nick-names, Ms Duane?" a prim voice asked and I walked into the fire-light, spotting the chair where my current client sat, round glasses perched precariously on his nose as he read from a book with worn pages. I bent to look at the spine and nodded, 'Don Quixote'. The man was small in height and build and wore dress pants, a button up dress shirt and vest done in green tweed and silk. He looked like a college professor, but I knew that he was much smarter than your average professor. His eyes had a calculating glance that you could have found on any mastermind behind a government coup. I didn't trust him, but I was certainly willing to take his money.

"I give everybody names. Makes things more interesting, Professor," I said. He glanced up at me over his glasses and I waved the box in front of him. "Got your diamonds."

There was silence but for the crackling of the fire as the Professor, as I had named him, closed his book softly and placed it on the table beside him. He stood and I felt awkward, towering over him by a good four inches. He walked over to me and smiled, a small gesture which set my heart fluttering nervously. I restrained from gulping in fear and held out the box. "Good. I trust there were no problems obtaining them?"

"Well, Scott knew you—or rather I—was coming and had two big bruisers waiting for me. Octavius and Brutus," I said, taking a step back to supposedly admire a crystal bird on the mantle as the Professor opened the box with a very small key covered in gold. He looked over the diamonds with a critical eye and nodded, satisfied.

"Octavius and Brutus? Appropriate," he said and gestured to Steve. The guard reached into his breast pocket and pulled out an envelope. He stomped over and handed it to me, and I counted the money carefully.

"All there," I said in confirmation, wondering if I should up my price for losing the two guards. Hazard pay, right?

"Good. I would walk you to the door, but..." the Professor stated and I decided against asking for more money. He scared me. I waved a hand and walked away.

"I got it, Professor," I said as I was followed to the door by Steve. "There are reputations to maintain."

"Correct, Ms Duane. Have a pleasant evening," he replied, returning to his chair and his book. I opened the door for myself and walked out.

"You, too, Mr Houtman," I called back and left, the envelope of money in my pocket, tired.

I could have called a cab and with my weary feet, I was inclined to. But I remembered my encounter earlier and ignored the impulse, putting back on my shoes and turning west. I walked past more alleys and the night people who roamed the darker parts of the city. Some knew me, others did not. I kept quiet, my hands in my pockets, head down.

It was nearing dawn when I finally made it back to my apartment building. It wasn't terribly tall, about six stories or so. I lived on the third floor, apartment 308B, and dutifully trudged up the stairs after glaring at the "Out of Order" sign on the ancient elevator, which hadn't worked since before I'd moved in.

My apartment was small. The studio wasn't more than a few hundred square feet and I had stuck my bed into an out of the way corner under a window, made neatly. The room, in my opinion, was comfortable and well decorated despite its size. I had a desk by the kitchen and a cedar chest at the foot of the bed. The kitchen had a couple of counters that stuck out from the wall, making it seem separate. There were two barstools next to one of the counters and a couch and coffee table in the remainder. Bookshelves lined the walls—mostly full—and there was no television.

I took out the money from my pocket and put it in a safe in my cedar chest, locking it with a combination and key which hung, most days, around my neck. I would take it to the bank tomorrow. I glanced at the clock and groaned. It was far past tomorrow. Tired from my exertions, I managed to brush my teeth in the closet-like bathroom before collapsing on my bed.

It didn't take me long to fall asleep and it felt like even less time before my alarm—curse me for buying that thing—went off. I tried to pick it up off my night-stand and throw it against the far wall, but failed. Wanting to see the reason for my failure, I opened my eyes blearily and saw that it had been bolted down. Right, I did that after I broke my thirteenth alarm clock in such a manner.

There remained nothing for me to do to the offending machine and so I simply turned it off and sat up. My mouth tasted funny and I was still wearing the clothes from the day before. I got up and meandered to the bathroom to take a shower and make general sense of my self. I threw on some yoga pants and a blue button-up shirt. The pants were too short and hit me about mid calf and the shirt was too big, but I didn't mind. I threw my hair into a scrappy bun and grabbed my money and satchel before trudging out the door.

My feet still hurt from all the running and walking.

I stopped at the bank first and then went to the

local coffee shop, grabbing one coffee, black, a chai latte with soy milk, and an iced cappuccino as well as two blueberry muffins and a piece of coffee cake. After the coffee shop, I went to my office, where I handed the iced cappuccino and one of the blueberry muffins to my door man and went down the hall to a small, independent photography agency where I delivered the coffee and coffee cake to the photographer, a scruffy looking man just out of college. He dug in his pocket and handed me a few bills, unlike the doorman who just paid me monthly for being an errand runner. I would go pick up his dry cleaning later.

"Thanks, Bailey," the photographer said through a mouthful of cake and I waved, shoving the bills into my pocket as I left.

"See ya, Charger," I said, and he grumbled after me through his breakfast. I had named him Charger after the car; he was full of spirit but wasn't much use in the real world. I was fond of him, though, and ignored the fact that he paid for his breakfast in fits and spurts at times.

Then, I was off to my office. Oh, my office was blissfully quiet and I had a nice couch where I could lay out and get some sleep. Often times, that was exactly what I did. Business wasn't wonderful when you advertised as a "go-fer", so most days were pretty darn slow.

My office was similar to my apartment in that I furnished it as simply as I could and tried to make it neat and tasteful. I had a desk facing in, with a large window behind it. There was a typewriter in one corner (because I like the way they sound when you type on them. All of my files were done on my computer and by typewriter. It kept me entertained when days were slow) and a fairly nice laptop in the other. In the centre was a notebook. There were bookshelves on either side of the door, also mostly full, and the couch I spoke of on the left wall if you were facing the door.

It wasn't much, but it was mine and I had hand-painted my entire business-card description on the door. I sat down and drank my chai while munching on my muffin. I checked my e-mail and updated my company's website. Then, blissful silence.

Chapter 2
In Which I Get A Job

Silence after a night of being chased by gun-waving thugs with a burning desire to kill you is really nice. Silence that lasts for hours after a night of being chased by gun-waving thugs with a burning desire to kill you starts to look an awful lot like a problem. Thankfully, I never made it that far.

I finished my breakfast and then went to the couch with the intention of taking a nap and catching up on my lost sleep. My plans were interrupted abruptly, quite unfairly if you ask me. I didn't want to reach paranoia levels of quiet, but I was quite content to take a nap.

I had just settled onto the couch when the door to my little office burst open. Without even a polite knock to see if I was available. In strolled two men, one ageing and stooped over with less than a full head of hair. His nose was long and overpowered the rest of his face and his eyes fairly twinkled. Truly. He wore what looked to be an old-fashioned suit, perhaps from the 1940s, a cane hanging over his arm and, I kid you not, spats on his feet. The other was tall and straight, wearing a more modern set of clothing that seemed to sit uncomfortably on his shoulders: simple black slacks, white button-up shirt, sports coat in grey. He had the wavy dark hair one would associate with a knight of King Arthur's court and he held himself in such a way that I wondered if he thought he was *from* King Arthur's court. He did not have a cane, but I could see a hint of a knife hilt sticking up from behind his jacket. It was better than guns, I supposed.

"She is not here," the younger one growled—did I mention that he did not look particularly pleased to be there? Honestly, I'd never heard anyone growl like that before.

"Then we will wait," the older said with perfect amicability. I sighed and stretched, standing. Both men jumped before turning to look at me, the younger one with a disappointed scowl, the other with a beaming smile. The older put a pocket watch in his pocket, the metal gleaming enough to catch the eye. Paying clients, then, rather than those looking for hopeful freebies.

"Right," I muttered, reaching up to fix my bun that was falling out of its tie. I did try to look somewhat professional for paying clients. "I'm Bailey Duane and I'm a professional gofer for hire. How can I help you, Fred, Gawain?" I said, indicating the older and younger in turn. Gawain looked at me with a confused, infuriated scowl, and I saw him mutter the word 'gofer' under his breath, drawing his brows together as he did so. People should actually *read* the door before they barge in. It makes explaining things much easier.

"Fred?" the older said. "I am not Fred. My name is James Webb."

"Fred," I said again, "As in Fred Astaire. What can I do for you? I will say that I do have a policy against working with goats. The last time was...destructive on my book collection."

"See how she acts?" Gawain said in a hushed tone to Fred. "Her services cannot be worth this disrespect."

"Hush, boy," Fred snapped, and turned back to me with a pleasant smile. I raised my eyebrows in question. Frankly, I wasn't amused, though I will admit to mild, objective curiosity. By which I mean that this was the most exciting thing to happen all day and I was fascinated. "We would like you to retrieve a document, please, Ms Duane."

"Okay," I said, going behind my desk to the notebook where I started a new page: Fred and Gawain. Document retrieval. I liked document retrieval. Document retrieval was comparatively simple. "So, is this document in a safe or filing cabinet somewhere? Because I have to have a really good incentive to resort to thievery."

"James, you cannot be considering this! We don't need help from a common thief," Gawain growled again, glaring at me. If you think I was one of those people to glare back, you'd be right. Except, in this case, they were potential customers and I really needed the money. Picking up breakfast doesn't pay the bills, no matter how much wishing I did. Besides, the Professor's money would only get me through the end of the month. That, and the fact that it wasn't the first time I had clients question my morality, and their need for my morality, in front of my face. It was why I always brought it up first time into a conversation, so the clients could get over themselves or leave. Stranger things have happened in my office—two of them involving racoons—so I kept quiet.

"Be quiet. You know that we need her help," Fred rumbled at Gawain, looking like a stern grandparent. Something in his voice must have struck a note of obedience in Gawain, because he simply curled his lip and fell into silence. "No," Fred said, answering my question, shaking his head and sitting in the small chair I kept for clients. Gawain sighed and sat on the couch (there was only room for one chair), glowering the whole time. "The document in question has been missing for two hundred years."

I wrote that bit of information down to hide my shock before sitting back in my chair and massaging my temple with my fingers. "Okay, not quite what I had in mind. Um, perhaps we should start at the beginning. What can you tell me about this document?"

Fred beamed again, looking like I'd just asked him how his six grandchildren were doing. I tried not to react and just took down notes.

"The document is a manuscript, written by Ambrose Madeline in the sixteenth century. It was never copied for reading by the masses, but changed hands many times. Upon Madeline's death, it was bequeathed to his granddaughter, who was kidnapped and killed three months later. The manuscript was stolen and came into the hands of some Catholic monks. Before they could properly copy it down, their monastery was ransacked and the manuscript taken, along with their precious jewels. After that, it showed up in the hands of a wealthy merchant who sold it to a lesser noble in the house of the Chinese Emperor. Then, it ended up lost when the noble was killed and appeared some ten years later in the hands of a private collector. He was killed and the manuscript was lost when his estate went up in flames."

I stared at him. Stupid, stupid Bailey. Never even *think* something is going to be simple until it's over and done with. "You know, it could have been destroyed. By the fire?"

Fred shook his head, quite firm. "No. It was not. There have been rumours of the Time Keeper—the manuscript's title—in many places. Iceland, Finland, Turkey, Russia, Egypt. It has survived."

"And you want me to find this Time Keeper book thing," I said, waving my pen around as I considered the fact that none of the places Fred had listed were in the States. Oh, goody. Fred nodded, smiling again. "Great. Good job, Bailey," I muttered quietly. "Find the book with the bloody and convoluted history that may be anywhere in the world."

Gawain grumbled, "If you don't want the job, we

can find someone else who will take it. Someone with more experience in these matters."

I flapped my hand at him. "Calm down, Gawain. I'll take the job. And I have plenty of experience in finding lost objects. But you're going to have to realise that I can't simply go gallivanting around the world in search for some document at the drop of a hat. I have other clients to take care of."

"Yes, buying breakfast," Fred said gravely, raising one bushy eyebrow at me. Sarcasm didn't suit his twinkling eyes and cheery disposition all that well. I slumped in my chair. I didn't even want to know how he knew my current schedule was wide open. Probably something to do with the calendar on the wall listing my current jobs. Which were all breakfast and dry-cleaning related.

"Right," I mumbled. "Buying breakfast. Fine. I can cancel any jobs until I find your document. But all travel expenses will be added to your bill. And I want half of my usual fee up front instead of being paid upon retrieval."

"Very well. There shall be no object to your payment. I have a file of information regarding the manuscript." Fred pulled out a packet of papers from his suit jacket and handed it to me. I was still a little stunned by his "no object to your payment" statement, but had enough professional capability to glance through the material a client gave me and keep my jaw off the floor.

I opened the dossier and flipped through a few of

the pages. For a simple document retrieval, he sure had a lot of information on the thing. Most of it was history, though, about the eras in which the document had been lost, which was fine except I really didn't need to know about shoe styles in nineteenth century Lebanon to find a document. I kept a groan back and instead took a deep breath. History really was not my thing. I mean, sure, I took the requisite classes and passed just like everyone else at university, but I was never a history buff. For goodness' sakes, I got a business degree doubled with a criminal science degree at Yale. I think I only took one history course and that was "History of Criminal Science." But the 'no object to your payment' thing was enticing. Really enticing. And Fred hadn't even asked what my price was, yet.

"Alright, alright," I grumbled. "I'll look over this file tonight and see what I can come up with. I'll let you know my next plan of action in the morning. If that's fine, then I'd like to go over some contracts and documents."

Fred beamed, quite literally, again. He nodded and held out his hand over the desk for me to shake. I hesitated for half-a-second then reluctantly took it. Something told me I was entering into a devil's bargain and doing it willingly. I pulled out one of my fill-in-the-blanks contracts and scrawled in a few lines, namely those concerning payment, before turning it over to Fred. It wasn't anything terribly fancy, just a statement of intent—find a document—and what I wasn't responsible for should I fail to find the thing. He, to his credit, read it thoroughly before signing 'James Webb' with a flourish. That was that. I nodded and Fred stood to go, Gawain standing as well, looking as pleased as peaches to be getting out of my office.

Fred shot Gawain a meaningful look and the younger man sighed, his posture slumping slightly before returning to its ramrod straight position. I wondered if that hurt, standing like that all the time. Personally, I liked a good, comfortable slouch. "I will be accompanying you wherever your travels lead," Gawain said. He turned to leave like the statement was a simple "goodbye." I folded my arms and raised my eyebrows.

"Whoa, whoa, whoa. How about no," I said, feeling a little silly standing up to this immaculately dressed man in my too-short pants with a shirt that fit like a sack.

"This is nonnegotiable," Fred said, fixing me with a stern look. Gosh, I felt like I was being scolded for being a wayward child, which was not unusual, considering my childhood. I grumbled and frowned and thought really hard about finances before finally nodded my assent; business had been slow and I needed the money. If putting up with the grumpy Gawain was the condition of my payment, fine. I'd done worse for clients than taking them on a ride-along. Such as my diamond stealing from the night before. Besides, document retrieval, what could possibly go wrong?

The two were about to leave, Fred checking the

time on his pocket watch and Gawain with his hand on my door knob when I realised something. "Hey, Gawain. What's your real name? For the files, you know?" He shot me a withering look and closed the door behind him. I leaned against my desk. "Alright then, Gawain it is."

So, turns out that when Fred was saying there had been rumours of the manuscript's existence, he forgot to mention that there had been nearly a hundred different rumours from all over the world, most overlapping each other in time. I read through the file I had been provided and, instead of my normal writing out of theories, I decided to buy an entire note-book. I wrote down everything I could think of, organising the dratted thing into different sections of the world, putting a map in and marking it with different colours of ink so I would know where the manuscript had actually been and where it was rumoured to have been. By the time dawn came around—Sleep? Pshaw— I had filled nearly a third of the book and I felt like some obsessed treasure hunter. And I hadn't even started on the internet side of the research or reached out to my sources in the world of desirable acquisitions.

I decided that the best place to start the actual search for this thing was in Finland, where the manuscript had last been officially sighted and owned by the private collector, one Jaska Aalto, before his estate had been burned. The estate was in a small town near the coast and the local people used it as a tourism sight when to supplement the fishing industry as a source of revenue. Not that there were ever many visitors. It was a good place to start and I could flesh out my plan on the go, maybe meet with some European contacts on the way.

In any case, I contacted Fred and Gawain and told them that I had booked two tickets to Finland via Iceland, where we could check out some other rumours. Also, Iceland has really good sushi. Then, I started packing, being liberal with my "potentially problematic situation" supplies. A couple of hours later, with my pack slung over my shoulders and a mug of tea in my hand, I shoved my way into my office and waited for the two to show up. I didn't have to wait long.

"Ms Duane," Fred said as he walked through the door, cane swinging over his arm, Gawain following along behind with his ever-present scowl. I had just set down my tea and was in the process of stuffing a muffin into my mouth before we started on our journey.

"Uhhewwo," I said through the muffin, which did not please Gawain. He shot me a withering, scum-of-the-earth look and dropped his own pack down. I was fairly surprised; his backpack looked to be well used and instead of slacks and a shirt, he was wearing a functional pair of jeans and a simple long-sleeved shirt. Perhaps having Gawain along wouldn't be quite as much work as I was expecting. I polished off my muffin and turned to business. "So, we're off to Finland..."

"A good place to start," Fred said, nodding his head. He slipped into the chair before my desk and looked up at me expectantly. I nodded.

"Finland," I said again, enunciating the syllables. Because after Finland, I had absolutely no idea where the heck I was going to end up and I needed to be prepared for every eventuality. There was a moment of awkward silence, and Gawain coughed pointedly. He looked at me as though I was a terrible person who set out with intent to kick puppies, then muttered something to Fred. Fred jerked and nodded belatedly.

"Right, of course. I have your money." Fred pulled out a pleasantly thick envelope and handed it to me. I painstakingly counted every bit, ignoring the incredulous look from Gawain and the slightly disappointed look from Fred—why he should seem surprised that I wanted confirmation of trust, I wasn't sure—then nodded. Half up front plus enough to cover general travel expenses. If he was willing to pay, I was willing to do the work.

"Thanks," I said, tucking the money away into my bag. "Plane leaves in an hour and a half. So, we've got to get going." I waited for Fred and Gawain to walk out of my office before closing the door and hanging up a sign: Out on Business. Be Back Eventually.

I walked past the two discussing something in earnest. Gawain was adamantly shaking his head while Fred muttered something quietly. I ignored both of them and went out to call a cab. First try, nada. Second try, nope. Third try, wait, stop! Finally, Gawain approached the curb and threw out his arm, and a cab stopped almost immediately. I glared at him and climbed into the taxi, saluting Fred as I did so.

The drive to the airport was pretty much the second most awkward trip of my life (the first being... well, I'm not really going to get into that, I think). Gawain said not a word except when I asked him about a few specifics regarding the document, though I tried to prod him into revealing something personal. Anything would do, really, but he was annoyingly silent. Until, that is, we passed the exit for the first major airport. He watched the sign go past and rounded on me. "The airport is over there," he said, pointing an accusing finger.

"Yes," I said, turning to look at the exit for the airport. "That is an airport."

"Driver," Gawain called, voice crackling with fury. I flapped my hand at the driver to continue on and, like any enterprising person, he obeyed the person most likely to pay. The Arthurian-looking man turned to face me with a scowl. I was beginning to think it was a permanent feature of his face. "So, we're not going to the airport. Which means, what, exactly? That you're going to take our money, kill me and dump me by the roadside somewhere?"

"I'm not a thief," I said. I frowned, considered and shrugged one shoulder. "I amend that statement. I don't steal from clients who pay me. And I'm not a murderer, so I'm not going to kill you. I'm just not allowed to go to that particular airport for another... five months. Or longer, depending on the review." I got a look of complete incredulity from my travelling companion.

"You were banned from the airport. From one specific airport," he stated flatly. I nodded and messed with my hair uncomfortably. It hadn't been my best job to date.

"Yeah. For releasing a flock of chickens at the terminal in order to get the security crew to postpone a flight so my client could stop his girlfriend from flying away and propose. I got paid for it, but security banned me and my client and his girlfriend from the airport for two years," I said. There might have been some other reasons why I got banned from the airport for an extra year, but I wasn't going to say anything about *that*. I was trying to run a business, not drive it into the ground. Gawain kept silent for the rest of the drive, giving me angry looks every now and again, but I, thankfully practised in the art of pointedly ignoring people, did not pay any attention.

The taxi dropped us off at the significantly smaller airport on the south end of town, and I gestured for Gawain to pay before stalking into the warehouse-like building. Hey, this was part of my travel expenses. At least I hadn't booked us at a five-star hotel in Finland. I did try to be conscious about spending client money. I had a shouting match with the lady at check-in and, after emptying my bag at security to prove that I did not actually have a knife in my bag, nor did I have any poultry or live animals, or anything resembling a rubber ducky, stomped over to the gate where I proceeded to slump into a chair and grumble my way into annoying Gawain. He was proving to be quite entertaining to annoy. As travel companions go, I could have had much worse. As time would soon show.

I was half-dozing, waiting for boarding to begin, when I heard a sound that made me freeze.

"Well, well, Bailey Duane. You're looking just as tired as ever," a woman's voice said. I straightened and spun around in my chair to stare in disbelief at the woman of about average height with curves where I was flat, wearing a flattering pair of grey trousers and matching jacket. She had her dark hair pulled back in a functional and severe tail and had a single travel bag at her side, her belt sporting a folded piece of leather that meant she was on official business rather than a coincidental pleasure-filled meeting. Though with Katelyn Dupont, coincidence didn't exist.

"Dupont," I said less than eagerly, making sure to put the French inflection on her name. "What are you doing here?"

Kate raised an eyebrow and tilted her head towards my backpack in answer. "Who is this?"

Gawain growled, turning from where he had been contentedly glaring at the floor. At least, I hoped he was content, because I hadn't had enough sleep in the last forty-eight hours to think about entertaining anybody. Judging by the glare he levelled upon Kate—

good to know it wasn't just me he glared at—he was far, far from content.

I sighed and shifted enough so I could see both angry people in my view. "Gawain, this is Dupont. Dupont, Gawain. Katelyn here works for the FBI and apparently gets notifications about my movements. Which you shouldn't, because we decided that the whole affair was really none of my fault."

Kate raised an eyebrow at me. "It was only circumstantially proved to not be your fault. And in case you don't remember, the last time you went out of the country—"

"Don't bring it up. It was an accident," I grumbled. "So, what, you're here because I decided to go to Finland? What if I were only going on holiday? I might have a thing for Finland. I hear people are happy there."

She folded her arms and cocked a hip at me. "Only going on holiday? With your 'friend' Gawain here? I don't think so. You're not his type. And since when did you last go on holiday? I got sent out here to supervise you wherever you go, be it Finland or Russia. Please tell me you're not going to Russia."

"Nyet," I pouted. Great, more supervision. But shaking Kate off was like telling a crocodile it couldn't eat your leg for lunch. I was not that brave. "Fine. Fine. But you realise that you have pretty much no sway overseas? The only jurisdiction you get is what the other governments grant you, and that all depends on how nice you are to them." I could tell by the look on her face that she didn't really care. I was an American citizen—half the time, at least—and therefore her responsibility. Goody. "Alright, so, what? You're coming with me while I do document retrieval? Do you even have your gun?"

"No," Kate said with a regretful frown. "But I know where to get one. Document retrieval, eh? With a bodyguard here?"

"I am not a bodyguard," Gawain protested. "And since Ms Duane is in my employ, I should be the one to say whether or not you go. And I say that you will not go. We do not need anyone else."

"That was the wrong thing to say," I said mildly to Gawain and moved backwards as Kate lunged forwards to grab Gawain by the collar. To his credit, the man didn't flinch as she glared at him (a truly frightening sight, take my word for it) and said nothing. Airport security gave us a casual glance and wisely kept going about their business.

"Listen here, bub. This isn't your call. I've been sent out here by the Bureau and by George, if I have to go back and say that some guy off the street said I couldn't come on the trip to Finland, I'll be out on my ass in ten seconds. So, whether you like it or not, I'm going," Kate snarled, her nose almost touching Gawain's to make her point clear. She released him a moment later and grabbed her travel bag, sitting in a chair next to mine, away from Gawain, arms folded.

"Dupont," Gawain said after her tantrum was over. He rolled the syllables over his tongue. "French?"

"Yeah," Kate said, still looking dark and angry. "My father is from Callais. Moved here after he married my mother and had me. I've got dual citizenship."

"I don't like the French," he muttered in reply. I groaned and put my head in my hands. It was going to be a very long job.

Chapter 3
In Which I Eat Some Fish

After preventing Kate from attacking Gawain for the French remark, we were allowed to board the plane. Being a very tiny airport, we had a layover in Canada before setting off for Iceland. The plane was barely half full and yet somehow, I was seated in the middle of the squabbling children under my supervision. I settled in for a very long forty-five minute flight.

"Comments like that," Kate said through a snarl as the flight attendants went through the safety talk—which I was *trying* to listen to and failing, mostly because it was better than the arguing between Dupont and Gawain—"make me think that you are either stupidly prejudicial, have some background with a very limited number of French people or are just English. Now, the likelihood of you being involved with a bad French-person is just ridiculous. We're delightful! And you don't have an English accent, so I can't assume that, either. Which leaves me with the option of you being stupidly prejudicial."

"Lovely speech," I grumbled. I doubt either heard me.

"I've had plenty of experience with the French," Gawain hissed in reply, leaning around me to jab his finger at Kate. "And I *am* English. Proud to be so, which I doubt you'd understand, being a half-breed."

"A half-breed?" Kate demanded incredulously. "You're toeing the line very close to racism, bub. But, fine. Fine. We'll play that game. If you're English, then where's your accent? Unless you enjoy putting on what passes for an American accent."

"Accents are," Gawain started, then swallowed the next words with a growl. He bared his teeth and sat back in his seat as the flight attendant went through doing a few last-minute checks. "Accents are different where I'm from."

"Oh, sure," Kate said with a snort, also sitting back in her seat. She folded her arms, though and glowered at the in-flight magazines in the seat pocket in front of her. "If you expect me to believe that, you must be a greater fool than I thought."

"Can we try not to kill each other before this trip starts?" I begged. I didn't bother to hide the sarcasm in my voice, though I was perfectly serious. "I don't need to fill out any paperwork as to why my client was killed by a Federal Agent who was meant to be keeping me *out* of trouble. And Gawain, really, cool it with the holier-than-thou attitude. This is a time of inclusiveness and you don't want me to drop you as a client for being a terrible person."

"I won't kill him," Kate snarled.

"Really?" I asked, "Because it seems an awful lot like you want to kill him. Just saying—"

"The worst that could happen would be maiming," she muttered, restraining a glare. It was said barely loud enough for me to make out the words, but I was still shocked. Katelyn Dupont was generally one of the most decent people I knew. I mean, I found her annoying as soggy toast, but that didn't mean she wasn't a good person. (Actually, the whole straight-and-narrow morality thing might have been part of the reason why I didn't get along with her all that well. It was one of those things that you don't really discuss with law-enforcement without a signed immunity agreement in place.) So the fact that she was considering hurting Gawain meant that she *really* didn't like him. Add another problem to solve to my expense list.

I did my best to keep the two from killing each other before we got off the ground. After that, it was the problem of the flight attendants. As a rule, written into my contract and and everything, I don't do work on planes. I have had more than one job that took place on a plane and it never turned out well. There was one where I had to transport a pure-bred Persian cat with a case of the grumps. The owner had purchased a seat on the plane and I sat between it and any harm. Except the man sitting next to me had a serious issue with cats and raised Dobermans. Let's just say that the flight attendants had to move the man to first class to prevent fur from flying. Literally. Then there was the time that I had been told to escort a "troubled teen" back home from military boarding school. It was more destructive than the cat and I didn't entirely blame the kid.

So, on this flight, I wasn't going to do zilch. Gawain and Kate were on their own. I was simply going to sit back, drink my free beverage and relax. Sort of.

Being tall means that there is generally not a lot of space on planes, or at restaurants, or in cars, or lots of places, for my long legs. So, on a twelve hour flight, I had to continuously shift and move about so that my legs wouldn't completely lose feeling. This annoyed both my travel companions, who had stopped fighting and were trying to sleep and ignore me. Oh, and did I mention that I have an incredibly hard time sleeping on planes? Something about the constant noise, and the light, and the fear of impending doom by cats and teenagers.

Despite the fact that I had hardly slept the night before what with going over the file given to me by Fred, and spent the night before that running about the city, I was wide awake on the flight to Iceland and knew that I would be in for some serious jet lag. Oh, goody. So, for the twelve hour flight, I read and re-red the file and the notebook I had made, ruling out some rumours as lies and cons and others as distinct possibilities. I decided that if we didn't find anything in Finland, that Egypt was next. I've always wanted to see the pyramids.

Getting to Iceland was fairly uneventful, apart from the bickering. It was what happened in Iceland that nearly gave me a heart attack. We signed into the hotel in Reykjavik and spent the first day just sleeping off jet lag and being completely oblivious to any sights or attractions. Which meant that I slept off jet lag while the other two sat around, bored and glaring at each other. The second day, though, was when we got to business.

The rumours surrounding the Time Keeper in Iceland centred around one of the smaller fringe towns near some of the glaciers and hot springs, so it was onto a bus and out of Reykjavik, just as the day was starting. I hadn't been to Iceland in ages and would have happily played tourist for a bit if it weren't for the fact that I was on a job. Still, the bus tour was nice, even if the landscape looked like something out of a sci-fi movie. We got to the town just as the bus was running out of gas and it clunked to a halt next to a small building just on the outskirts of town. I shouldered my pack and looked cheerfully at the others. "Well, that's not ominous at all. Come on, let's go see what we can dig up."

Gawain glared at me and Kate sighed. "I really hate those department people. I should be back at home, sipping a nice cup of coffee and reading the newspaper right now. Not following a maniac out here in Iceland. Where, by the way, it is rather cold."

I beamed at her—if they were going to be grumpy,

then I was going to be cheerful—and set a brisk pace into town, "Isn't it great!"

If you've never been to Iceland, then know this: it is a beautiful and forbidding country. The land has been formed primarily by volcanoes, which are still alarmingly active. There are hot springs, glaciers, mountains, and vast fields of landscape that is under-girded by volcanic rock. The plant life is small but hardy and wood is an astonishingly valuable resource. The houses, therefore, are made from concrete and rock and look surprisingly modern. The language is closer to Old Norse than any modern language, and the people are friendly, if a bit aloof, like they hold the harshness of the land inside them. Thankfully, it is a country which also has an extremely large tourist industry, so people are used to clueless foreigners wandering about and getting lost. This made our direction-asking much, much easier.

I was looking for a family by the surname Vilhjal-masson, which, despite the many languages I could muddle through, I tried to pronounce and failed. Gawain took over the asking after the third mispronunciation. Eventually, we were pointed by wary looking townspeople to a low-set house near the open land beyond the town, set a distance away from the other houses. I approached and knocked cheerfully on the door. Bad idea.

The door swung open a few moments after I knocked and I came face to face with an angry looking old man who was wielding a shot-gun, pointed right at my nose. I stared down the barrel nervously, my most recent run-in with guns fresh in my head. Octavius and Brutus had wielded guns and, luckily for me, I was quick enough to be out of range for them to accurately shoot me. With a shot-gun up my nose, though, I had little to no chance. "Uh, hi," I started. "Is this the family Vilhjalmasson house?"

The man shouted what sounded like obscenities in Icelandic at me and waved the gun in my face. I blinked and swallowed, turning to Kate and Gawain. "You wouldn't happen to speak Icelandic, would you?" Kate shook her head adamantly and Gawain muttered a brief no. "Great," I said and turned back to the old man, clapping my hands together and putting on my determined face.

I grabbed the barrel of the gun and pushed it away from me, holding onto it so I could pull the old man forwards and twist the gun out of his hands, turning it on him. "Bailey!" Kate snapped at me.

"Relax, Dupont," I said as the old man held up his hands, muttering at me. I waggled the gun in front of him, indicating for him to go back into the house. He harrumphed at me and led the three of us inside. The house was low (ow, my poor head) and cluttered with furniture and odd tidbits that looked like torture instruments and furs. Lots of furs. I quite liked it. Gawain seemed to be more relaxed as well, but that could have just been the lighting. Kate, on the other hand, was looking distinctly uncomfortable and annoyed, at me mostly. I set the gun on the table where the man immediately snatched it away and cradled it against his chest.

"What want you?" he barked out in broken English.

I pulled out my notebook and a pen and prepared for a long interview, though I desperately hoped that he would have the document in question and just hand it over nicely. Somehow, I doubted that was the case. "Have you heard of the Time Keeper?" I asked. Vilhjalmasson looked at me blankly. I made a face and turned to Gawain. "It wouldn't happen to have another name, would it?"

Gawain blinked, "It was written by Ambrose Madeline. He was French. Called it the Chronométreur."

That got a reaction out of our angry Icelandic friend. His eyes widened and he started muttering in French, "Chronométreur." He started waving about his hands rapidly and speaking in French. I looked desperately to Kate who blinked and replied to the man, holding her hands up for him to slow down.

"He says that the Chronométreur was lost to his family many years ago, when his great-grandmother was married. Her husband sold it off to a wealthy foreigner from Italy and it vanished. He says because of that his family was cursed and now he is losing money on his livestock to the cat-men," Kate said. "He says that the cat-men watch him and that he should not be talking to us. I'm not entirely sure he's sane, Bailey."

"Could your translation be wrong?" I asked.

She glared at me.

"Right."

I wrote down everything the man said and put a big question mark next to cat-men before looking at Gawain. He had gone a bit pale and his jawline was tight. Tighter than usual, I mean. "Cat-men? Who or what are the cat-men?" To my surprise, the normally stoic (or just very angry) man shivered and rose from the table.

"We should leave. Now," he said, his tone brooking no argument. "If they are watching, we should not be here."

"Who's watching?" I asked, standing and following Gawain to the door while Kate said hurried apologies to the man and followed after us. I received no answer from Gawain and resorted to running after the man to get back to the bus. The rest of the tour was off at an eiderdown factory tour, which left us there to wait with the driver, who was engrossed in a novel. We slumped against the vehicle and Kate looked at me in confusion. I shrugged, similarly lost, and our straight-backed escort looked around nervously. He moved to the bus driver and asked him something.

"We won't get out of here for a while, I shouldn't think," the man said, kicking the bus in derision before turning back to his novel. "It's broken. It'll take a few hours for us to get another one out here."

Gawain scowled and nodded brusquely before marching back to us. "We shall find a place to eat, out of the way."

I was all for that, it being lunch time and every-thing, but mostly, I wanted answers. I couldn't do my job without answers and I was really annoyed that they had been kept from me in the first place. We found a small shop willing to serve us sandwiches and settled down with warm cups of tea.

"So, what do you think it is?" I asked, poking at my sandwich. Iceland was very good about having recognisable food, catering to the million or so tourists who came each year, but every now and again, I wasn't sure what I was eating. This one was some sort of fish, but I didn't know which and I wasn't certain I wanted to know.

"I don't know," Kate said, "but the sauce is very good."

"It's halibut," Gawain grumbled, half-throwing his plate onto the table and sitting before his tea. He considered the food then picked up his tea and let out an infuriated huff before sipping.

"So. What was that all about? You just freaked out back there and gave us no information. I need to know what's going on, Gawain, or I can't do my job," I snapped, sandwich halfway to my mouth. Kate picked at her own food, looking around nervously and I wondered if perhaps I should be nervous as well. I mean, Kate had FBI instincts and Gawain, well, he was just angry and brooding. But I didn't feel in any real danger, or any danger at all, and I had been in danger enough times in my life to have developed some sort of sense for the thing. So I just continued eating and stared Gawain down. He kept my gaze for a few moments then blinked, frowned, and looked away, sipping at his tea.

"James and I are not the only ones looking for the document," he said as if the news were groundbreaking. I blinked and rolled my eyes.

"Well, duh. I figured that. You're willing to pay my price, no questions asked, and came to me in the first place. For retrieval jobs, usually that means you're not on the level or that you're competing against someone else," I said. He looked at me with confusion then turned to Kate.

"On the level?" he said.

"Legal. Bailey here does work for some.. unsavoury people," Kate said, giving me a hard look with her dark eyes. I gave her a sheepish smile. "Which puts her on our radar in the first place. But she hasn't broken any laws that we are willing to contest. For now."

"Gee, thanks for that," I said darkly. Kate shrugged and smiled wanly and I reminded myself why I didn't like working with officials. Or detectives. Of which Kate was both. "Anyways, I figured you weren't the only ones after this thing. But what *I'm* interested in is whether I should be worried about the competition. Is this like a knitting club that has a fondness for rare books, or a society of secret ninjas that want to rule the world?"

Gawain took his time before answering which made me nervous. If he needed to figure out how to phrase his words about something so essential, I had to be careful around him and around whoever was also searching. "They are...dangerous. Willing to cause great pain and go to great lengths to get what they want. They have killed many before now."

"Killed many," I said slowly. "Great. So, who died last time you tried to find this thing? The person you hired? Cause I didn't sign up to be put in the line of fire. I charge extra for that."

"We already said that we would pay," Gawain snarled at me, anger suddenly written on his features. He clenched his fists and glared daggers at my face. "Are you so greedy that money is all you care about? I have known many like you, mercenaries who care nothing but for the coin in their pocket, no—" he broke off and ground his teeth to keep from saying any more.

I had dealt with the argument before, though I had never seen anyone so angry at the prospect. Indignant, yes. Concerned, yes. Frustrated, yes. But not angry. I picked my words carefully. "I like what I do. It's a job where I can do almost anything. But I have a life to live and I'm not doing things for nothing. Money matters in this world, whether you like it or not. So, yeah, call me greedy. But I'm also smart and I get what I want. It's basic business."

"You're nothing but an immoral mercenary who doesn't care what sort of blood gets on your hands as long as you get your money. You disgust me," Gawain hissed.

"That's your problem," I said easily. "I am what I am. Moral, immoral, however you want to look at me. I don't care as long as you're in my employ. Of course, if you want to cut the contract short, that's your issue."

Gawain looked as though he wanted to hit me, violently and repeatedly. Instead, he gripped his mug of tea dangerously hard and snarled at the table. "You will finish this job. The sooner the better."

"As you say," I said. Truth be told, Gawain's words bothered me some. I mean, sure, I work for some pretty iffy sorts of people. I've also done some iffy sorts of things—most of which involved theft of items stolen from iffy people, so there was no breaking of the law, just amending it. But I'm not as despicable as Gawain or Kate would believe. I have very strong guidelines which I will not break. I will not renege on a job, no matter how much of a bribe people try to offer to get me out of it. While I am on a job, everything I have including my life is at my client's disposal. I will not betray any of my former clients to current clients or law-enforcement (which is where Kate Dupont's real issue with me lay, I think. Though there was that time with the balloons filled with flour).

Sure, I was doing all of that for money, but it wasn't for love of money that I was doing it. It was to survive so I could continue to do my job. I shook my head subtly, ridding myself of such thoughts. It didn't matter how Gawain thought of me as long as I continued to be what I was. Still, it hurt some.

Kate rolled her eyes at me and ate her sandwich. Gawain looked like he wanted to say something but remained quiet and looked around as if on guard. I finished my lunch and wrote in a few more notes into my notebook, specifically 'cat-men: dangerous. Probably very' next to the question mark I had previously scribbled. "So," I said after a few more minutes of silence. "Why did Vilhyel—Vilhjyl—Villy call them cat-men? Are they a cat-lover's club? Cat-human hybrids? Fans of catnip?"

Gawain sighed and rubbed his head (I must say, giving people head-aches is one of my favourite pastimes. I'm getting quite good at it, too). "They call themselves Leonum Temporis. The Lions--"

"The Lions of Time," I said. "I took Latin in college. For about a month. What is it with you people and time?" Gawain said nothing. "So, what, you guys are like the Scarecrows of the Past? Or maybe something else, like the lion hunters."

"Bailey," Kate warned and I sighed. "Be nice."

"What are you here for exactly?" I snapped. Kate just shot me a look and I turned away, fidgeting uncomfortably under her death-glare.

"Leonum Temporis isn't an organisation to be trifled with," Gawain said. "They are extremely fierce and follow the rituals of the originators. The organisation started in the times of the Romans, when gladiators were matched with near-starved lions. The victors and their patrons of the Consulate started the Leonum Temporis as a... profitable organisation. They gained power and voices in governments throughout history and their members grew incredibly rich."

"So why are they after the Time Keeper? For a rich

organisation, it seems like they could just do without the thing," I said, glancing out the window to check on the bus. Another one was pulling up just then and the drivers were conferring with a lot of poking at the engines and gestures towards town. The other passengers that had been on the bus with us were milling about near the bus, looking hopeful.

"It is the basis of their beliefs," Gawain said, going back to being a man of few words. Unhelpful words, too. I raised my eyebrows at him.

"I thought that they started in the Roman times. Madeline didn't write the manuscript until the sixteenth century," I said. Gawain shifted and finished off his tea.

"He was the first to write the beliefs of the Leonum Temporis onto paper in their entirety," Gawain explained. I shrugged and we walked outside to the bus where people were beginning to board the second bus. Kate climbed onto the thing first, followed by Gawain. I looked about a bit and saw, standing in the shadows of one of the buildings, shot-gun in hand, angry expression on his face, Vilhjalmasson. He had a sweater with a hood pulled over his head and gestured at me emphatically.

I muttered an excuse to the bus driver and trotted over to the man, looking about to see if anyone was watching. "What are you doing?" I asked, though I was doubtful he could understand me.

He didn't say anything but pressed a small, leather bound notebook into my hands then pushed me away, raising his shot-gun to point at the other shadows. I rolled my eyes at his paranoia but slipped the notebook into my pocket with a hurried thanks and ran back to the bus, climbing on and giving the driver, who frowned at me, a smile. I was American, by accent if not by birth. I was born British and grew up between the States, England, and much of Europe. I could get away with a bit of tardiness. At least, the dumb American tourist schtick certainly helped my cause. There was so much more leeway if people saw you as annoying, dumb, but mostly harmless.

I slipped into the seat next to Gawain and pulled out the notebook. It was, joy of joys, in Icelandic, which was really no help. But by the slanting, feminine hand, and the date written on the inside cover, I figured it was from Vilhjalmasson's great-grandmother who had been the last in the family to own the document. "See," I said, waving the diary in front of Gawain. "Iceland wasn't completely useless!"

He ignored me.

Chapter 4
In Which I Outsmart Some People

It turns out that, once again, I was wrong. We may have got a journal from a woman who had held the Time Keeper, but I couldn't make heads or tails of it. My smattering of European languages didn't extend to Icelandic. And I wasn't about to hand it off to someone who could translate it and get back to me, because now there was competition for the book. That was the second part of my being wrong. I'll get to that in a bit.

"I didn't hire you to go shopping," Gawain snarled as we walked around Reykjavik. I wondered if he were capable of talking in a normal voice to me, or if I would forever be putting up with the undeserved anger. (Okay, some of it might have been deserved.) We were in the centre of town, where all of the shops that catered to tourists were. So far, I had stopped to get some chocolate—on my own dime, thank you very much—and Kate had forced us to wait while she bought a sweater, complaining about the cold.

"No, you hired me to find this document. It just so happens that I need to go shopping to find this document. Unless you want me to march up to the University and hand this journal over to anyone who speaks or writes Icelandic so your Leonum Temporis-ites can find out what we wanted translated by asking? No? I didn't think so. Which is why we're looking for—" I said, turning in a circle. I brightened and pointed to a store across the street. "That."

"A book store," Kate said. She made it sound as though my idea were crazy. Or stupid. Or both.

"Yes, a book store," I retorted. "They hold such wonderful things. Mysteries. Travel guides. *Dictionaries.*"

Gawain made a sound in the back of his throat which I took to be one of understanding, though it could have been a cough just as easily. Kate, to her credit, nodded and gestured to the door. "Just don't dawdle," she said. "It's getting late and I want to be back at the hotel before the streets clear." I thought of the multitudes of books on my shelves back in the states and laughed. It came out rather nervous and sarcastic.

"Dawdle? In a book store? You must be joking," I said, throwing open the door to the book store. "And don't be paranoid, Dupont. We're far too early into this game to be paranoid."

"I'd feel better if I had a gun," Kate muttered. I

ignored that statement and the three of us went inside the book store. To my credit, I didn't dawdle. I hadn't really planned on needing to spend much money, as Gawain and his friend Fred were taking care of all my travel expenses. I also had packed light, lightly enough to pick up a few things along the way, but not lightly enough to be able to buy books. So, I didn't. That didn't mean I didn't look, though.

Thirty minutes later and we walked out, me clutching the dictionary in my hand and Gawain looking annoyed. Again. Or, rather, still. Kate was feeding her paranoia by jumping at every sound that didn't come from one of us. Considering the number of people around, she jumped a lot. "Seriously," I said at last. "You're driving me crazy. Can't you just relax? You're going to get whiplash."

"No, she's right," Gawain said. "We are being followed."

I blinked. How would he know? He looked as calm as ever, meaning he wore a glower and practised scowling with his ramrod straight posture, and he hadn't been looking around. So how would he know we were being followed? I chalked it up to some supernatural sense that had come with his perpetual bad mood. Then, I looked around and tried to figure out who was following us.

Give me some credit; I was discreet. I may not have had the instincts of an FBI agent or the apparently supernatural senses of my client, but I had been doing this job for a while, and in that while, I had done some work for some pretty interesting characters. I'd picked up a few skills that you don't learn at university. At least, not the university I attended. I started taking an interest in the store fronts we passed, pretending to look at the merchandise while really catching the reflections of those around us. And, annoyingly, Kate and Gawain were right.

Whoever it was, was good. He stayed back about thirty feet and looked just like any other tourist. He had a phone that he pointed at various buildings and horizons, snapping pictures, many of them with us in the frame. He wore a hat and a sweater that had been made specifically with tourists in mind. He ambled along, the tail of a receipt sticking out of his trousers' pocket. The only difference between him and the other tourists around were his shoes. They were efficient. They were the type of shoe that you can wear in any climate or over any landscape and not feel bothered. The laces went high around the ankle and the soles were thick and durable, meant to spread his weight out over the entire shoe. And they had obviously seen use.

"Goodie," I said. "We're being followed."

"We should lose him," Kate said. "Split up and head back to the hotel via different routes."

"Splitting up is a bad idea," Gawain said immediately, tensing up. "We stick together."

"Splitting up is our safest option. There's only one of him and three of us. He can't tail all of us," Kate argued. "Meet back at the hotel in an hour."

"Do. Not. Separate," Gawain snarled. "This man,

these men, they are so much more dangerous than you realise. If we separate, all of us will be killed."

"I'm a huge fan of avoiding death," I put in, raising my hand like a school child. Considering my height, I think I only managed to look ridiculous. "There are other ways to get rid of him."

"We're not going to kill him," Kate hissed at me, a hand reaching towards her waistband where I suspected she was keeping a knife. The movement was not unnoticed by Gawain and he curled his lip in disdain.

"No," I said, "we're not. I have no plans to become a murderer, thank you very much. And it just warms the cockles of my heart to know that you think I am capable of such things, my dear Kate. I was thinking more along the lines of distract him and tie him up." I caught the look that both Kate and Gawain threw at me and heaved a dramatic sigh. "Not literally."

"What would you suggest?" Gawain growled, the sound something slightly more calm than what I would have expected considering the circumstances. "Push him into the harbour?"

"Tempting," I said, "but no. Come on, this way." I immediately spun around and marched back down the street we had just walked up, feeling slightly petulant and also amused as I watched our tail widen his eyes in surprise and do his best to look busy and unobtrusive. As soon as he started trying was when he failed. Now that I had seen him, too, I wasn't going to lose him.

Until I lost him. Ah, English, a language that never makes things easy.

We marched down the hill and into the centre of town where, despite the late hour, tour busses were still loading up and preparing to go out on excursions, perhaps to watch the northern lights or something. I found a bus that looked big enough and full enough and walked up to the bored looking tour guide. "Hi there," I said. "I have ten thousand Icelandic Kroners here if you'll do me a favour and let us get on, sit for a few minutes and get back off. And then leave more or less immediately."

The man looked at me like I was insane then looked at Gawain and Kate who stood at my shoulders. I did my best to look friendly and not to tower imposingly over the guy, which was rather difficult given that I did, actually, tower over the man. I'm not sure that it worked. But the offer of money was rather hard to resist, even given the relatively small amount, and he took it. The three of us traipsed onto the bus and waited for our tail to climb on with us. He was forced to buy a rather more expensive ticket, which had me feeling smug again. The tour guide then climbed on board, exchanged a few words with the driver and shot me a significant look. I took the cue, stood, and fairly dashed off the bus, my two travel companions close behind. The doors swung shut behind us and I watched as the bus started to drive off. In one of the windows, I saw the enraged features of our tail. I waved.

"Righty-ho, then," I said, turning back and walking towards the hotel. "Who's up for some tea?"

"That was pretty clever, Bailey," Kate admitted, though the compliment was obviously grudging, and she still checked over her shoulder every now and again to make sure we hadn't picked up another tag-along. "With your history, I figured you'd do something really complicated and outlandish. The tour bus was a good call."

"Why thank you, Mademoiselle Dupont," I said in my best French accent, which is really bad. "You underestimate me. Or overestimate me, I guess. If there's a simple way of getting rid of someone, I'll go for it. I am an inherently lazy person and I hate being forced to run or do things requiring effort. I mean, just the other day I was forced to run from these two thugs Octavius and Brutus and pfft... that was annoying. I should have told the Professor to add to my fee, but he isn't the sort of guy you just...I shouldn't be telling you this."

"Octavius and Brutus? The Professor?" Gawain asked, making it sound like the words were foreign to him. I sighed dramatically.

"You know, Shakespeare? They gang up and kill Julius Caesar because he's too high-and-mighty for them," I said. "Geez, you should get out more. Or, I suppose, stay in and read more."

"Yes, yes," Kate cut in. "You're very clever. Now stop preening and tell us what the next step is. Because this is *your* game, Bailey. I'm along for catastrophe management on behalf of the American government and Gawain here is along to monitor his investment. You're the one who actually has to find this thing."

"I don't need the reminder," I said, frowning. I was becoming increasingly annoyed with these two. Gawain was a superior know-it-all-except-when-he-didn't and Kate, well, she was being awfully pushy. "And I'm working on it, alright? From the file that you gave me, I've got a whole heck of a lot of information to slough through. Rumours abound."

"The sooner you find this book the better," Kate muttered. Gawain hunched his shoulders, an odd sight given his constantly straight posture, and grumbled something which sounded an awful lot like an agreement. "I don't like competition."

"You think I do?" I said. "Gee, how else am I meant to make my business survive if I don't beat out the competition? Not to mention I don't like having guns waved in my face or people tailing me. I like having all the information before I start a job, but in the not-so-rare event that doesn't happen, I like to be able to do things without having my life in danger."

"James and I did not think that the Leonum Temporis would be able to track us. They have obviously... adapted their methods," Gawain snapped. "They are only after you because you are looking for the Time Keeper. Once you deliver it to me, they will no longer be an issue."

"Fine. Whatever," I said. "I can deal with competition. I don't like it, but I can deal with it. The bit I have serious issue with is being kept in the dark. If there's anything else you haven't told me about this Time Keeper, your order or the Leonum Temporis, now would be the time to tell me."

Gawain frowned. It wasn't the sort of 'how dare you, you insolent little employee' frown that I normally got from him. It was a frown of consideration. He was actually going to tell me all of the information I hadn't been given. While I wasn't surprised that there were more details, I was slightly irked. It was irksome. His eyes flashed darkly and he shook his head before striding forwards and into the hotel. I tried to exchange a hopeless look with Kate but she didn't get the memo and sighed once before heading off to our shared room. I settled with looking at a young boy who was holding a toy and frowning at my height.

"Just because you're good at investigating, doesn't mean that you want to do it all the time," I told him. He blinked at me and called something over his shoulder in what sounded like German. I sighed and moved on. It just wasn't my day. I checked with the hotel clerk, just in case something had happened that I needed to know about. I haven't yet had anything happen that the clerk needs to tell me about, but I keep hoping. Then, I trudged up the stairs and turned to see Kate and Gawain standing in the doorway to our room.

"Hey, guys, um, can I just get in there? I have sleeping to attend to. Updating the logs, getting to some translating, too, but you know. Sleep," I said. Kate grabbed my shirt and pulled me forwards to look at the mess that was our room. "Ah," I said. "Now that would be a different sort of issue."

The hotel room was trashed. Well, actually, that's not quite true. The hotel room had been left in pristine condition. Our belongings, on the other hand, had been trashed. Kate and I had absolutely nothing left that was serviceable. Our clothing had been slashed, our toiletries had been emptied and thrown about, everything that we had left in the hotel room had been completely destroyed. Kate and I had left our larger packs in the room in anticipation of returning to the room that evening. I had been smart enough to take my notebook, phone, and computer with me, as well as my usual wallet and other necessary supplies in my satchel. Kate had only a small backpack with a water bottle, her identification and a few other knick-knacks.

"I thought this hotel was secure," Kate hissed, stepping forwards and picking up the sad remains of what looked to have been a silk negligee.

"I really hope that was yours," I said. "Because I definitely didn't pack anything quite that revealing."

"Can you be a little bit more offensive?" Kate snarled, rounding on me and glaring up into my face. I took a step back. Just because I'm tall doesn't mean that I am not cautious. Kate could kick my tail.

"I respond to problems with sarcasm," I said. "And snark."

"Well cut it out," Kate said.

"Would you two please be quiet," Gawain snapped. "We have a more pressing matter. Did you lose anything important? Any of the papers that James gave you, any of the speculation, any information about where we're going next?"

"I'm more interested in who could have done this," I said. "The guy tailing us wasn't the only one in on this. He's been behind us for most of the day. He can't have got in here and searched our things. He'd have needed help."

"We knew that the Leonum Temporis was working to search for this book," Gawain said. "Of course there was more than one person."

"Not my point," I answered, moving some of my shredded clothes off of the bed so I could sit down. "I mean that I only bought tickets for Iceland two days ago. We've only been here a day. And this was only a stopover on our way to Finland. So these people must have been following me since *before* we left the States. And I'd only got your job about twenty-four hours before leaving for Iceland. These people have moved very quickly. Abnormally quickly. Even if they'd been following you, Gawain, they'd have needed some heads up. These guys are connected. Way too connected."

"I keep telling you," Gawain said. "These people are very dangerous. Connected, as you say, and very dangerous."

"You're missing my point," I said again, my temper beginning to rise. "But I'm too tired to explain it to you and you won't bother to listen anyways. So."

Gawain growled and began to look rather murder-ous. He seemed to puff up like an offended cat, and began to bear down on me, though, considering how angry he always and how dangerous he had the potential to be, I would say lion over your typical domestic house cat. I stared him down, using my height against him. It's a lot harder to bear down on someone who is the same size as you are. Actually, I'm a lot skinnier and knobbier than he is but I think I could take him. Kate, not so much, but Gawain, probably.

"I am fed up with you," Gawain said, voice low, dangerous. "You have no right to insult my intelligence and my honour. I am doing the best I can to assist you, but *you* were the one hired to find the Time Keeper and if you cannot do that, then please let me know right now and we will turn around. James can find someone else. Anyone else."

"I didn't say I couldn't find the book," I retorted, putting an extra amount of snark in my voice. "I'm just making a note of how complicated things are beginning to look."

Gawain looked like he was going to say something else, then he swallowed his words and a myriad of angry-type emotions flashed over his face. He took a deep breath and forced himself to relax. Kate watched all of this without a word and one quietly raised eyebrow. I gave it a count of thirty before speaking.

"Have you checked your room?" I asked. The question came out rather more weary than I had intended and, to my surprise, Kate began to rub her neck, mirroring my feelings. Even Gawain began to look tired.

"I did," he said. "But there was nothing for the intruders to search." I nodded; he had been carrying his pack the whole day. It was small enough to not be a hassle to carry and I had figured that he was merely being paranoid. Now, he was cautious. Funny how things change. "Is there anything left that is still serviceable?"

"I think they left my unmentionables intact," I muttered—mostly to Kate—while I dug through the remains of my pack. Gawain made a sound in the back of his throat and pointedly looked away. Kate snorted and shook her head.

"Mine are all ruined," she said, loud enough that there was no question of Gawain's hearing. He shifted uncomfortably and made a point of watching the door. "But I do have some socks that are still in one piece. My case has been trashed."

"Mine, too. Look, Gawain," I said, standing. "I'm sorry to do this to you, but Kate and I are going to need to get new supplies tomorrow. I don't have the funds to do this on my own."

"I said I would pay all travel expenses, didn't I?" he snarled, rounding on me. Once again, I held my own, staring him straight in the eye. He held my gaze for a good ten seconds before turning away. "I appreciate the consideration," he muttered.

"No problem," I said. "I like getting paid, but I'm not cruel. Or greedy." Gawain snorted and I shrugged. "Believe me, don't believe me, but I'm not in the business of lying. Oh, one more thing. Dupont and I shouldn't stay here tonight. If our intruder comes back, we should stick together. It's a lot more difficult to get rid of three people than it is two."

"I'll sleep on the floor," Gawain said, sounding absolutely thrilled by the proposition. Kate and I salvaged as much as we could then walked down the hall to Gawain's room. It was basically the same as ours but much cleaner and there was only one bed. I made a call to the clerk, complained about the mess in our room in the hope that they would panic and cough up the funds to replace our belongings, though I doubted it. Then, just about as exhausted as I could be after a day of arguing and traipsing around trying to get information out of people who were rather opposed to giving out information, I kicked my shoes off, brushed my teeth with the top-half of my toothbrush and fell into bed.

"If you kick me," Kate said groggily, "I'm buying a gun and shooting you."

"Good to know," I said, moving as close to the edge of the bed as I could. The bed wasn't all that big, meant for use by a couple not two people with an aversion to one another. Especially not when one of those people was as tall as I was. Kate snuggled into the bed, pulling the covers around her and leaving me with a scrap of blanket and sheet. Gawain was already asleep on the floor, a pillow propped up beneath his head and a blanket wrapped around his shoulders. I sighed, rubbed my eyes and did my best to get to sleep.

I had a fairly fitful night, waking and jumping at

every sound and freezing my toes off while Kate and Gawain kept warm with Icelandic wool blankets. Eventually, somewhere around four in the morning, I gave up and crawled out of bed. I made myself generally presentable with a shower and a finger-combing of my hair. I grabbed the leather journal and the Icelandic dictionary then slung my satchel over my shoulder and went down to the hotel bar in the hopes that I could get a very large cup of coffee.

"Coffee," I begged the weary looking bartender. He pulled out an average-sized mug and I shook my head. "No, no, larger than that. And lots of sugar. With cream." The man looked at me before shaking his head very subtly and making the drink to my specifications. He handed me the mug and I handed over the money then took the coffee to a table. I looked around, making sure that there were no cameras looking over my shoulder. Then, I sat with my back to a corner and facing the door, just so that no one could sneak up on me.

"Great," I muttered to myself. "I'm inheriting Gawain's paranoia." The bartender raised his eyebrows in my general direction and pretended to be very busy with wiping down the bar. Again. I ignored him and opened the notebook I had filled with the information given to me on the Time Keeper. I narrowed down the rumour centring in Iceland and put a tick next to the name Vilhjallmasson. I noted the information received and added an entry about the Leonum Temporis, making a note that it had been left out of the initial information provided. Once that was done, and my coffee had been given time to do its magic, I pulled the dictionary towards me and began the very painstaking business of translating.

Let me give you a little professional advice: if you ever have to translate a handwritten journal that's about a century old and you don't know the language, give it to someone else. It took me an hour just to get through the first page. I had to look up every word, write out each "translated" sentence, figure out the grammatical inconsistencies and then change it into actual, understandable English. Of course, even with that being done, it was still choppy and unprofessional. I was sorely tempted to foist the journal onto a professor at the University, or even the bartender who spoke Icelandic. I knew I couldn't, not with Gawain and the Lions of Time looking over my shoulder. With that thought, I did a quick check around the room to make sure that no one could actually be looking over my shoulder. There was a woman sitting at a table on the far side of the room that I didn't remember being there before, but otherwise it was clear.

I glanced at the clock, looked at the piddly amount of work that I had completed and sighed in annoyance. I had only figured out that the woman's name was Anja and that, at the time she started the journal, she was eighteen, engaged to a man from another village and had two younger brothers. There was no mention of the Chronometreur or Time Keeper or even creepy guys hanging around with an obvious "I'm going to hurt you" air. I needed a different strategy. I turned to the dictionary, looked up the words for Time Keeper. I didn't have a French dictionary, so it would have to do. Then, I began skimming the journal.

I stopped after three pages, looking at the words written across the top. Then, I looked at my notebook and saw exactly what I had thought I would find. "This doesn't make any sense," I muttered.

Chapter 5
In Which I Flee the Country

"What doesn't make sense?" Gawain asked, sitting across from me and startling about fifty years of my life out of me. I jumped, violently, upsetting my now-empty coffee mug and staring at him as if he had tried to kill me. Given the hour of the morning and the fact that he showed up just as I was discovering something, I shouldn't have been all that surprised. Of course that's when he would appear. He replied to my panic with a frown and a raised eyebrow.

"Are you *trying* to kill me?" I demanded. Gawain blinked pointedly and sipped at the tea that he had carried over. There was a good five second pause before anything happened and I didn't move, still trying to calm my racing heart.

"Of course not. That's what the Leonum Temporis are for," he said in a low voice. I narrowed my eyes. Was it just me or was that an actual attempt at humour? As far as I knew, Gawain didn't have a sense of humour. At all. He hadn't laughed or cracked a smile in the entirety of our acquaintance (granted, I had argued with him for most of that, but still) and here he was, making a joke.

"Since when are you funny?" I snapped, righting my empty mug and putting my notes in order. Don't be fooled. It was all a front to give myself time to get my panic under control. More than anything, more, even, than detectives and law enforcement, I hate people sneaking up on me. It's just about the meanest thing you can do, short of shooting me. But at least with shooting, it's hard to sneak about. Anyways. "That was a joke, right? Or are you resorting to making overt threats against me in the knowledge that I can do nothing to stop you because I am under contract?"

"If I wanted to kill you, I would hardly resort to trickery to do so," Gawain replied, sounding calmer than I had ever heard him. Maybe he was a morning person and just got grumpier as the day progressed. Who knew? "I came down here because you were not in the room."

"Couldn't sleep," I defended instantly. "Dupont has a bad habit of stealing the covers and I don't tend to get a good night's sleep when the thought of people digging through my things keeps running around my head. So I figured I'd get some work done."

"That was my conclusion as well." Gawain nodded to my notes. "Hence why I am here. We should not split up."

"Says the guy who left Dupont alone in the hotel room. Asleep, I might add," I said. The concern Gawain was showing was strange and unnatural and I didn't like it. I'm a huge fan of people behaving as they have previously behaved. When they go changing on me, I start thinking "Conspiracy! Conspiracy!"

"The French woman is not under my employ," Gawain replied. I paused, trying to come up with a smart retort and failing. Curse him and his logic. Gawain watched me in silence, sipping at his tea and behaving, for all the world, as if he had always been generally pleasant to me. Or, at least not biting my head off.

"Touché," I said. "Though, I can take care of myself. But, as you're going to argue with that point and I'm running on about three hours of sleep right now, I'll concede the point." Gawain smirked and shook his head.

"I am not quite as argumentative and cruel as you seem to believe, Ms Duane," he said. I snorted in reply and a touch of anger flashed over his features. "I am not used to working under such circumstances as I find myself in and I did not want to be on this job in the first place. James insisted."

"Couldn't you argue back? I mean, come on. Document retrieval seems a bit... demeaning," I said. "I'm happy to do it, but that's because I'm okay with doing the demeaning, undemanding work that people want to hire out."

"I am, as you would say, under contract," Gawain said.

I furrowed my brows and considered that. From the start, I had been assuming that Fred Astaire and Gawain were partners, with Fred being the senior partner and Gawain the junior. But if he was just another employee, that would mean the organisation behind this job was much, much more complicated than I had previously assumed.

Gawain seemed to sense my confusion and mistrust because he began clarifying, willingly offering information for the first time since I'd known him. "My working relationship with James is beneficial to us both, but it is a temporary measure. I was hired under the expectation that I work out... some issues."

That explained so much.

"I think you may have to work on that a bit more," I muttered, trying to get back to our familiar and comfortable state of biting each other's head off. Sure, it was much easier dealing with Gawain when he was not yelling, but it was odd. It was as though he were actually a decent person and that meant I needed to detach myself. I did not want to end up being friends with this guy. Or any of my clients, really. It was on my list of "things not to do in this business" that I had in a drawer back at my office.

Gawain curled his lip in annoyance but didn't say anything, instead sipping his tea to hide the fact that he had suddenly grown very tense. "What exactly doesn't make sense?" he asked after a moment. I blinked in confusion. "When I came down, you said something doesn't make sense. What is it?"

"Ah, now you're striking on something interesting," I answered. I looked around again to make sure that we weren't being spied upon. There was only the woman and the exhausted looking bartender. I leaned in closer and turned the journal so Gawain could read it. "Look at that," I said, pointing.

"The date," he said flatly. "What about it?"

"Read it out," I said. Gawain grumbled, but did as I asked.

"The seventeenth of September 1862. I don't see what the problem is," Gawain said. "We knew this journal was over a century old. How is this relevant to finding the--"

"Let's try *not* to say that out loud, just in case people are listening in, please," I snapped. For once, I was the more cautious one, but Gawain conceded. Maybe being targeted by a very large, very old, very dangerous organisation had something to do with it. Or it could be the fact that I was running on next to no sleep. Yeah, let's go with that. "What's interesting, Sir Gawain," I growled, "is that the manuscript was in the hands of a private collector in *Spain* in 1862. Very publicly in the hands of the collector. But that's not the only discrepancy. Look! I thought that this was just a mistake, but the manuscript is said to have been in Egypt and in China simultaneously, during the eighteenth century. Now, is there any way that the information James gave me is false? No? I didn't think so. Then you have a serious problem."

"And what would that be," Gawain asked, suddenly looking pale. He finished off his tea with a fierce jerk of his head and had the look of a man who wanted something quite a lot stronger than tea. He set the mug on the table very carefully, very precisely.

"You have two manuscripts floating around," I said. He looked at me and I saw a flicker of relief on his features, which could mean only one thing: he knew that to be inaccurate. And if I was wrong, then the only other explanation I had come up with must be the truth. So saith Sherlock Holmes and so say I. When you take away all other possibilities, the only thing that remains, however improbable, must be the truth. "If that's not the case—and I'm still not convinced it isn't. If Madeline didn't write two copies of this book, then someone is passing around forgeries. Very good forgeries. And your opposing organisation would not appear to want any copies, fake or otherwise, to be floating around."

Gawain looked around, taking a page from my book of paranoia. Then, he turned back to me and made a big show of arranging his now empty mug exactly next to mine. "I know for a fact that there are no forgeries of the manuscript."

"You can't know that," I snarled in reply. I was tired of being fed false information. I was never a huge fan of being kept in the dark which, I suppose, is why I got into the business of getting into other people's business. But this stuff with Gawain, it was beyond annoying. I was being misled at every turn and if I didn't start getting some real answers, soon, I was going to have something more than words to say to my employer. "There is no possible way that you can know that. Unless you've been with the manuscript at every point in history, which is impossible by the way, then you can't know that."

"I can," Gawain snapped in reply. Our truce from earlier, even the semi-apology from a few minutes ago, that was all null and void. I opened my mouth to reply and Gawain raised a hand, effectively cutting me off. "I can assure you that there are no copies of the manuscript and that there are no forgeries," he said, making a visible effort to be calm. I frowned and raised my eyebrows. Gawain sighed and looked me straight in the eye. "Can you just trust me on this?"

"I don't know how I'm meant to do that," I answered, my voice quiet and barely carrying the few inches between us. "You haven't really given much basis for trust, you know."

Gawain struggled with silence for a few moments, looking as though he desperately wanted to say something, to tell me just what the dickens was going on. He swallowed whatever he had been about to say and shook his head instead. "I can't..."

"Can't what?" I asked. He shook his head once more and I glared. I gathered my notes together and closed the notebook with a *snap*. The leather journal and dictionary followed the notebook into my satchel and I stood. "Fine. Well, you hired me to do this job, Gawain, so I'm going to do it. But don't expect any favours from me. And stop trying to look pitiful to gain my sympathies. It won't get you anywhere."

"Won't get who where?" Kate asked, choosing that moment to waltz into the dining area. She looked well-rested and even though she was wearing the same clothes as the day before, she exuded an air of cleanliness and confidence. I wanted to stalk over to her and rub my hands over her hair until it was as messy and annoying as mine felt. The shower earlier hadn't done much to clear my head or make me feel any better. Compared to the FBI agent, I was the abominable snowman. (Read: grumpy and unkempt and mostly made up of roars and cold air.)

"Sleep well?" I jabbed at her. She raised her eyebrows and, without a trace of shame, smiled.

"I did, thank you. I take it you didn't?" she purred, walking over to the bartender. He dutifully served her a cup of coffee and she smiled her way into his good graces. Curses on curvy women who have been trained to make full use of their looks and feminine wiles. The best training I had received was in the theatre department at one of the public schools I attended. When I was twelve. And boys still had cooties.

"You're cruel," I said. "Drink up. We leave for the airport in twenty minutes."

"What?" Gawain and Kate said simultaneously. I shifted my satchel on my shoulder and put my nose in the air.

"Oh, didn't I tell you? I cancelled our flight to Finland. We're going to Egypt. And the flight leaves in two and a half hours. So, we leave for Keflavik airport in, hmm, seventeen minutes to be precise. Don't forget to pack your toothbrush," I sang. All of my belongings that hadn't been destroyed were in the satchel on my shoulder. I had received a lump sum from the hotel in lieu of a formal apology for letting our belongings get trashed. I had considered handing it over to Gawain and changed my mind when he started being very difficult. So I would exchange it for Egyptian pounds and purchase the necessary supplies in Cairo.

"You know," I heard Kate say as I stalked out of the bar area. "I think she's annoyed at us."

"She's been annoyed with me since I met her. What's your excuse?" Gawain grumbled in reply. Kate chuckled darkly and said something in response which I didn't quite catch, considering I was half-way to the lobby. It might have been 'she's just like that' or 'her tabby cat.' I can't be sure, as we had both been involved in a situation involving a very mangy tabby cat and a roll of aluminium foil. That was a weird day.

Exactly seventeen-and-three-quarters minutes later, Kate, Gawain and I traipsed onto the bus to the airport. Gawain had paid and I had heard the shouting match from outside. Apparently, Sir Knight had objected to paying for a room that had been broken into and not slept in. The hotel claimed that they had already paid me a sum as recompense for supplies, but that didn't seem to appease Gawain. The shouting match was ferocious. He won. Then, he cornered me on the bus, making me sit next to the window and demanding to know why I hadn't told him about the payment.

"Because you were being an insufferable know-it-all-and-won't-tell-you this morning," I said. "And because there's no point in giving it to you as Kate and I will be using it to buy clothing and supplies."

"Don't you think it would have been, oh I don't know, *courteous* to let me know that the hotel had already paid you?" Gawain snarled. I shrugged.

"Courteous is as courteous does," I said. "You will get courtesy when I get some. Tell me what's going on."

"I can't," Gawain hissed while Kate turned to us from across the aisle, looking very interested. I shrugged and looked out the window at the barren, mysterious landscape that flashed past us. We sat the rest of the trip in silence.

Keflavik airport was surprisingly busy given how early it was. We managed to get all of our tickets and belongings sorted out without too much difficulty and then made our way through security and to the gate. After the incident with the hotel, none of us were willing to give up our bags, so we carried them with us. Then, we waited some ten minutes before boarding started and half-an-hour after that, we were in the air and on our way.

Remember how I said that I don't do any work on planes? Well, disregard that. See, ten minutes into the flight, I got a prickly feeling on the back of my neck. It was the kind that you get when you've been pointedly not stared at but very carefully observed for a period of time. That was the kind that only came from professionals. I was sitting in the aisle seat—Kate and Gawain had stopped arguing enough that I could allow them to sit together for the sake of my legs—so it wasn't too difficult for me to start rubbernecking around and seeing what sort of professionals I could spot.

I spotted Steve. Er, Jon, whom I called Steve. The guy who worked for the Professor or Mr Houtman. The guy whose illegal un-cut diamonds I retrieved. Yeah... that guy. I turned back to face forwards in my seat, hoping that Steve hadn't seen me looking at him. "Well, bother," I said.

"What is it this time?" Kate asked. She was sitting in the middle to save herself from listening Gawain and I argue as we had been doing on the way to the airport and the entirety of the day before. That and I think she lost a coin toss for the window seat, though, considering she was quite a bit shorter than Gawain or myself, she should have given it up anyways.

"Um... you know that guy that you wanted me to testify against in exchange for immunity for crimes that you could never actually prove I committed?" I said. Kate frowned and gave a heated glare to the tray table in front of her.

"There have been a few, Bailey," she said. "Why don't you be a little more specific?"

"Think smuggling," I said, trying to be helpful. I knew that even though we were out of the States, she was still an FBI agent and still trying to get me to either incriminate myself or give up information on my previous clients so that she could arrest them. I wasn't going to oblige her (hopefully).

"Houtman. Charles Houtman. That the guy?" Kate asked, enunciating her words. I nodded.

"Right, that's the one. Well, his bodyguard is sitting three rows behind us doing his best not to make it obvious that he's watching us. Me. Watching me. I can't be certain, but I think that the Professor—that's Houtman to you—is sitting with him. I couldn't see behind that chairs without leaning completely out of my seat and I don't want to get on the bad side of Steve there," I said.

"Steve?" Kate asked. She was looking very interested and I think my words had even roused Gawain from his feigned sleep because he was shifting in his seat as though prepared to look around, though he wouldn't be able to do much from the window.

"Real name Jon something-or-other," I said. "I never caught the last name. But, I would feel pretty confident in hazarding a guess that he's following us. Me. Us. Don't know. But he's probably after the manuscript." This last part was directed at Gawain and his gaze flashed like steel when he comprehended what I had said. Not that shiny stainless steel, either, but the kind that swords are made out of that have been used in battle a few times but kept up and sharpened because they are meant to wield death.

"Are you sure? Could be that you just cheated him

out of some product," Kate said. I recalled the last time I had seen the Professor and shuddered. He had looked so cosy in his fire-lit flat, the Queen Anne décor lending an old and dangerous tone to the room. With his first edition books and that clever smile, there was no doubt in my mind.

"Yeah," I said. "I'm sure. There's no way I'd risk cheating that man. He's dangerous."

"Which is why we've been trying to get you to—"

"You don't understand me, Dupont. He's dangerous. Think of all those people that you want to get your hands on but wouldn't ever dare to approach for fear they would reach back and bite your heads off. Then add in the intelligence of a master chess player and someone with absolutely no reserve. Then you might, *might*, be able to grasp just how dangerous the Professor actually is," I said, speaking in an undertone so that no one else would be able to hear me over the roar of the engines. Kate blinked and Gawain stilled his movements to stare at me. He snorted and shook his head.

"He is nowhere near as dangerous as Leonum Temporis," Gawain said. I shook my head.

"Buster, from what I've seen of your Lions, they've got nothing on the Professor. Heck, for all I know, he could be leading the charge and your Leonum Temporis guys are just piggybacked along. We have to lose this guy. When we land to change planes in Glasgow, we are losing this man. I don't care how," I said. Kate shoved an elbow in my ribs and I shrugged. "Ow.

And seriously, Dupont. I don't care if you lock me up for this. I want him gone."

"How do you plan on doing that?" Gawain hissed, narrowing his eyes as one of the flight attendants walked past, wearing her fake smile and asking about drinks. I ordered some tonic water to soothe my nerves and was not entirely surprised when Kate ordered a vodka and orange juice. Gawain ignored the flight attendant.

"Well," I said, thinking furiously. "How do you two feel about boats?"

"I don't know what you mean," Kate said, frowning. Gawain actually looked slightly more calm than she did, which I found surprising. After all, wouldn't expediency be a boon in this game? Maybe he had my problems with flying (minus the cats and angry teens and so forth).

"Think tramp steamers," I answered. "Because I think I'm going to get us kicked out of the airport again."

"You don't have access to chickens," Gawain pointed out. I pinched the bridge of my nose and did my best to remain calm. Did he really think me that incapable?

"I don't need chickens to cause a ruckus. It just so happened that that particular job involved chickens. I am perfectly capable of getting us kicked out of the airport without resorting to throwing live birds at the security. Unless you two can think of something else to get rid of these two tag-alongs, then we're going to have to give up on flying to Egypt," I said. "I know some guys in Glasgow that could get us on a ship no problem."

"Couldn't we just lose them in Cairo?" Kate grumbled. "The sooner we can get this job over with, the better. I have mounds of paperwork to do back in the States."

"You're welcome to leave anytime you wish," Gawain snapped back. "I am not employing you to come along with. Things would be easier with two of us."

"I've been charged with not leaving Bailey here alone in a foreign country. Any foreign country," Kate growled. "So whether you like it or not, I'm stuck with her."

I held up my hands as a desperate attempt for peace. "We're putting up with you, Dupont. But this job is going to take as long as it's going to take. There's nothing I can do if the Professor and Steve want to follow us onto the plane. I'm not about to stage a coup and force the flight attendants to open the door so we can shove them out." Kate looked as though she wanted to argue but kept her mouth shut. She had probably learned that I wasn't the best person to argue with; I tended to be more stubborn and annoying than just about everyone and so I often won. Instead, she sank into the seat and took her drink from the flight attendant. I took a sip of my own tonic water and the three of us sat in silence for a few minutes.

I could feel the non-staring of Steve very acutely

now, and it was getting worse by the minute. The temptation to do something about it sooner rather than later was growing. I took another sip of the tonic water and told myself that it was only two hours to Glasgow. I could manage. I had to manage.

Once again, the image of the Professor's smiling filled my head and I shuddered. I was happy to work for him and take his money, but now I was on the other end of things. Now I was being targeted and he wasn't sending someone like me after Gawain, Kate and I. He was coming personally. I didn't know whether I should be flattered or terrified. I went with a mix of both. I needed a distraction.

My eyes slipped to where Kate was drowning the last of her vodka and orange juice. She set her face in a grimace and bared her teeth in a wolfish snarl.

"Oh, and by the way, there's no point in following me around the UK. I'm a citizen there. I have rights."

"Stuff it," Kate said. I shrugged and did my best to relax. Two hours was going to take forever.

Chapter 6
In Which I Meet Some Old Friends

Glasgow. Ah, how I love Glasgow. Well, just about all of Great Britain is great, if you ask me, apart from a very strange alleyway in Reading where I once... never mind, you don't need to know that. Glasgow has rain and culture and tea; what more could a person ask for? I was in the middle of expounding on all of the wonders of Scotland and specific traits which Glasgow held when Kate thwacked me over the head.

"Ow," I said, hunching my shoulders slightly to go through the plane door. I'm not actually *that* tall, but I feel perilously close to knocking my head on the frame each time I walk through, so I bend anyways. "What did you do that for?"

Gawain made a show of rolling his eyes. He was really checking up on our tail. I swallowed nervously. My hope of it being only Steve that had been sent after us was dashed into the ground when the Professor himself stepped into the line of people trying to file off the plane. He was discreet, blending in with just about every other person there, so I pretended I didn't notice him and hoped that would be enough to make my plan work.

"If you like the UK all that much, why is your *business* in the States? For that matter, why did you attend an American University?" Kate asked, her tone sharp. Her accent was standing out in this land of Scottish burrs and English murmurs. Perfect.

"Because I am enterprising. And there are a few too few calls for my line of work among the independent and capable Brits," I said. "That and Yale gave me a scholarship."

"So you're saying that you work in the States because Americans are lazy and incapable of doing anything for themselves?" Kate asked. This time, the question wasn't a ruse. She was honestly curious and honestly looking quite annoyed. I nodded, fully aware of the peril that I was in. "I've had just about enough of your judgemental attitude," she snarled, pushing me forwards through the walkway. Gawain tagged along behind, looking just about as calm as can be while still wearing his habitual scowl.

"Oi," I grumbled, "I'm not on American soil. You can't push me around like that."

"Watch me," Kate hissed, shoving me backwards. At this point, the airport security was getting very interested in what was going on. They began to move closer, speaking into their radios and looking all sorts of shifty. I reminded myself that I was getting paid and that I would much rather be thrown out of the airport than dead. Then, I stepped up to Kate and glared down at her.

"Look here, Dupont," I said, "If you think you can just push me about because you're some sort of 'authority' back in the States, you've got another thing coming. So why don't you go back to your desk and your paperwork and leave the real work to people who are better suited for investigating, okay?" I jabbed my finger into her chest as I said this and, even though she was fully aware that I was playing a ruse, I could see the flash of shock and pain in Kate's eyes. Then, they became like steel and I knew that what was coming next wasn't going to be faked at all. It was going to hurt.

Kate shifted her stance and in a fraction of a second, sent her fist flying at my jaw. It hit with a loud crack that registered before the pain. I stumbled backwards, straight into the unwilling arms of Gawain. My vision went spotty for a few seconds and my face felt as though it was on fire. Apparently teaching people how to hit was in the FBI training course. Kate had, obviously, passed with flying colours. I rubbed my jaw experimentally and as I straightened up, the three of us were surrounded by security. Just as planned.

"Ma'am," the leader of the security said. If he wasn't the leader, then he was taking rather a risk by stepping up. Then again, none of his team seemed to want to get involved. "I think you need to come with us."

"I work for the United States Federal Bureau of Investigation," Kate hissed, pulling out her badge and flashing it about impressively. "I'm not going anywhere with you until she is arrested and thrown in the darkest jail that you Brits have."

"What has she done?" the security man asked, reaching for a collapsable bully stick at his belt. I tensed and felt Gawain tighten his grip on my shoulder. Kate needed to make her act not quite so convincing. The last thing I needed was a beating from Glaswegians. The Scottish are a lovely people, one of my favourites in fact, but you don't mess with them. I then realised that Gawain was still holding onto me. I shifted and pulled away and he didn't try to stop me. I guess we were both too busy watching the show to recall our situation. In another circumstance, that would have been fatal.

"Done?" Kate asked incredulously. "I'm sure she's done all sorts of things. But we can't find any hard evidence, so I'm stuck with following her around the world on a stupid job of hers so I can catch her when she slips up and make sure that she doesn't go vanishing in France or wherever. I don't really care what she's done, I just want her gone."

"Ma'am, I really think you should come with me," the security man said, holding out his hand insistently. Kate said something very rude and then things went along quite nicely. In less than an hour, with absolutely no sign of our tail, Gawain, Kate and I were thrown onto our rear ends on the curb outside the airport, banned for the next two months.

"Great acting, Dupont," I grinned, throwing my hand out for a taxi. The driver ignored me and I grumbled in annoyance. Something about me must make me invisible to taxi drivers, because Gawain held out his hand and had no less than two cars stopping for him. "How do you do that?" I asked as we clambered into the vehicle. Gawain shrugged.

"Acting?" Kate muttered once we were on our way. "I have no idea what you're talking about."

Wince. Well, it was my fault for jabbing below her belt. And it wasn't like the two of us actually got along in general. Every encounter I had with Katelyn Dupont prior to this job was her throwing me in handcuffs after her picking me up in what was possibly a very incriminating situation. None of the evidence panned out and my stories were rock-solid. It didn't stop the Bureau from flagging me as a target. Look where that had landed me: I try to go out of the country on what was meant to be a simple document retrieval job and I have my own personal FBI noose around my neck. So what if I lashed out a bit?

"The shipping yards," I said to the taxi driver, pointedly ignoring the tension that Kate had created. It was partly my fault, but I wasn't in the mood to argue with her. Especially not after she had hit me quite squarely across the jaw. I could already feel a bruise forming.

"Are you sure this person is going to be there?"

Gawain asked. I nodded and clutched my leather satchel closer.

"Oh, yeah. Ask anyone," I said. The driver shifted at this and I demonstrated my point. "Hey, does Samir Ozolonish still run freighters out of the ports?"

"Ozolonish? Oh, certainly. He's got quite the reputation at the pubs in the area and he's been known to throw a good party," the driver chuckled. I raised my eyebrows pointedly at Gawain and he shrugged. The driver then proceeded to go into a monologue about Samir Ozolonish until we got to the shipping yards. Gawain paid the man and Kate and I walked to the entrance gate. I waved to one of the guards and sauntered over.

"Do you have an appointment?" the man asked with a look at my single bag and rather rag-tag appearance (getting hit probably didn't help).

"Not exactly," I said. The guard tensed and I held up my hand. "Relax. Just tell Samir Ozolonish that the stork he used to run around London with is here to see him. Oh, and that he still owes me twenty pounds. Plus interest."

For that, I got an incredulous look from the guard. He stared at me for a good five seconds to make sure that I was serious. I waved my hand at him and he curled his lip before lifting his radio and speaking into it in a murmuring voice, his eyes fixed suspiciously on me. We stood there for fifteen seconds, the guard quite obviously blocking my way, I demanding entrance. It was quiet enough that we could hear the sound of the ocean from the other side of the shipping yards. Gawain shifted behind me and I could just imagine Kate looking around and expecting an ambush. Then, startling all of us but me, as I had known it was coming, came the sound of the radio crackling to life.

I could barely understand what was said, but there was little doubt that it was an order to let us in. The guard raised his eyebrows and asked it the person on the other end of the radio was sure. The distorted voice came quicker this time, sharper and more distinct. The guard nodded and pushed the button that would open the gates and let us in, not meeting my gaze. "Mr Ozolonish is expecting you. Just follow this path to the right and you'll come on the offices in a couple of minutes. Good day."

"Thank you," I said primly and stepped through the gates. Gawain and Kate followed close behind me. I heard the clang of the gates swinging shut as we entered the yards and did my best not to shudder. It was a sound of being trapped and I didn't much appreciate it. I've had bad experiences in shipping yards and I didn't much care to return. Needs must. The three of us followed the path the guard had set us on and I hunched my shoulders, feeling the skeletons of old ships and large containers looming up around me as if caving in.

"What is it?" Gawain asked in an undertone. He must have picked up on my distress and was looking about for whatever ghosts might be lying around the shipping yards. I shook my head.

"I don't like these places. Ships, sure. Boats, fine. Ports, marinas, whatever. But shipping yards, no thank you," I grumbled under my breath. Gawain furrowed his brows and looked at me in surprise.

"Then why are you here?" he asked. "Surely there are other ways to get to Cairo."

"Yeah, but this is safe. As safe as can be when trying to run from an international organisation with a desire to kill me or, at the very least, seriously injure me." I spotted the offices and hurried forwards. "Come on, let's go. I want to get out of the open."

Gawain muttered something to Kate and she muttered something back. I couldn't catch what was said, but I didn't especially like the unease that laced their voices. I opened the door to the offices and did my very best to ignore them. After a few seconds, that became much easier because I was pulled into the office. A man with more wiry strength in his arms than sheer physical force wrapped an arm around my neck and pulled me close, putting me in a half-nelson hold. I reacted instinctively and jabbed my elbow into his side, using my outside arm to loosen the hold and then I buckled his knee, dropping him to the floor.

As I turned to face my attacker, I was met with breathless laughing, the kind that was whole-hearted and absolutely free by nature. I straightened and tugged at the hem of my shirt—which, by the way, I had been wearing since very early the day before. "Could you *be* more idiotic?" I demanded.

Samir Ozolonish took a good, long look at my

expression and started laughing even harder. I scowled in reply, taking a page from Gawain's book. Samir was a medium-sized man with dark golden skin despite living permanently in a Scottish climate. He had that thick, dark hair that was signature of people of Middle Eastern descent and had the chiselled features that attracted all sorts of attention, most of it feminine. I know that he hid a great number of scars and tattoos under the neat black sweater and jeans he wore and the smirk he habitually wore was a mask for danger.

I opened my mouth to chastise him more when I felt Gawain step closer to my shoulder, Kate not far behind him. Immediately, Samir stopped laughing and jumped to his feet, his sense that he could be in danger as impeccable as ever. "Goodness, Bailey, I didn't realise you were so touchy," Samir said in a perfectly cultured Oxfordian accent.

"Introductions?" Gawain growled in my ear. I shrugged my shoulder in annoyance and Samir raised an eyebrow ever-so-slightly. I took a deliberate step away from both parties, distancing myself from any possible altercation that could arise from this situation.

"Right. Gawain, this is Carlos. Carlos, Gawain. Oh, and Katelyn Dupont," I said, indicating each in turn. Samir raised both his eyebrows at the two names and Gawain growled something unintelligible. "I'm currently working for Gawain here and Dupont is my watchdog."

"Since when have you needed a watchdog?" Samir asked, appraising both of my companions expertly.

"Since the world decided that I needed to be watched," I said, making him chuckle again. Samir held out his hand to Gawain, who waited half a beat longer than was strictly polite and returned the shake.

"Samir Ozolonish," the man said, nodding his head. "The lovely Bailey here is convinced that the entire world needs to be rewritten into her nicknames."

"She does at that," Gawain said, not giving his real name, which did not go unnoticed by Samir. I've come to the realisation that the people I spend my time with are far more dangerous than the average citizen. I think I need to re-think my life choices. "Where does yours come from?"

"The Robert Ludlum novels. Carlos is an assassin against which the protagonist is pitted. Have you read them?" Samir said. Gawain shook his head, looking around at the offices as he did so, taking in all of the exits and layout of the furniture. Or so I imagine. I mean, for all I knew, he could be admiring the décor, or shaking off a head-ache, but I rather thought he was taking the world in.

"I can't say that I have," Gawain said.

"And you, oh watchdog," Samir said, bowing his head to Kate even as he took in her curves and sharp eyes. "Where does your nickname come from?"

"It's not a nickname," Kate said, barely suppressing a snarl. Samir took a step backwards in surprise and looked at me as if I had suddenly sprouted two heads. Who knows, maybe I had. Kate stood for a few moments, taking in the staring as if she had been trained to it. Then, taking into consideration her actual training (meaning staying behind the scenes and keeping unnoticed), she started getting annoyed. "Enough. Can we just get on with this?"

"Get on with what?" Samir asked. He folded his arms very carefully and precisely and looked at me. I shrugged and fiddled with my shirt again, remembering all the times back in my London days that we had got into trouble following one of Samir's looks. One time, the two of us had been lounging in a park and it started raining. Samir thought it would be entertaining to go and find a nice flat with a fire to cosy up in while we waited out the rain. Of course, the flat he had chosen belonged to a civil servant on holiday. When Samir's father got the notice of that little event, he nearly had out heads. Samir talked us out of any trouble and we got off with apologising to the man, who looked shifty enough that he couldn't *just* be a civil servant. Then, there was the time with the brawl in the pub. Actually, there were many pub brawls.

Anyways.

"We need to get to Cairo, preferably inconspicuously and rather unofficially. Just so that our names don't appear on the register for a couple of days," I said. "I was thinking tramp steamer."

"You want to get a head start," Samir said. I shrugged, avoiding saying the obvious. The fewer people that knew of our plans, the better. And, no matter that I knew Samir very well, I wasn't about to trust him with something of this nature. He shook his head good-naturedly. "That's just like you, Bailey. Always wanting to get ahead of the game, always playing with a different set of rules."

I shrugged. "What can I say? I'm not good with conventionalities."

Samir laughed outright at this. Then, his expression turned serious. "I have a ship leaving for Alexandria in a few hours. I can't get you any closer than that by ship, but I know a few people in that area and I can tell the captain to introduce you."

"Alexandria is fine," I said. "We can make our way from there." Gawain breathed something impossible to make out and I did my best to ignore the nagging feeling that he thought I wasn't doing things properly. Kate took a step closer to Gawain and shifted her grasp on her bag. Gawain wasn't the only one uneasy with the situation. "Look, Carlos, I know this is all very sudden and such, but—"

"Bailey, I haven't heard from you in years. I never expected to. But we've been through too many things to be enemies now," Samir said. His words weren't really meant for everyone to hear, but there also weren't going to be many other opportunities to say them. I would make sure of that. "You blame me for what happened. But you also came to me for help. That shows a degree of trust, right?"

I wrapped a hand around the strap of my satchel and let it rest as casually as I could. Then, taking a deep breath, I looked at the ceiling. "Do you know why I call you Carlos?"

"Admiration for my obvious cunning," Samir said, a smile behind the words. It vanished when I lowered my gaze from the ceiling to his eyes. He set his expression in a neutral position and waited, outwardly patient. I knew better.

"I call you Carlos because I've seen you do all manner of dangerous things for the sake of money and furthering your own career. We ran around London and a good part of Europe for sport as children while your father met officials for various conferences and hush-hush sort of events. But you were doing a lot more than running around; you were educating yourself on the workings of the underworld. Don't bother giving me that look, alright? I've seen you do enough criminal acts to send you away for a very long time," I said. "And, yeah, I blamed you for a long time for what happened. I don't know if coming here means that I've forgiven you, though. I'm still working on that."

"I will hope that it has happened," Samir said, his voice matching his neutral expression. "Because we have been friends a very long time."

"Right," I said, not looking away. "*That's* what we were." Samir recoiled as if I'd hit him with my best right-hook. Then, he growled out a monosyllable and marched to his desk. He scrawled something on a piece of paper and stalked back over to me, thrusting it into my hands.

"Consider us even, Bailey Duane. Next time, find another way to Egypt." Samir pointedly turned his back on us and I led the party out of the offices. Kate walked at my shoulder, Gawain behind us two to watch our backs. He didn't believe anymore than I did that Samir would let a little thing like personal history stand between him and money.

"What's the deal with him?" Kate asked, stepping close enough to brush her shoulder against mine. It was the most comforting, friendly thing I had ever seen her do, especially with me. It took me aback a bit and I had to wait a few moments before I could even consider answering. Then, I took a few more moments to try and figure out how to explain my past with Samir.

"I grew up in the foster care system, half-way adopted by Carlos' father, a diplomat who lived—essentially—in the States and in London, while travelling around in Europe. He was involved in the world of high finance and I was merely a ploy to gain support with some of the more difficult factions. Carlos—Samir—was meant to be his father's legacy. He was looking for absolute perfection. Samir and I got along very well and we would often go tearing around London. I spent half of my school years at a London boarding school and we were inseparable. Then, we became more aware of the world. Samir was caught up in trying to impress his father. He wanted to build an empire, first to please the unpleasable man and then to surpass him. He did that, but with the creatures of the underworld. Drug dealing was first—easy enough to get into. Then he expanded until he had control of some of the finer manufacturing spots. Then smuggling across borders, which brought to his attention the shipping industry.

That became his legitimate front for his dirty business. He got into all sorts of crimes: money laundering, arms shipping, even bounty hunting. I watched. He didn't think I saw, but I did. And then I saw him kill the man that I had thought myself to be in love with. It was, officially, an accident at the shipping yards. My boyfriend fell into the water just as one of the tug boats was bringing a freighter into port. The freighter crushed him," I said. My voice wasn't quite matter-of-fact, but it was close.

"Bailey," Kate whispered. I shrugged off the hand she placed on my shoulder and pointed to a ship.

"That's the one we want. *Storm Runner*. She's heading for Alexandria," I said. Kate tried to put her hand on my shoulder again, as if she were my friend. Before the incident at the airport, I might have thought that were the case, but now? I couldn't forget what stood between us. I was on the wrong side of the line and she wanted to penalise me for it. "Stop it, okay? I was sixteen. That was years ago."

"It doesn't change the fact that your friend killed your boyfriend," Kate said.

"You know what? Maybe that's the difference between you law-enforcement types and people like me. We tend to think of things differently than you do. Samir—Carlos—made a mistake. Time passes. We get over it," I snarled. Kate pulled back, her face hard. I loped over to *Storm Runner* and talked with one of the people loading her up. I was ushered onto the deck and a few moments later, Kate and Gawain joined me.

"We're going to be holed up in the Section B hold. First mate said he'd bring us meals, but otherwise we're to remain out of sight."

"Fine," Kate hissed. She walked to the stairs leading below-decks and was pointed in the direction of Section B hold. I was inches away from following her when Gawain put a hand to my shoulder and stopped me.

"You're lying," he said flatly, for once not looking at me with a sneer or anger or disgust. It was odd, but I thought he was looking at me sort of like I was a human being. "No matter what you say, someone you know kills someone you love, you don't forget. It stares you in the face every time you see your reflection." With that, he walked after Kate, as annoying and enigmatic as ever.

"Yeah, thanks for that, Mr Cheerful," I grumbled under my breath, wondering once again, just what I had got myself into. Little did I know that things were about to get, well, weird. Er.

Chapter 7
In Which I Scream, A Lot

Sitting in the hold of a ship which was meant for transport rather than comfort wasn't exactly the best travelling experience of my life. Granted, I've had worse, but it was certainly up there. The hold was mostly full of crates and things anyways, so we were in fairly close quarters. I decided that being squashed up next to Gawain was better than being squashed up next to Kate. I really wasn't in the mood for dealing with emotional baggage. For some reason, people think that they need to support me in my time of need. Except I'm not actually needing.

It was only forty minutes or so before the ship got under way and then we were in for a long, long wait. Travelling by cargo ship isn't the fastest method in the world. Again, I've had worse, but still. About three hours into the ride, I pulled out the notebook with all of my theories about the Time Keeper and started to go through it again. "I'm still not convinced that there aren't any forgeries or other manuscripts out there," I said once I had gone through the discrepancies in the dates three times.

"It's the truth," Gawain said. "I am absolutely, completely certain about this."

"That's a stupid thing to say," Kate said. She sounded grumpier than usual. Hmm. "No one can be absolutely, completely certain about anything. People who claim to be are fools." That was harsh, even coming from the tough-as-beans FBI agent. I wondered if that was meant to be a dig at me for rebuking her comfort and decided against it. No, this ran deeper than that.

"So those people who believe in God, they're fools?" Gawain snapped back. Ah, right. Just what we needed. A philosophical debate about the nature of the universe. I stood and shoved my notebook into my satchel, forcing the two of them to move or get stepped on.

"Okay, that's enough of *that*," I said. "I'm going to go find the head or the loo or whatever and when I get back, you two had better have hashed our your differences. If not, I'm going to find somewhere else to spend the trip." Kate snarled a wordless statement and Gawain did his best to get comfortable. I took a precious five seconds to glare at the both of them before marching out of the storage hold to go have a wander about.

The ship was a big place and the storage hold where the three of us were waiting out the trip was far away from any place where crew members were living. That meant that finding a head was not all that productive. I spent a good ten minutes trying to find one before I gave up and decided to head up to the deck and ask someone. I was met by the first-mate who looked rather livid.

"I thought that you were given orders to stay out of sight," he growled. I shrugged and sidestepped the hand that he reached out to grab my shoulder with.

"I would love to stay out of your way, but I need the bathroom," I said. The man curled his lip and muttered something in Turkish. He turned and began leading me across the deck to another set of stairs that led below. "Seriously, you guys should have more signs about. People can get lost in a place like this." He growled in response. I spotted the room that I was looking for and thanked the man as politely as I could. Which is to say, I didn't say anything at all. Otherwise, I would have snapped at him. And he was our ride to Alexandria.

By the time I made it back to the deck (golly, these things are big. Have I mentioned that?) it was pretty plain that we were heading for a storm. The wind was whipping up and the sky was getting dark. Wonderful. I hunched my shoulders and wished that I had bought a sweater or something in Iceland; it was getting cold, fast.

"Bailey," Kate called, trudging over to me. Gawain was close behind her, looking around at the various people on deck who were checking the straps on the cargo containers. She looked less than thrilled and, like me, was wrapping her arms around her body. "Couldn't you have checked the weather before we set out?"

"I'm sorry," I grumbled. "I didn't bother to check the weather considering that we needed to get out of there sooner rather than later. I should have looked at the registry of tramp steamers and found one that was leaving tomorrow. I'm sure the Leonum Temporis would have waited to follow us."

"I think we weren't fast enough," Gawain said in an undertone, scowling into the wind as he looked at the crew. The first-mate threw the three of us a look and shouted something in our general direction. The words were snapped up by the wind, but I got the impression that they were not friendly and obliging. "We're being followed."

"It's pretty hard not to follow us or notice us on a ship. I mean, the thing is big, but it's not *that* big," I said. "And we did promise the first-mate that we would stay below decks, so it's no wonder that he's mad."

"That's not what I meant," Gawain said. "There are three agents of Leonum Temporis on this ship. They're the ones who look like they're doing work but aren't." I looked over my shoulder and did just what you're not meant to do in such an instance: I stared at the people following us. Gawain snarled at me, "And now they know we're on to them."

"Well, gee," I said. "How terrible. Come on, there's no way that those people could be Leonum Temporis.

We got on this ship way before they could have even figured out where we'd gone. They're probably just annoyed that we've showed our heads on deck."

"Oh, sure," Kate said, wrapping her arms tighter around her. The storm was picking up speed and she wasn't looking all that well. The ship was big enough that it wouldn't be capsized or anything by the storm, but even we wouldn't get away without feeling it. It showed. "Maybe they're just really cranky workers."

"Was that sarcasm?" I asked. I turned and got another look at the people who weren't working. They were all built on the same line as the guy we had lost in Reykjavik: nondescript, powerful and probably very dangerous. That wasn't a terribly encouraging sign. "So, fine. These people may be after us. But that doesn't mean they're Leonum Temporis. They couldn't have known that we were on this ship."

"I've been telling you not to underestimate these people. They are extremely resourceful," Gawain said. "We should get out of the open."

"The open is probably the best place for us," I grumbled. "There are more witnesses about. And I haven't been underestimating these people. But I'm telling you, it's just not *possible* for them to be here on this ship. They would have to be magic. Or time travellers. Or something."

Gawain said nothing, though a vein popped in his neck. He struggled to control himself for a moment and I wondered if this was one of those things that he wanted to tell me about what was going on but couldn't. That had been happening quite a lot lately and I was moving well past annoyed and into pure anger territory.

"As long as we're staying up here," Kate started, "can we stand closer to the edge. I think I'm going to be sick."

She finished her words and widened her eyes. She put one hand to her mouth and dashed to the side of the ship, grabbing onto the chain fencing that kept people from going over. It wasn't the most secure defence and it looked as though it had been rusted a bit, but it was strong enough for Kate to hold on to while she emptied her stomach. Only, there was one problem.

The guys Gawain had spotted and claimed were Leonum Temporis were moving towards her. Fast.

"Crap," I said and started towards Kate, Gawain hot on my tail. One of the guys pulled something out of his pocket and pointed it towards her. I couldn't tell what it was but anyone who looked as dangerous as that and who was—as it seemed now—following us with hostile intentions, would definitely be carrying a gun. "Crap," I said again for good measure.

Kate came up for air and I saw my chance. Unfortunately, so did the Leonum Temporis agent. I was tall and had long legs and I was pretty good at running. But this guy had a head start and I wasn't carrying a gun. I put on an extra burst of speed, desperate to reach her before the other guy. "Dupont!" I shouted. "*Kate!*"

She turned to look at me and saw the man rushing

her. In a normal circumstance, I figured that Kate would have pulled her service weapon and shot the man. Except she was sick and didn't have a gun. The man barrelled into her, the two of them struggling at the edge for a moment. Kate fought back, kicking the guy where it hurts most and wrestling for whatever it was in his hands. I saw her snarl something at him, but before I could help, Kate bent backwards, the man pressing down on her. The chain broke and the two went over.

I screamed.

Gawain grabbed me around the waist and stopped me from making the same move as Kate. I was inches away from the edge and looked desperately for any sign of a splash. Instead, I saw the remains of a white, fog-like substance. Perhaps the spray from the ocean or the beginnings of rain. Either way, it didn't matter. She was gone.

"Damn it," I cursed, banging my fist on the remaining pieces of fence.

"Bailey, there's nothing you can do," Gawain said. I turned to glare at him. He looked the most concerned I had ever seen him; there was actual pain in his eyes. "She's gone."

I was going to do my best to scream at him and demand that we find her, but in turning my head, I saw that the second Leonum Temporis man was drawing upon us. He wasn't running as hard as his compatriot, but he was looking quite a bit angrier. Gawain must have seen the alarm in my eyes because he pivoted and met the attacker with brute force, his brows drawing down into fury.

The Leonum Temporis man swung his fist, but it was just a distraction. He reached into his pocket and pulled out something that looked similar to whatever it was the other man had used against Kate. It was round and could fit into the palm of a man's hand. Gawain saw this object and began to attack with redoubled efforts.

"Oh, no you don't," he hissed. The man fought back, countering Gawain's strikes and driving him backwards. I turned, determined to stop this before this document retrieval could end before any real progress could begin. Kate was gone. I was pissed.

"Get away from him," I challenged, lunging into the fray.

"Bailey, no!" Gawain said. The Leonum Temporis agent replied with a toothy grin and raised whatever the object was. I felt Gawain's hand on my arm and a stinging, resonating pain surged through my body. My vision went white and a moment later, my senses faded into oblivion.

I figured that was what death felt like. It was nice. Calming. There was no pain, no worry, nothing at all. All that I had to do was lay back and enjoy the quiet sound of the wind through the long grasses of the field, their soft stalks cushioning my body, the sun warming my skin. I slowly drifted back into my body, became weighted again, perfectly calm and peaceful.

Until my head started splitting in agony. I let out

some sort of animalistic cry and brought my hands up to my head. Somehow, I rolled to my knees and was able to bend over, cradling my head as best I could.

"Bailey." Through the pain, it sounded as though someone was calling my name. That's funny.

"Bailey." There it was again. My head wasn't pounding quite as much and I managed to grasp that single point of reality.

Suddenly, the events of the last minute or so came back to me. Kate went overboard. People were attacking us. Gawain grabbing me. Did we go over? Had we been rescued? Was this some sort of hospital? I opened my eyes, the light that had felt so nice on my skin now piercing my eyes and making my headache worse. What I saw wasn't encouraging.

I was in a field surrounded by trees. I had thought I felt grass and it turned out to be true. It was perfectly green and completely isolated. Definitely not a hospital and definitely not the ocean.

"Bailey." There was that voice again. This time I recognised it as Gawain's voice that was speaking and I managed to respond with a groan. "Bailey, are you okay?"

"What just happened?" I asked. My voice sounded foreign and odd to my ears, as though I was speaking with an accent that I had never before used. I swallowed and looked up again, confirming that I was, truly, in a field. "Where are we? How did we get here? And why do I sound funny?"

"Answer my question, first. Are you okay?"

Gawain asked. He moved into my field of vision and put his hands against my head. Immediately, there was a sense of cool relief. I straightened slightly and rubbed the heel of my palm against my eyes.

"I think I'm fine. My head doesn't hurt quite so badly," I said. "What's going on? Where are we? The last thing I remember, we were on the ship, fighting that guy."

"Ah, yes," Gawain said, sounding wary. Now that I thought about it, *he* sounded funny, too. Something fishy was going on and I'd be a hanged woman if I wasn't going to find out what. "Bailey, promise you won't freak out, okay?"

"If you don't tell me what is going on, I'll show you freaking out," I snarled. My response seemed to encourage Gawain—or maybe he was just relieved that I was acting normally again. He sat back on his heels and took a deep breath.

"I'm a time traveller," he said, releasing the breath. I blinked. Scratched my nose. Looked about at the field that we were in. Then nodded. I figured that as soon as I started talking, my brain would start working and then things would go pear shaped. So I just sat there.

"It was the only way that I could get us off the ship safely. The Leonum Temporis agent was about to send you somewhere and I couldn't comb through history to try and find you. It would be ages before I would be able to pick up any traces of your time stream and then by the time I got to you, it could be too late. Relatively speaking. So I took us both through the stream and, well, here we are."

I nodded again, processing the facts as best I could. Gawain didn't seem all that deterred by my lack of speech and forged ahead as if the floodgates had been broken and he could say all the things that he hadn't been able to say before.

"This is how the Time Keeper has been able to be in multiple different places all around the world. It's one of the only things that is allowed to exist in multiple places at the same point in time. Other things can't cross their own time stream, even if there is no direct contact, so they can't exist. That's how I know that there are no copies or forgeries. They just couldn't exist. But I can exist at multiple points in the same time because I've been given a Timer. It's like a watch, except it controls the time streams instead of recording them. I'm sorry I couldn't tell you sooner, but James made me sign a contract that would ensure that I didn't tell you until you figured it out yourself or I was forced to take you through time. Does this make sense? Bailey? Bailey?"

I stared at Gawain for another moment or so. Then, I snapped.

"Aaaaaaaaahhhhhhh," I said, my scream carrying the length and breadth of the field. Gawain slapped his hand over my mouth and looked around as though he expected people to jump out at us from the grass. A moment later and he carefully withdrew his hand. I had stopped screaming, but I think my panic showed in my expression.

"I *told* James that this would end badly. I wanted to tell you as soon as things started getting suspicious, but I couldn't. Actually, I didn't want to involve you at all," Gawain grumbled. That brought me out of my quiet panic for a moment. I remembered that. He had been whispering to Fred Astaire the whole time that he didn't want me involved, that I was an uppity and annoying derelict that couldn't figure anything out. Apparently he was right, because here I was, sitting in a field some indeterminate amount of time away from my life and things were looking, um, bad.

Time travel indeed. I definitely hadn't figured out this particular wrinkle. So much for my much-prized intelligence.

"Why did you then?" I snarled in return. "And would you please explain to me why my voice sounds funny!"

"That's an effect of the Timer. You've adopted the native accent and tongue. It sounds strange because you're translating it instead of just naturally speaking," Gawain said. "And we involved you because... you were necessary."

"That's not creepy at all," I grumbled. I was moments away from pulling my hair out in shock and horror. "This cannot be happening!"

"James, once again, didn't want me to tell you this unless it was absolutely necessary." I frowned and crawled over to Gawain as my legs didn't feel quite stable enough to stand. I jabbed my finger into his face and snarled.

"From where I'm sitting, imbecile, it's absolutely necessary. I mean, I could understand you people being some crime organisation, looking out for your financial interests. I could even understand you people being mercenaries. But *time travellers?* That's a bit too far fetched. Only I'm looking at the evidence and there's pretty much no way to deny what just happened! And that only makes it perfectly clear to me that you are going to explain what the heck is going on and that includes why I'm involved. So, start explaining. Now!"

Gawain moved backwards enough to show he understood that I meant business. I was feeling pretty violent, given that my entire life had folded inside out and then imploded. You did not want to mess with me when I felt violent.

"Bailey, relax, okay?" Gawain raised his hands and spoke in a soothing voice. It didn't help. "There might be some residual effects of jumping the time stream that could act up if you get aggravated."

"Then keep me from getting aggravated," I snarled. "Explain everything. Now."

"Fine. But don't say I didn't warn you," Gawain growled. "You first came to the attention of the Ordo Noctuae—"

"The Order of the Owl, seriously?" I cut in. "Geez, you guys give yourselves strange names."

"We did not name ourselves. We were named by

the founder's daughter, who saw people coming and going from the order headquarters at odd hours of the night. Hence, Ordo Noctuae. Are you going to let me explain or will you just keep interrupting every few words?" Gawain snapped. I folded my arms and slouched, thoroughly annoyed. He nodded in satisfaction. "You first came to the attention of the Ordo Noctuae when we found a record of your existence in three different time periods. Only you had never been a member of the Order—we have records of all past and future members before you ask. It's one of the benefits of time travel. How could someone like you, a normal, be present in multiple time streams? It didn't make sense."

"Well, it hasn't happened. Won't happen, whatever," I said. "I haven't and won't show up in your different time streams. I'm not a crazy time traveller, whatever you say."

My life as a person who helped people with theirs, sometimes to very strange extremes, was feeling very normal, now.

"And yet you've ended up in my time," Gawain said.

"You *brought* me with you," I pointed out. "It's not my fault."

"Just one thing, though, the Timer only lets one person through. It isn't powerful enough to pull two through," Gawain said. I blinked. "That's what was so interesting. You seem naturally in tune with the time streams, able to jump from one to another without much difficulty. Don't ask me how because I don't know. As far as the Order is concerned, I'm nothing more than a low-level lackey. But your natural ability made you perfect for seeking out the Time Keeper. It could jump across history and it wouldn't matter. You would still be able to track it and find it because you are naturally in tune with the time streams. So you were the one we needed."

"Let me get this straight," I said, pressing a hand to my head, which had begun to hurt again, though I didn't think it was from jumping through time. "You need me to find a book that you lost somewhere in history or the future because I'm a natural time traveller?"

"Something like that."

"This is insane! Couldn't you people just jump to whenever you found the book and pulled it back?" I asked.

Gawain shook his head and took another deep breath. This was going to be a longer conversation, I just knew it.

"The thing about time travel is that you can't just skip events. Things still have to happen for them to take place in history. Certain individuals can jump around because they are less grounded in the fixed events of history than otherwise. But we can only participate in things, not change the outcome or jump forwards and bring things back, bypassing all the things that had to happen for us to have that moment to jump to. History happens. We can do our best to change things, but whatever we do only ensures that history continues to happen. Change something now and the future might be different, but history will still happen. Understand?" Gawain asked.

"Not really, but I'm working on it," I said. "Keep going. Next thing you're going to tell me magic is real and you're all really dragons or something."

"Shh," Gawain answered, suddenly tense. I frowned. We were pretty alone in this field. It wasn't like the Leonum Temporis people could have followed us if the Timer-thingy was only able to pull one person through at a time. Though the time-travel aspect did explain a whole lot about how those people were able to be on our tail before we had made a move. Actually, it cleared a whole lot of things up, despite my determination to pretend none of this was happening. Anyways.

"There's no one here," I said. "We're in a big empty field in whenever your natural time is."

"Shut up," Gawain snarled. He ducked down below the level of the grass and pulled me down next to him. I listened but still didn't hear anything. A moment later, though, and I was proven wrong yet again. The shaking of the ground was the first indication that things were approaching. A dull thumping came next, growing louder by the moment. In a few seconds and Gawain and I were surrounded. By what, I was having a hard time believing. I mean, if I hadn't believed the whole time-travel schtick a moment ago, it was hard to deny it now. Because we were surrounded by—I kid you not—a group of men on horses, pointing swords at us and looking as though they'd come straight out of the early days of England's history. The slightly past Roman-invasion early days of England's history.

"Who are you vagrants that dare trespass on our land?" the leader of the band asked. He had reddish-gold hair that was long enough to be considered girly in my time but was definitely *not* girly the way he wore it. Around his neck was a metal collar-type-thing with some sort of insignia on it. He wore a green shirt and brown buckskin breeches (seriously). He had a leather vest and various straps and belts and things which held sheaths for knives and the very long sword that he was currently pointing at me. If that wasn't enough, the scars on his face and hands certainly didn't help me feel any better.

"We're going to die," I whimpered. "We're really going to die."

Gawain, idiot that he was, stood and addressed these people with his hands outstretched, the normal haughty tone to his voice magnified tenfold.

"Do you not recognise your sire and King?" he challenged the leader, tossing his head. The man on the horse stared hard, tightening his grip on the sword. I figured I could probably escape the circle of horsemen but I doubted I could outrun them. Gawain's plan, whatever it was, had better be a good one.

Turns out, it was. Because a moment later and the man had jumped from the horse and run to Gawain, wrapping his arms around him with a great laugh. "Arthur! You're back!"

I'd just discovered time travel existed and still thought that this reaction was weirder than anything I'd seen yet. And this was only the beginning.

Chapter 8
In Which I Am Too Tall for History

The leader of this band of horsemen, the one that had called Gawain "Arthur" embraced my surly companion once again before stepping backwards and letting the others of the group get to him. A few moments later and the entire situation had changed from "I'm about to die" to a giant hug-fest. I was feeling a little weirded out by this. Not to mention that somewhere in the back of my mind, my synapses had put together the whole King-and-sire thing with the Arthur thing. At this point, I figured I had two options: consider myself insane and this as the product of my fantasy or accept all that had been told to me.

I was still working on which one to go with.

"Arthur, you've been gone far too long. Where have you been?" the leader asked, once again slinging his arm around Gawain's shoulders. Gawain winced and ran his fingers through his hair, which only brought it to the attention of the horseman. "And what are you wearing? Your hair is cut like a child's! The last we heard, you were being ferried away to Avalon so that the Three Sisters could heal you."

"Ah, well," Gawain managed before another man cut in. This one had blonde hair as long as the first horseman as well as a beard streaked with brown. He was attired similarly to the first and was wearing a hopeful scowl.

"We searched for the body of that traitor Mordred but—"

"Men, the battle at Camlan has passed. I am returned and curious to know what has happened in my absence, but the fewer questions that are asked the better. The Ordo—the Three Sisters of Avalon request it," Gawain said. The leader of the group slapped Gawain on the back and began to lead the King to the horses.

"Of course," he said. "We are not far from my castle. You shall have my finest mead and meat from the best of my herds. We will call our bards and hear of all that has passed in your absence."

"That sounds wonderful, Gawain," Gawain—Arthur said. I was wrenching my eyes between the two of them and felt my mouth go dry at the realisation that I had been calling Arthur by this man's name the entirety of our acquaintance. Worse than that, he hadn't said anything. I was going to have to come up with a new nickname, and fast. "I cannot tell you how I have missed this place. How long has it been since I've been gone?"

The real Gawain frowned and the second man who had spoken stepped up once again. "Three years. Things have been... chaotic since you left. But that will change now that the rightful King has returned. Your throne at Caerleon will once again be yours. You will once more reign strong over this land," the man said. I was beginning to feel as though I was in a reenactment of those times, which were generally considered myth by modern historians, with lots of hopeful hurrahs and drinking and over-the-top heroes.

I decided to break things up before my mind exploded. I coughed pointedly, still crouching on the ground. It was time that Arthur remembered I was there.

Immediately, I was surrounded with lots of pointy swords and even a bow was nocked with an arrow pointed straight at my heart. I was on my feet faster than you could sneeze and decided that I would prefer being chased by goons with guns than being threatened with angry looking knights with swords. "Right," I said, holding up my hands and giving a little wave. The swords got closer.

"Enough," Arthur said, his voice crackling with authority. The men hesitated and he repeated the order. "Lower your weapons. She is with me."

"What sort of joke is this, Arthur?" the blonde man asked, gesturing at me in what seemed like a very rude manner. "You come back here after years of being gone and bring this...harlot with you?"

Okay, I was out of my element, but in my element or not, I don't take kindly to being called a harlot. I straightened to my full, imposing height—which, thank you very much, was just about equal to that of Blondie—and glared. "Come closer and say that again," I growled. The man looked as though he were about to take me up on that offer. He threw the sword he was holding into its sheath and stepped forwards, reaching out his hands. I settled into the fighting stance I had learned as a necessity to years of running around with Carlos.

"Kay, stop it," Arthur snapped, stepping between us. He stared at the man for a moment before Blondie looked away. "This is the Lady Bailey Duane. Customs in her land require a different sort of attire than what you are used to, but she is no harlot. Nor will I allow any of you to treat her as such. Understand?"

Lady? I was far from a Lady, but I supposed it was better than being called a harlot. The moment's hesitation from the men gathered around seemed to grate on Arthur's nerves.

"Do you understand?" he snarled, some of his typical Gawain-like temper showing through.

At this point, my head began to spin. I was having to take in too many things too quickly and my brain didn't think it was up to the task. I lowered my hands, more to keep my balance than anything. Kay must have seen it as a concession to his authority because he stepped back and nodded. He wasn't going to attack me. I was thrilled. The men muttered uneasily for a moment then a third man, who had not spoken before and looked younger than the rest, bowed to me.

"It is an honour, Lady Bailey," the man said. I glanced desperately at Arthur—Art? Artie?—in the hopes that he would tell me what to do. He just watched. Some help. I nodded and sort of returned the bow combined with a half curtsy. That's what people did, right? Arthur winced and shrugged it off and the other men did their best to hide their snickers behind beards and hands.

"Right, great," I said. "Um... so what now?"

"Now," Arthur said, climbing on the horse that Gawain held the reins to, "we go to Gawain's castle. Have a rest and some decent food. I will hear all that has been happening in my absence and then we can figure out what to do next."

"Plans can wait until tomorrow," Gawain said. The younger man, a darker auburn than Gawain, held out his hand to me and I took the pointed look from Arthur to mean that I was going to accept and follow. Because I was out of my element. Right. I took the hand and was led to a horse who eyed me with as much skepticism as I did it. "For tonight, we celebrate the return of our King!"

"Would you like assistance?" the young man asked, gesturing to the horse. Oh, he wanted me to get on the beast. I frowned and glared at the horse who snorted in reply. Then, in a move that I had practised vaulting over fences of school grounds, I clambered onto the horse. The creature looked alarmed and did its best to move out of the way before I was properly seated. I held on, much to its consternation.

"I'll manage," I replied through gritted teeth once the young man got the horse under control. He grinned cheekily at me and before I could protest, climbed on behind me. I nearly jabbed an elbow into his soft spots when Arthur shot me a look that told me to comply. I saw that he was double seated with Gawain and figured that this was acceptable. To them, maybe, but I was quickly growing annoyed. Things had gone way beyond my control and though there was nothing I could really do, I was beginning to feel like it was time to take that control back. For now, though, I would keep my head down. I had been in many a dangerous situation; I knew when to bide my time.

The man sitting behind me wrapped his arms around me and, once again, before I could protest, the whole group of horsemen had turned and began galloping somewhere to the west. I held in a squeal and did my best to relax. Just in case you were wondering, it is rather difficult to relax while on a horse that is constantly moving and moving at a decent clip over uneven ground. I began to panic—which meant hyper-ventilating—and when I felt the man's arms tightening around me as we turned slightly, I knew I was inches away from having a full mental break down. I forced myself not to struggle, but it was looking to be hopeless. I focused, instead, on keeping my muscles as relaxed as

I could manage. Breathe in, relax. Breathe out, relax. Relax. Don't fight, Bailey. Relax.

Twenty minutes of this later and we slowed to a trot, the gait bouncier and somehow less threatening than the gallop. I opened my eyes and saw that we were riding up to a—yes really—castle. This wasn't the sort of castle that young girls dream of having, but the square, fortified stone castle that was meant to stand up to an assault by an army before hosting a party, with some elements of Roman design and a lot of moss and lichen growing over the stones and wood. The party rode through the gates and we were met with general commotion as the servants and stable hands and pages rushed forwards to help the various knights off of the horses and lead them away. My escort dismounted and held out his hand to me, still looking cheerful and far too hopeful. Despite the fact that I was sorely tempted to wipe that cheeky grin off his face, I accepted the hand and slid to the ground.

My legs held me, barely.

There was some organisation to be done with all of the men returning earlier than expected and the return of their King plus one very tall, very angry woman. Gawain started giving orders and the rest of us were left to ourselves for a few moments. I managed to get close enough to Arthur for the first time since this whole business had begun to hold a decent conversation. It began with, "What just happened? Who are you? I thought this whole thing was a myth!"

"Bailey, you don't look so well," Arthur said,

putting a hand on my shoulder. I was struck with a sudden feeling of how *real* this man felt. Sure, we had touched before, casually brushed up against one another and I had definitely got close enough to hit him a few times (though I had abstained), but this was different. It was as though I was floating and he was solid, trying to ground me in whatever reality we had landed in. Given my wobbly legs, my headache and the stress that I was experiencing, it was too much. I managed a painful sound in the back of my throat before collapsing to the all-too-solid stones on the ground.

I woke with a cool cloth resting on my forehead and the sense that I was being watched. I did my best to turn my head and look around for the source of my unease and managed only a groan. Since when did all the muscles in my body feel like water?

"You're awake."

Gee, what sort of genius could think of a statement like that? I forced myself to turn and look at the man sitting on the stool next to the bed where I was laid up. Arthur stared at me, wearing some clothes that looked like the ones his retinue wore with his apparently-too-short hair looking cleaner than it had for a couple of days. He also sported a scruffy sort of stubble which meant he either hadn't slept properly and therefore cleaned up properly or he was fitting into the fashion of the day. I suspected the latter.

Whatever sleep I had got seemed to have only solidified my situation, because now my mind wasn't even trying to reject it.

"Artie. Ugh. Yes, I'm awake," I managed, my mouth raspy and dry. Arthur picked up a wooden cup and tipped it towards my mouth. I drank, coughing it up a moment later when I realised it was wine and not water that was being given to me. "What was that?" I demanded, ignoring the protesting of my muscles and sitting up in the bed. "Are you trying to give me a heart attack?"

"I would not suggest drinking the water around here unless you find a pure spring. I would also not suggest calling me Artie around the inhabitants of this place," Arthur said wryly. I was really going to strangle this guy. I curled my lip in annoyance but accepted another sip of the wine. I didn't cough nearly as badly and the sweet flavour of the drink seemed to do me some good. I groaned.

"Ow," I muttered. Arthur reached forwards and I instinctively pulled back. When all he did was take the damp cloth and set it beside a basin on a small table, I felt incredibly stupid. He hadn't hurt me, though we had yelled at one another a few times. More than a few times. I was pretty sure there was no lost love between us, though he did seem less ornery here. "Okay, so... I think it's probably about time that you started explaining things."

"I told you, I brought you to my time," he said, looking as though he were desperate that it be enough to sate me. It wasn't.

"Yeah. Sure, fine. Except you failed to mention that your time happens to be that of King Arthur—which is *you*, by the way—and that there are a few more details that might have been important to my survival. One of which is the fact that, oh, I don't know, King Arthur is a myth?" I glared at him and he sighed.

"Not a myth, per se, just lost to history. It happens, even with travellers keeping history alive and remembered. Honestly, if I'd told you before now, would you have believed me?" he asked, staring me straight in the eye. I looked back and saw an entirely different character from the sulking, grumbling one that had been accompanying me on my trip thus far. This man was regal and carried the weight of the world on his shoulders, and he did it well. I looked away and picked at the wool blanket.

"Probably not," I sighed. "But anything would have been better than the misinformation or lack of information that you fed me. I'm not an idiot. Sure, you hired me to do a job and I don't mind being kept in the dark about some things, but when it gets me into trouble, I like to know. Geez, you could have told me your real name, for one."

"It was easier for you and me to work under the nickname you provided," Arthur said. Then he sat back on the stool and looked at the ceiling, a myriad of stone and wooden beams. "Besides, it was easier for me to bear the name of one of my most loyal and honoured knights than that of my own."

"Which means..." I prompted. Arthur shot me a look which bordered on frustration and I shrugged, wincing when my muscles protested. "I've had enough with secrets. If I'm going to fit into this society for however long we are to remain here, then I'm going to need a history lesson."

"Surely you know the legends," he said. I frowned. "Fine. Fine. I will spare you the beginning of my story, about how I drew the sword from the stone and became King, but some other details are more pertinent. My half-sister, Morganna, was as the stories proclaim, power-hungry and determined to keep the old ways alive, even when they had been lost to the mists of time—there are some things that even us travellers cannot prevent from being lost. And there are some things that are better that way—but my nephew—and son, for those stories are true as well—Mordred, was the real danger. He inherited his mother's lust for power and my determination and skill in battle. When he learned the truth, it became his personal vendetta to have me killed. At the point of his attack, I was just..."

"Keep going," I demanded. Arthur shot me another look, this one significantly more frustrated, but nodded.

"Lancelot, my best friend, and my beloved Guinevere, ran off together. I threw myself into the battle—Camlan. My grief was overwhelming, though, and many died. This is where the legends diverge, though. Some say that all my knights were lost and the kingdom thrown into chaos. What was actually the case was that my armies were decimated and *I* was lost, my friends scattered to their respective domains. I was taken, supposedly, by the Three Sisters of Avalon to be healed until needed again. In actuality, this is where my contract with the Ordo Noctuae began."

"Let me guess," I interrupted. "They offered you a chance to atone for your mistakes and make a difference in the world—future and past—if you would join them."

"Yes," Arthur said. "How did you--"

"That's the calling card for just about every gang, mob and cult out there. They probably got it from your precious organisation putting their fingers into too many historical pies," I grumbled. "Fine. So you vanish for three years—"

"More like twenty," he said, wincing. "On my end."

"You don't look like an old man," I said, which only made him scowl. See, who says that I can't make everyone feel like their normal, cheerful selves? I have a special talent in that area.

"Ageing works differently when you're a traveller," he said. I shrugged, not wanting to think of the implications of such a thing.

"Fine, whatever. You vanish for an indeterminate amount of time and now you're back, saying that the Three Sisters released you? For goodness sakes, why don't you just go about saying that Merlin brought you back from the dead?" I asked, folding my arms and swallowing a groan as I did so.

"Ah, Merlin was a traveller," Arthur said, hunching his shoulders.

I sighed. "Of course he was."

We sat in silence for a few minutes. I was processing and feeling like I had been hit by a truck. Arthur was doing his best not to look completely distraught by reliving his past. Twenty years, three years, one year, it didn't matter. People betray you and you don't just forget. I should know. "So... why do I hurt so much? Is that some sort of side effect of this travelling thing?"

"Occasionally, if the jump is violent," Arthur agreed. "Though in your case, I would venture a guess that it is merely because you haven't jumped before. You probably just grabbed onto the energy that my Timer uses and hitched a ride. I don't imagine that's the most comfortable way to go about travelling."

"No," I said. "It isn't."

"I have to admit, you're taking this better than I expected." When I raised a querulous eyebrow, Arthur winced and clarified. "I had imagined quite a lot more sarcasm and protesting. And another bout of screaming. Complete denial, perhaps. But you don't seem to be, well, freaking out all that much, to use a colloquial term."

"Ha," I said. "You're just hilarious. I'm not freaking out because it's sort of hard to deny the fact that one minute I was inches away from falling off a boat and now I'm sitting in a castle. The way I figure, I can accept your time travel theory or I am dead. I'd rather live. I'm fond of living."

Arthur nodded, but he didn't do much more than that. I figured that he was tired, too. I mean, I was thrown into an unfamiliar time, but he had been brought back after having expected never to see it again. What a trip. It was, by my reckoning, past time for the both of us to get some sleep. And no, being unconscious doesn't actually count.

"We should figure out what happens next," I said. Arthur looked at me in surprise. "Hey, I've been hired to do a job. I don't quit halfway through just because I've been sent to another time. That's like saying I was too lazy to get out of bed, so sorry, I can't find your document."

"You do realise that now the Timers have been used, the Time Keeper could be anywhere?" Arthur asked. I gave him a look. "The Time Keeper is only bound to a history as long as it is in someone's possession. Those times when it does not have an owner, it only remains in a history as long as people go without using a Timer during that history. Say that the manuscript was in the year 1854 and I wanted to jump somewhere. If I were in 1854, I couldn't jump times without the manuscript jumping times as well. But if I were just a year later or earlier and I could jump without the manuscript jumping. Whoever was looking for it could find it."

"That's quite the intelligent book." I scowled. Arthur shrugged.

"That's, apparently, what happens when you put the ideologies of a time travelling organisation onto paper with a Timer nearby. The very nature of the thing makes it unstable. It's been to nearly every point in history—before some things have been changed and after—and that means its been imbued with certain... properties," he said.

"I got it. Book jumps, gets jumper capabilities. Sort of annoying, really. But fancy bookwork aside, you're saying that it could be in any point in history?" I asked. Arthur nodded and stood so he could pace around. Obviously, this was sort of stressful for the guy. I could understand that. It was stressful for me, too.

"That's the main reason why we needed you along," he said. "I mean, you're good at finding things that people don't want found, so that was one aspect. But the fact that you seem to be more in tune with the time streams means that you can figure out where the book is. You just have to hone in on it and figure out where it is and we'll jump to it."

"I see one flaw with your plan," I said, holding up a hand and wincing while I did. Man, I really needed some sleep to recover from travelling or dying or whatever. "I don't know how to do that. The last time, I had to 'tune in' to your Timer and I basically just hitched a ride, like sticking out my thumb. I don't know how to manipulate these time streams. I don't know how to do this fancy jumper-traveller-thing. Frankly, I'm not quite sure I can. I think your Timer glitched and just pulled me along."

"Glitched..." Arthur said, looking at me strangely. He had paused in the middle of his pacing and I was the sole focus of his attention. It was slightly unnerving.

"Wigged out. Went on the fritz. Had a bug. Was broken. It doesn't matter how you say it," I said. The man looked at me oddly for a few more seconds then went back to his pacing, rubbing a hand over his jaw, as though he was unfamiliar with the feeling of stubble.

"I can teach you the art of manipulating the time streams," he said. "It might take time, but that is not something of which we are in short supply. No, I am more worried about the various people of my time that you are going to offend while we have your lessons."

"Pfft," I said, waving a dismissive hand. "I'm good at assimilation. Just give me the basic rundown and I'll fit right in. Just go with the flow, right?"

Arthur winced and tugged at the tunic that went over his shirt. For the first time, I noticed that it was one size too big and fit him like it belonged to a man with broader shoulders and more muscle mass. Things had changed for the both of us. This was a King, reduced to wearing clothes that didn't fit and living in a place that didn't belong to him. And there was me, ready to 'go with the flow.'

"That," Arthur said, "is what I'm worried about."

Chapter 9
In Which I Meet Different Old Friends

"Here." Arthur thrust a bundle of fabric into my hands. It was a full day and a half after our conversation. I had been tired from everything that had happened and slept for a good eighteen hours. Apparently the muscle weakness was from using my ability to align with the time streams for the first time. At least, that was the working theory. Now I had been through a bath—assisted by two very helpful maids who persisted even when I protested—and was dressed in a linen shift.

"I had to explain to the store masters that you were a warrior from the land where you hail and were, therefore, allowed and even required to wear breeches and a shirt as men do. Try not to mess that image up, okay? And for heaven's sake, don't accept any offers to spar."

"I'm not a bad fighter," I grumbled, taking the clothes and examining them. The pants looked as though they were long enough to fit me and were made out of a material that didn't look too scratchy. I pulled them on under the shift and pointedly stared at Arthur until he turned around before putting the shirt on. It was too big and hung awkwardly down to the middle of my thighs.

"Well, I suppose it could be worse," Arthur said once I had given him the all clear. "At least none of my men will be distracted by your shapely figure."

"Hey!" I protested. "It's not my fault I happen to be skinny. I blame an exercise regimen which consists of running from one end of the city to the other while jumping fences and so forth. You try it some time."

"At least put a tunic over the shirt," the king said, handing me another piece of fabric. This was a dark green piece which had no sleeves and hung to nearly my knees. I cinched the belt handed to me around my waist and held out my arms for a second appraisal. "From a distance, you could pass as an unusually tall page. It will have to do."

"I'm not trying to be one of your knights, okay? I'm not muscly enough and I can't grow a beard," I said, doing my best to examine myself without the aid of a mirror. My hair hung in wet strands around my face, as I had refused the maids' help in putting it up, and I imagined that I still looked tired. Between that and the too-big shirt and tunic (though the breeches did actually fit), I probably looked like a mess. But as Arthur said, it could be worse. "Look on the bright side. At least I'm not trying to act like an actual lady."

Arthur winced and, despite of the grumpy mood

he had displayed thus far, chuckled. I suspected he was still hungover from whatever celebration had gone on the night before, and therefore not in full grasp of his faculties. "Lady Kay would have torn you to pieces," he said.

"My point exactly," I answered. "Great. So now that I'm properly attired, what's the plan?"

"As I said before, we must work to get you attuned to the time streams so that you can jump at will. Then we can find the Time Keeper. Once that's done—"

"Yeah, yeah, we can go back to our normal lives, me as a gofer for hire, you as a... dead king guy who travels in time," I finished. "I meant, what is the *actual* plan? As in, now we're going to go downstairs and have something to eat. And then we're going to go find an open place to practise, which involves steps one through seven. Logistically. With lots of details. You know, that sort of plan."

"I liked you better when you were asleep," Arthur grumbled. "Come on, we'll go get some food and then get some horses. I have no doubt Gawain will be pleased to lend them to me for the day."

"Great! I'm starving," I said.

Arthur growled something under his breath and stalked to the door, looking distinctly annoyed at me. I beamed; it was a good start to the day. Walking through the castle, I was doing my best not to bounce around. After sleeping for so long, my muscles were feeling wound up from lack of use and I was eager to get around to doing something. Not doing something would mean that I had resigned myself to staying in...whatever time period this was. I wasn't going to give up without a fight and Arthur's plan, as crazy as it might have sounded two days ago, was the only option. He knew about this time stream thing. I didn't. I would do whatever it took to get back to my quiet office and my job of errand-runner/stolen goods retrievals expert/gofer for hire.

With that in mind, I was still stunned when we emerged into the great hall which served as a dining room for the many people that were staying in the castle. Most of whom were the knights that had brought us thither the day before. It wasn't all that early in the morning, but there were still a number of people lingering over breakfast. Everyone paused when Arthur and I entered and I swallowed the urge to give a sarcastic wave and a "hey."

"Arthur!" Gawain called, striding across the hall. He clapped the king on the shoulder in a good-natured sort of way. "Are you feeling well after last night? You were looking rather piqued after the third horn of ale."

"I haven't tasted such good ale for what seems like twenty years, my friend. It was merely the shock of the flavour which made me seem out of sorts," Arthur said in a silver-tongued manner. I hid a snort behind a surreptitious glance around the hall.

"As eloquent as ever," Gawain laughed. "Come, come, we'll get some food into you and the lovely Lady Bailey here and you can figure out your next steps.

Perhaps we should plan a tour of the kingdom, see what has befallen the land in your absence."

I happily followed Gawain to a wooden table and bench at the far end of the hall. Arthur was offered the seat at the head of the table and I was given a spot at his left. Gawain took the seat at his right and with a wave of his hand, servants appeared with platters of food.

"I would love a tour, old friend," Arthur said.

Gawain grinned, "Then we shall prepare immediately! Where would you like to start? The old centre of the kingdom? Caerleon? Or perhaps the border regions?"

"I cannot," Arthur said. Immediately, the cheerful countenance of the knight vanished. He frowned and drew his brows together, taking a long sip of whatever was in his cup. Arthur looked at the table and traced some of the patterns in the wood.

"You vanish for three years and now you're back and you can't even... why not? Are we that terrible? Have you not forgiven us for our sins?" Gawain asked. Seemed a bit harsh to me.. Couldn't the guy understand that his friend and king had been taken by a time travelling agency and spent twenty years or so messing about with history? Well, okay, perhaps not. Still.

"I forgave you long ago," Arthur murmured. "But my time here is not my own. I must assist Lady Bailey in her efforts here and then, as the Three Sisters demand, I will be gone. I cannot stay."

"But you are our King," Gawain insisted, slamming

his fist on the table. "This land has been so diminished since you left. Now you're here and everything can be better than before and you're simply refusing? Don't you care about the future of your kingdom?"

"I fear not for the future of this kingdom," Arthur retorted. I nodded to myself; the guy would know, all things considered. Gawain reared his head and I got the impression that he was going to chew Arthur out. But the king raised a hand and the knight subsided. "Gawain, think not that I do not care simply because I cannot be what I once was. You, my greatest friends, and my kingdom are the most important things in my life. I must, however, do what I have been called to do. That is to assist Lady Bailey. I am sorry, old friend."

Gawain glared at Arthur for a moment then looked away, shaking his head in annoyance and disgust. "I would have thought that your duty to your people would have been all that mattered to you. It seems as though I was wrong."

"My people are well cared for. My time is over," Arthur said. He reached for his cup and was going to drink when Gawain put his hand around Arthur's wrist. Immediately, the temperature in the air dropped ten degrees. Arthur raised his head ever so subtly and Gawain backed down, pulling his hand back and lowering his head. I wasn't quite sure what I had just seen, but it seemed to have something to do with power. Real, blooded power. Added to what I had previously seen of Arthur, that was just terrifying.

"Brr," I mumbled, receiving a sharp look from my

travelling companion. I answered with a cheeky grin and proceeded to stuff a roll with sausage into my mouth. Arthur made an annoyed sound in the back of his throat and proceeded to eat his breakfast in silence. When we were done and the servants had taken the empty platters away, Arthur stood and looked at his now-sullen knight.

"Gawain, I have need of a pair of horses for the day," Arthur said regally. "We will return by the evening meal."

"What belongs to me is yours, *your Majesty*," Gawain sneered.

"Many thanks," I said in my best uppity voice, feeling that it was about time I intervened. "That's awfully nice of you."

The knight threw me a look that was at first annoyed—probably with my insolence. I have that effect on people—then contrite and finally settled on confused. Somewhere in there, I figured he had remembered the fact that I was a woman and was trying his best to reconcile that image with the tall, gangly person who stood before him with snark readily on the tongue.

"It is my pleasure, Lady," Gawain said, this time rising and giving me a slight bow. I was pretty sure he was snubbing me, but I couldn't be absolutely certain. These people were practitioners of different expectations when it came to giving the cut direct, as it were, so who could tell.

I decided that the best solution was to be as

cheerful as possible and follow Arthur and Gawain out to the stables. We waited until two horses were saddled and brought to us and, as before, I refused the help offered me, instead choosing to humiliate myself in trying to clamber onto the horse. I made it and it wasn't too terrible, but the look that Gawain threw me was enough to make me shift and grumble in annoyance. Arthur looked down at his knight and extended a hand.

"It is good to know that you care as you do," he said. "I only wish things were different. But that cannot be."

Gawain clasped the hand but did not meet Arthur's gaze. "I wish things were different as well. I will be sure to keep reports of your return from spreading."

"Thank you," Arthur said. He dug his heels into the horse's sides and the creature leapt off, my horse following by example. I tightened my fists around the reins and did my best to keep my seat for the sake of all watching our departure. Only when we were about a mile out from the castle did I loosen my grip and allow my legs to relax. We rode for a few more minutes until there was no chance that someone would have followed us and all signs of civilisation, what little there was, had vanished from view.

"I've been to Wales before," I said at last, dismounting the horse as Arthur did. He took the reins of my beast and didn't say anything. "It's amazing how different everything looks."

"Time changes things. If anything, my time as a

traveller has taught me that. People would love to believe that their lives are significant and enduring, but that's just not the case," Arthur replied. "Compared to history, our lives are nothing more than a blink of an eye."

"Wow, you know, that doesn't really help," I said with a scowl. Just for good measure, I kicked at some dirt and did my best not to feel annoyed when nothing more than a cloud of dust appeared for my efforts.

"The thing is, Bailey, that even though people's lives are just a blip in time, they do wonderful things with the time they have. You just have to look at the advance of technology to see that. Then there's art and music and philosophical thought."

"And wars and plagues and advances in weapons technology and unspeakable horrors that people have committed," I countered.

"Now who's being depressing?" Arthur snapped in return. I growled under my breath and folded my arms. Maybe it was the fact that the people here didn't seem to like me. What can I say? Return with the long lost king and prevent him from doing what they want? You're going to bring up rather a lot of animosity.

Arthur watched me for a moment, then shook his head. "Okay, let's get started. Have a seat."

"What?" I asked, looking at him in surprise. He was already sitting on the ground, settling in as comfortably as possible. I frowned but complied, sitting across from him. Arthur pulled out his Timer and handed it to me. I took it tentatively, not wanting to appear in a different time and be on my own, then turned it over in my hands. "It's a pocket watch."

"Not quite. Look at the hands," Arthur said. I did so and frowned. They were...not marking time. The hands were fixed at a certain point on the watch, which looked like a bunch of gibberish to me, and though they flickered every now and again, did nothing significant. "Those will only move when you access the time stream through the Timer. When you decide on a point, they'll become fixed and then you are pulled through the streams to that point."

"Why are they flickering?" I asked. Arthur leaned forwards and looked at the Timer in curiosity. Not a good sign, to my thinking.

"I think it's because you're a natural Timer. It's getting confused by the signals that you're sending or something. I don't know," he said. I snorted but didn't deign that with a response. "Scoff all you want, but it could be useful. We're going to start with, um, focusing on the feel of the stream. Hold the Timer tight and try to think about the passage of time."

I did as he told, wrapping the Timer in my hand and closing my eyes. After a decent five minutes of trying to think about the passage of time, I was feeling stupid and had got nothing accomplished. "I think you're just doing this to annoy me," I said, eyes still closed.

"Okay, fine. We'll take a short jump, then, or at least initiate one. Then you can see exactly how it's done," Arthur said. It lacked the finesse of proper teaching, but I suspected he wanted me to figure this out as quickly as possible, not necessarily do it correctly. Then, I doubted that travelling in time was quite like learning tae kwon do. Or whatever.

I handed over the Timer and watched as he wrapped it in his hand, taking on a look of severe concentration. I was about to make a snarky comment when the world started to shift. It didn't look much different at first, but I could *feel* it. It was like the ground began to change under my feet, becoming at once more solid and more fluid. If I wanted, I could reach out and take hold of that feeling, bend it to my will. I waited, though, watching as the world took on a bright white tinge and then re-solidified. My head was hurting slightly from having that feeling of rightness snatched away, but it wasn't as bad as jumping the first time. At least, I assumed we had jumped, though nothing looked any different.

"So... when are we?" I asked, slightly proud of myself for asking the proper question.

"About an hour later than when we were. I'm not sensitive enough to be able to do smaller jumps, so the Timer does the best it can," Arthur replied. He looked somewhat out of sorts, but a moment later and he blinked; the emotion was gone. "So, what was it like? Do you think you can duplicate it?"

"I think so," I said. Arthur handed over the Timer and I closed my fingers around it. The confidence I had felt a moment ago vanished and I was left with a desperation. I needed to get this to work. It was our only way out of here unless Arthur somehow figured out how to get the both of us to jump again. And even that would be no guarantee that we could find the manuscript. I closed my eyes and remembered the feeling of change that had occurred. There had to be some way to initiate it, some way to start it without Arthur's help. Was it centred around the Timer?

There! A nodule of space that was different than the rest of the world. It was something other than the unchanging reality in which I found myself. I touched it, physically or mentally I couldn't tell, and the nodule reacted.

"Bailey!" Arthur yelled, but it was too late. I was already widening the different space, making it bigger so that I could grasp onto it and change it.

"Bailey, stop!" Arthur called again, his voice sounding farther away.

Why should I? I was good at this. I was a natural. And it felt right. I shaped the space, pulling it, moving it to my whims until a question popped into my mind. It wasn't my voice, or Arthur's or anyone that I had ever heard before.

When? The voice asked. It sounded gleeful and a little curious. I shrugged.

"I don't know," I said. "I'm just playing around, trying to see how this works."

But you can go anywhere you want. Anytime in the whole of history. You could see the beginning. The end. You could go home or to a point in your past. You could save your love from the hands of Carlos. The voice was soothing and tempting and presented enough of a challenge to me that I wanted to try, to prove that I could. And I wanted, desperately, to go back and save John from the hands of my childhood friend. It was a desperate need so strong that I nearly reached out and did just as the voice asked. Then, I paused. What had Arthur said? History happens.

You think that the rules of time apply to you? You are special, Bailey. You can change history. You can do whatever you want. That soothing cadence had slipped away, leaving the glee again. It was the voice of someone who enjoyed chaos and order in equal measure and was thrilled when someone appeared to change things. It was...ancient and terrible and young and full of potential. It—*he*—was the point around which the entire time stream swirled. And in listening to the voice, I felt like I could easily get lost in the mists of time.

"I'll think about it," I growled, forcing myself to think in the moment. "But for now, a few seconds will do."

Very well, the voice said. The world around me resorted itself and began to feel more solid and unchangeable. The white tinge that had appeared vanished and I found myself sitting just as I had been, Arthur right in the middle of calling my name for a third time. I blinked and the world fell back into the place, dead centre in my head.

"Oh, crap," I said, leaning forwards to cradle my head in my hands. It was splitting and pounding and throbbing all at the same time, something which I had never experienced quite so badly, though there was one time when I had been out drinking to keep a client company so he wouldn't call his ex-girlfriend. Gofer for hire. Get hired for all sorts of things. And no, he didn't call; he bought a hamster.

The next thing I knew and Arthur was putting his hands on my shoulders, forcing me to sit up and look at him. The world was too bright for that so I growled and buried my head again. "Could you not do that?" I demanded.

"Are you okay?" he asked.

"Just peachy. That's what you call a terrible headache, right?" I snarled. He sat back and made a satisfied sort of sound.

"You're fine. The effects of messing around with time will wear off and the more you use it, the less it will happen until you can jump no problem," he said.

"You're annoying," I retorted. I forced myself to take three deep breaths and sat up, holding my eyes closed until the light that filtered through my eyelids didn't kill me. Then, very carefully, I opened my eyes and waited for the world to adjust. Curses, he was right. The headache was already starting to lessen to a steady throbbing and splitting instead of throbbing and pounding and splitting. "Okay, what happened?"

"You tell me," Arthur said. I narrowed my eyes at him and curled my lip in annoyance. He shrugged— such a *kingly* gesture, that—and kicked at a rock with the toe of his boot. "You jumped, there's no doubt about that. Only ten seconds or so, but it was a true jump. Actually, I'm surprised you managed such a controlled jump the first time around. Most people end up jumping hours, days or weeks at a time."

"I told it—*him*—that I wanted a few seconds," I answered, doing my best to sound as nonchalant as Arthur did. It was pretty difficult to manage given that I had just: a) travelled in time; b) been spoken to by a creepy non-corporeal voice, and c) returned to the world with the worst headache in the history of headaches.

"Told... it? Him?" Arthur asked. I shrugged. The shrug was my attempt at concealing the moment of panic that filled my mind. He didn't hear a non-corporeal voice when he jumped, asking when he wanted to go? Did that mean I was crazy? Or just, as the voice had suggested, special?

"The voice. Started asking me when I wanted to go. Offered me a whole bunch of choices and didn't seem to like that I was only going a few seconds. I think it wanted me to play around in history a bit. Would you stop looking at me like that? It's freaking me out," I said, pointing a finger at him. He shook his head, but the wide-eyes and fearful look remained.

"I've just... I've never heard of anyone actually communicating with the, well, Time. Normally, you have to hold the time you want to go to in your head and you jump. What did he sound like?" he asked, his skepticism showing through. I shook my head.

"Oh, no," I growled. "I'm not crazy. I'll show you.

Take my hand and I'll initiate the jump and I'll prove it to you."

"Bailey, it's not that I don't doubt you," Arthur said, raising his hands carefully, as I would do when dealing with a crazy person who was about to fly off the handle. "But no one has ever talked with Time. It can't happen. Not in this realm, though there are rumours that a realm of magic exist where such things might be possible. And even if you want to prove it to me, we've jumped enough for one day. Given the probable state of your head, another jump could rupture an artery or something. We need to get back to the castle and relax, okay?"

I bit my lip and considered the ground. My head was splitting. I was exhausted. And the fear that I was, indeed, crazy was filling my mind in a very convincing manner. I nodded. Arthur visibly relaxed and we stood, walking over to the horses, mounting and riding back to the low stone castle. We didn't talk much on the way.

"Your majesty," one of the servants said, bowing to Arthur as we arrived. "Welcome back."

"Thank you. Tell Gawain that I wish to see him," Arthur ordered. The servant froze and did his best not to look panicked. He stuttered for a moment and Arthur sighed, looking the boy in the eye. "What is the matter?"

"Sir Gawain is busy with his—" the servant started. If he finished his sentence, I didn't notice, because at that moment, the doors burst open and two people stormed out. One was Gawain, looking fiery and rearing for a fight. The other was a woman dressed in very fine clothes for the time, looking properly curvaceous and with dark hair spilling over her shoulders and around her waist.

"I don't have time for your arguments, wife," Gawain yelled at the woman, hair flying and making him look, well, fierce.

"I return from a week away and you say I cannot sleep in my own bed because what? Someone that you refuse to tell me about is here that forces me to be removed from my bedchambers?" she yelled back, giving just as good as she got.

"Don't get me wrong," I muttered out of the corner of my mouth, "but I thought that women of this time were, um, demure."

"Most are," Arthur said. Gawain drew closer which, in turn, brought his wife closer. Then I understood what it was that made her seem so out of place and yet familiar at the same time.

I knew her.

"Kate?" I said, staring openly. In the back of my mind, I heard a voice chuckle morbidly.

Chapter 10
In Which I Resort to Snark

"There's no way that you can be alive," I said after everyone in the near vicinity fell silent. It was, of course, the absolute perfect time to say such things and in return, Kate gave me one of her signature death glares. Except it felt off. I mean, here was this person who I didn't really like but who I wasn't completely opposed to, who had died right in front of my eyes. Only she was standing right there. Wearing the dress of a noblewoman. Apparently the wife of—wait a moment.

"You're...you mean he and you...will someone please explain to me what is going on?" I asked. I didn't mean to sound hysterical. It just happened.

"I would agree," Sir Gawain said, looking between Kate and myself. "Wife, I did not know that you knew our guests."

"I only returned today, husband," Kate said. "I did not know we even had guests." There was no guile in her voice when she addressed Gawain, nor anger or, well, anything but affection. They really were married. I didn't understand how and considering the day I was having, I was unsurprised to feel my headache returning.

"But you do know them," Gawain said, pointing at us. Well, me, mostly, but Arthur was included in that as well. Kate turned her gaze towards us and appraised us for a good ten seconds, saying nothing. Her eyes took in every inch of Arthur and myself and while her expression gave nothing away, her eyes were stormy and filled with bitterness and rage. Oh, dear. Finally, she gave a terse nod.

"I know them," she said. "We met years ago, before I came to this place. I didn't expect to...see them again."

Oh, wince. There was malice in those words, meant to bite and sting. Well, they did just that and I wasn't all too keen on it.

"Nor did we," Arthur cut in, somehow sounding completely calm and even pleased to see Kate. She stiffened at his words and turned her head, stepping closer to Gawain who, in turn, wrapped a protective arm around her waist. Great. We had already alienated the knight, and now we were getting even worse marks in his book. I did my best not to scowl at my day.

"Perhaps we should talk inside," Gawain said with an alarming amount of forbearance. I seized on that eagerly and nodded my assent. Kate curled a lip and turned without a word, stalking into the castle, her head held high. Arthur and I followed, and Gawain made up the rear. He was stopped a moment later by a young servant who needed his attention. Arthur paused, looking back.

"Go on," Gawain said. "I will deal with my responsibilities."

This time it was Arthur's turn to wince. He was still being attacked for now taking up his mantle of kingship again. I was beginning to think that the sooner we got out of this place, the better it would be for all of us. Arthur turned back towards the castle and we walked inside in silence.

Kate was waiting for us.

"Come with me," she snarled, spinning on her heel and leading us into a secluded room that, in something more modern, might be considered a study. She waited until the door was closed before letting loose, for which I was thankful. Kate can yell when she wants to. Take my word for it. "Do you have any *idea* what I've been through?" she yelled.

"We thought you were dead," Arthur said, barely able to cut through her fury.

"We saw you fall off the side of the ship," I added, making her turn towards me. I expected an explanation of what had happened to her but instead, she just pulled her arm back and released it, punching me square in the jaw. I, to my credit, didn't land on my bum. I landed, instead, on my shoulder, fairly certain that I had just had a few teeth knocked loose. Kate turned towards Arthur and looked as through she were about to do the same thing.

"How about you explain what happened," Arthur said, holding up his hands.

"What happened?" Kate hissed. "What happened was that I grabbed this *thing* out of the hand of the Leonum Temporis agent that was trying his level best to kill me and then poof, next thing I know, I'm in some mysterious field where people are running about beating the living daylights out of each other. They were about to kill me, too, but I know how to handle myself in a fight and I got out of there as quickly as possible. It took me all of an hour to figure out that I'd either died or travelled in time somehow and I figured that you would follow me. But no! It's been two bloody, dirt-infested years since I came here and I haven't heard hide nor hair of you two. The only good thing that happened to me here was that I met Gawain—the real one, you bastard—and he kept me from being raped or killed or worse by the various people that are running about this country, tearing it to pieces. *Two years.* Do you have any idea what I've been through?"

By the time that Kate had finished ranting at us, she had dropped into a chair and was looking rather the worse for wear. She hadn't gone into much detail, but I wasn't sure I wanted her to. I had only been in this time for a couple of days and I was struggling. Kate, absolutely rigid in her lifestyle and used to people acting a certain way, had been thrust into a world where things were completely different.

I wasn't surprised she was angry and bitter.

"Kate," Arthur said, kneeling before her and tentatively putting his hand on her knee. "I'm *sorry*." She curled her lip, looking like she might want to hit him (or me). Instead, she buried her face in her hands and began to cry. I had never seen Kate cry before. I looked away.

"You had no idea I was here, did you?" Kate asked. Arthur shook his head.

"You have been here for two years. For us, you've been gone a matter of days. We jumped mere seconds after you did and landed years later," Arthur said. "And I'm sorry."

Obviously, it was the wrong thing to say. Kate's anger returned in a flash and she stood, glaring down at Arthur. "You bastard," she snarled. "You *knew* about this time travelling crap and you didn't think to *mention* it to me? I nearly went crazy! It nearly cost me my life!"

"Join the club," I muttered. She rounded on me and I shrank back. Stupid mouth. It has no filter.

"You! Did you know about this? Did you know what sort of problems you were getting me into?" Kate challenged, stepping towards me and curling her hands into fists. I drew back, happy to keep my safe, defensive position on the floor.

"Nope," I said, wondering why my voice sounded higher than usual. "Not a clue until we jumped here. I knew something wonky was going on, but this idiot wouldn't explain what it was." I jerked my thumb in the direction of our third companion.

"It was to protect you," he defended, and poorly, I might add.

"Of course it was," Kate said, mouth twisting in a sneer. I was, in this matter, on her side. Keeping something like being a time traveller secret was what got us into this mess in the first place. Actually, no. It was me being stupid and taking the job that got *me* into this. Kate was following me. So everything could, in probability, be blamed on me. I didn't mention this thought out loud, instead deciding that discretion was the better part of valour and that I needed my brain to shut up.

"Listen, Kate," Arthur said. "I'm sorry. If I had known, if I had even been *able* to tell you about any of this, I would have. I was obliged not to."

"Oh, sure, like I'll believe that," Kate snarled, stepping forwards and looking as though she were seriously going to fight Arthur.

"It's true," Arthur said. "I may have had power here once, but in the Ordo Noctuae, my organisation, I was —am—little more than a blunt instrument. I didn't have the authority to reveal any of this to you. I can't stress how sorry I am that any of this happened, but there's nothing I could have done."

Kate opened her mouth to yell some more and was interrupted by the opening of the door and the admission of her, dare I say it, husband. The real Gawain stepped into the room—he was probably drawn to it by the loud voices shouting at each other from inside— and, upon encountering the tension in the air, immediately stepped close to Kate and glared at Arthur and myself. She didn't resist him twining his arm around her waist and even, to my surprise, leaned into the embrace. I was expecting anger to remain in her eyes as she glared at Arthur and I, but all I saw was weariness and mild annoyance. Interesting.

"Will someone please explain to me what is going on?" Gawain asked, looking between Arthur and me. I pulled myself off the floor and did my best not to look like a fool. I think I only half-succeeded.

"We met your wife during our travels, some time ago," Arthur said, tugging at his shirt and straightening into a stance that I imagined worked very well when he had been king. Only, he wasn't a king now and that stance only served to remind Gawain of the fact.

"I thought that you were in Avalon with the Three Sisters, *Your Majesty*," Gawain snarled.

Kate stiffened, stared, narrowed her eyes, considered and finally slipped out of Gawain's grasp to go sit in the chair. She made a noise in the back of her throat and looked at me, mouthing, *"You have got to be kidding me."*

I shrugged and shook my head. Nope, no kidding.

"The sisters had tasks for me," Arthur said. "I know that this must be difficult for you, Gawain, but you must understand. I am still beholden to the Three Sisters. I am still not allowed to return to my rightful place. There is nothing I can do."

"Then you should not have come here," Gawain said, pinching the bridge of his nose. "You should have just stayed on your island or done your travels or what-ever, but you should not have returned here. It would have been easier for all of us. Now I must explain to the people here why you are choosing to give up your throne when your kingdom needs you most."

"I have told you, it is *not my choice*," Arthur growled in reply, tensing as though he were about to leap at Gawain. I seriously hoped he wouldn't; I didn't need more issues at the moment.

"Then if you had a choice in the matter, you wouldn't return here at all?" Gawain asked, his voice suddenly gone quiet.

"Yes—no—I would return in a heartbeat," Arthur said. "I wish with all my being that things could be the way they were. We cannot pretend that the past hasn't happened. That is one thing I have learned in my time in Avalon. History happens. It cannot change. And, no matter how much I wish it..."

"Lancelot betrayed you and Guinevere is gone," Gawain finished. Arthur tightened his mouth but nodded. I heard that annoying voice in the back of my mind again, chuckling. My headache began to return as well.

Could you just shut up, I snarled inwardly, hoping that there was an actual entity to whom I was speaking and not just a product of possible schizophrenia. The voice laughed even louder in return.

The naïve fools. They jump around from time to time and think they know everything. History happens. The past cannot change. Pah. They know nothing of what it means to be a traveller, the voice replied, sounding pleased with his words. I wanted him to be corporeal so that I could give him a good thwack about the head, but there was not much I could do about that.

So history can *be changed?* I asked, making sure to pay some attention to what was going on in the room around me. Gawain was currently pinching the bridge of his nose between his hands and Arthur was looking mournful.

Of course. What fun would things be otherwise? The voice subsided into quiet chuckles and noises at the direction of the conversation. Great, I thought. I had a subversive, bored entity in my head and he was interrupting at all the wrong moments..

"I guess I just thought that you had come back to fix things and that things would get better," Gawain said. "I *missed* you, Arthur. You were my best friend and then suddenly you were gone. You gave me *Excalibur* to return to the lady at the lake. You told me you could not return until this was done! The promise that you would come back got me through the day. Everything else was irrelevant and I was inches away from despair." He paused and took a deep breath, "Then I met Kate and things sort of fell back into place. Now I've learned that you knew her before we met and it's like you've just taken another part of my life. How am I supposed to live with that?"

"I don't know," Arthur said.

Gawain peered at the king and shook his head. "You have changed. The Arthur I knew would never have said such a thing. He would have turned to Merlin, perhaps, turned to us for advice, but never actually said that he didn't know. It's like you've become two different people."

"Perhaps I have," Arthur replied. I decided that this was a good time to intercede and raised my hand. Almost instantaneously, I received a look from Arthur that stated very plainly I was performing an anachronism, and a look from Kate that was something along the lines of "I can't believe I have to put up with this again." Gawain just raised his eyebrows.

"So, I'm thinking that this all very nice and all," I said, hearing my voice do the odd noise thing which meant that my words were being translated. Even so, I saw Arthur wince and was mildly pleased with myself for that. "But I was wondering if we might get some food and then call it a night or something. I have rather a lot of work to do in the morning..."

"What is it exactly that you are helping Lady Bailey with, Arthur?" Gawain asked with an incredulous tone. I'm fairly used to incredulous in my line of work, so this was nothing new. That meant I was happy to simply stand there and wait for someone else to either speak or answer my request.

"It's a long story. She is searching for an artefact and I must help her retrieve it," Arthur said. I was tempted to throw in a comment along the lines of "not so long a story" but didn't. That would be rude. And Bailey Duane isn't rude. Not without cause, that is.

"Not so long a story," I muttered, garnering another

look from Kate and Arthur. Gawain, once again, just raised his eyebrows.

"There's quite a bit to it," Arthur grumbled, curling his lip in my direction. I shrugged. "And it is turning out to be harder work than I was expecting. Which is why I agree with *Lady* Bailey; we should get something to eat and have an early night. I apologise for intruding on your hospitality."

"Oh," Gawain said. He looked downcast for a moment before turning a sly eye on Kate. "I had planned a feast for the return of my wife and was hoping that you would join us."

"A feast?" Kate asked incredulously. "I've only been gone a short whi—"

"She is so modest," Gawain said. "But it is also drawing near to the day of her birth and, well, I was thinking that you would enjoy a celebration after your time on Avalon. Last night was merely drinks, after all."

Well, bother. This was exactly the thing to say to get an honour-bound, annoyed-at-me king-from-a-different-time to attend a party. That meant I had to attend as well and if there was one thing that I had proven, it was that I was absolutely hopeless at the finer points of culture involved with fitting into this time. So, either I was going to have to get some training or there were going to be rather a lot of questions asked of me.

Questions I could not answer.

"Gawain," Kate said, half-growling. "It is unnecessary to throw a party in my honour. And I'm sure our guests are tired after their day and wish to retire early."

"Come now, Kate!" Gawain said, turning on her with a hopeful look that was a cross between puppy and adorable child. It was working on me and I didn't even like the guy all that much. Kate was married to him. "It will be fun."

"Fun," she said, obviously wavering. She sighed and shook her head. "Fine. Fine. You can have your feast, party, whatever. I'll let you discuss the details with the king and Lady Bailey and I will go get ready. I'm sure she would like a bath after a hot day."

"What?" I asked, realising too late what was in store for me. In one fluid motion, Kate rose, snatched my arm and dragged me from the room. I had absolutely no choice but to follow, and follow I did. I was rather fond of the arm currently being pulled from my socket. As we travelled through the castle, her grip grew tighter on my arm until I had to forcibly extricate myself from her grasp. "Relax, will you?"

"Sorry," Kate hissed, pulling me into the room where I had been staying, and which was apparently *her* room. "I'm having a hard time reconciling your presence with the last two years of my life. You'll have to give me a few minutes."

"Right," I muttered, standing awkwardly by the window and rubbing my arm where her nails had dug into it. She glared at me for a moment before sticking her head out the door and ordering a bath to be drawn and a basin of water to be brought. Then, with a pout that was completely unlike the Kate Dupont that I had known, she sat on the bed and crossed her arms.

"You don't have to be so reasonable," she grumbled. I shrugged.

"Sorry? I could snarl and hiss, but there doesn't seem like much point. Besides, I'm glad to see you're not dead," I said, moving to join her. A sharp look stopped that advance, but didn't prevent me from sitting in a chair.

"I want to hate you so badly," Kate said, sighing and reaching up to undo the coil of hair at the nape of her neck. "But I can't. Don't get me wrong," she snapped as I straightened in surprise, "I'm still angry, but I don't hate you."

"Gee, thanks, Dupont. I don't hate you either," I said. Kate glared and finished undoing her hair in silence. A few minutes later and a servant knocked, announcing through the wooden door that the bath was prepared and could she enter with the basin. Permission was granted and the poor thing dashed in and set the basin and cloth down and scurried away as though she were terrified of Kate. I was right there with her.

"You wash up here and I'll go take a bath. I'll return shortly," Kate said, rising primly.

"Uh, I thought I was the one who was meant to take a bath," I pointed out.

"I've been travelling for two weeks, I'm annoyed and I'm not in the mood for an argument. I'm taking a bath and that's that. Got it?" Kate asked. I nodded fervently and relaxed only when she left the room, the door rattling in the frame after her. I sighed and sat on the bed where Kate had been a moment before.

"See?" I muttered. "This is what happens when you mess with time."

She would have been angry at you whether or not she had travelled here. She is meant for safe offices and arguments with unarmed people. Travelling does not suit her. Was it my imagination or was the voice getting more snarky? I frowned.

"You're to blame for that, then, Casper," I said, standing and stalking over to the wash basin. I drenched the cloth, rang it out and proceeded to give myself a bird bath, wishing that I had something more suitable for washing my rat's nest of hair. I settled for the comb on the vanity and attacked it with dogged determination.

Casper? I should think not. The voice grumbled.

"Well, I can't simply keep calling you the voice and since I can't see you, I'm going to have to give you a proper ghost name. So Casper it is," I snapped, wrenching the comb through my hair and wincing at the strands that were pulled out.

Surely you can come up with a better nickname, if one is even necessary. It's degrading to be reduced to something so... juvenile. You may call me Time, for that is what—and who—I am. Good, I was getting on his nerves. Now I could reciprocate some of the annoyances that had been paid me.

"No, I'm pretty sure that Casper suits you. You're

the one who got me into this mess, so no complaining, got it? *Casper?*" I said.

Time subsided into silence broken by a few word-less grumbles every now and again. I grinned and finished attacking my hair. I managed to get it into some semblance of control by the time Kate returned. So when she took one look at me and burst out laughing, I was feeling a little hurt.

"There's no way I'm letting you go into public looking like that. And besides, you're dressed like a man. There must be something we can find that will fit you," she said, striding over to her wardrobe. I noticed that her hair was primly done and she was wearing a new dress that was much more elegant and plainly meant for a party rather than day-to-day wear.

"I'm too tall," I pointed out gladly. "And no one has complained about my needing to dress like a man before. Besides, you used to wear trousers, too."

"And then I came here," Kate said. "The only reason that no one has pointed anything out is because you're meant to be a foreign dignitary who gets special privileges for being more savage. That and you are living in a house of men. So if you want to eat tonight, you will wear a dress and you will like it. Am I clear?"

"Yes, Mistress." I scowled.

Kate bared her teeth at me and I shut up, tromping meekly over to the wardrobe where Kate proceeded to hold up just about every dress she owned to me. All of them were too short, so she eventually called a seam-stress into the room, ordering that something be done about letting the hems down so I might have something decent to wear. The old woman stared in surprise at me, but did as she was asked, letting the hems down until there was nothing else to let down. Even then, the garment was about an inch too short for me. I was going to point that out to Kate in the form of a snarky comment when she twitched her lip at me. I remained silent and put on the dress.

It wasn't terrible. Even tall and knobbly, I wasn't completely hopeless when it came to wearing dresses. At least, *I* thought so. But Kate made a face and Casper laughed in the back of my head. I tugged at the skirt, wriggled in the bodice and put on my best grimace. "If we're done playing dress up, can we go eat, now?"

"You haven't changed at all," Kate said, raising her nose ever so slightly.

"I'm doing my best to stay as static as possible. Now, let's go. I'm starving."

Chapter 11
In Which I Travel In Time

The trimmings for a feast had been laid out during the time that Kate and I were washing up and talking. Apparently, men didn't need to bathe before a party if they'd only been out wandering for a day, so Arthur and Gawain were as before: casually dressed and slightly smelly. Kate didn't bother lingering at the door to the great hall, though, wrinkling her nose at her husband and my travelling companion as I might have expected. She merely strode forwards, going directly to Gawain and greeting him with a healthy kiss. I remained in the doorway, feeling out of place.

Arthur was laughing, a tankard of something in his hand, another one of his knights at his side, illustrating a story with his hands. The king laughed again, drawing Gawain's attention and, inevitably, Kate's along with it. The two moved to Arthur and joined in the conversation. I stood in the doorway, fingering my dress. It was ill-fitting and something I was unused to wearing. I hadn't worn a dress in, well, I couldn't remember the last time. Now here I was, in a foreign time which might have as well been a foreign country, trying my best to fit in when I knew that there was no chance of that. Hmph.

I winced as another peal of laughter rang out. Then, noticing a servant carrying a tray of drinks behind me, got out of the way for the man and put into practise something which I had been practising for years. I made myself scarce.

Where are you going? Time asked just as soon as I'd slipped through a door which looked under-used. Under-used doors, just in case you are wondering, are the best kind for hiding. People don't use them (duh) and they expect that others won't use them, either, just because they themselves don't. It's like the customer in the store. They exist for the moment you're staring at them, but as soon as you look away, they never existed and never could have existed just because your thoughts are diverted. Depressing, sure. But it was useful for trying to stay away from people.

Just another one of those tricks I learned from Carlos.

"Anywhere but there," I replied, finding myself at the top of a stairway filled in with cobwebs and about as dark as I'll get out. The only light was coming from behind me and I knew that I had to close the door if I wanted to really be out of the way. "Any chance of a light?"

I am in control of all Time. You think a light is out of the question for me? Time asked, pretending to sound offended. I say pretending because there was a definite tone of arrogance in his voice. I shrugged and closed the door, expecting to be plunged into darkness. Instead, my hand lit up like a torch and I could see everything perfectly. The light was reminisce of the whiteness that came about whenever I had jumped through time and it gave me a slight pain in my head, but it did the trick. I took several deep breaths to prevent a panic attack at the sight of my left hand glowing like a LED light.

This was just one more piece of evidence that my life was very strange, indeed. Now I was dealing with magic, not just jumping through time. I wondered what else I had missed in my ordinary life until now. Dragons? That would be very cool, I decided.

Besides, Time put in, *I am not the one you should be questioning, oh traveller. You're the one who can do the jumping and playing around with history. I am merely here for the conversation.*

"Says the voice hitching a ride in my head," I muttered, going down the stairs while trying my best to keep the spiders in possession of the cobwebs from getting in my hair.

I'm only here because you let me in. I have no control over what you do. I can only advise and assist. You're the one who initiates events, Time said with a sniff. I growled and yelped quietly when a stone slipped out from beneath my feet. Well, it looks like the castles were falling apart even during their prime.

"If that's meant to make me feel better, it's not," I snapped. By this time, I had reached the bottom of the staircase and was more inclined to look around than argue with a voice in my head. At least with the light pouring out of my hand, I could be pretty sure that I wasn't just crazy.

You ran away... to a larder? Time said. I frowned, but there was no point in disagreeing. A larder—and a seemingly forgotten one at that—was exactly where I was. There were crates of smoked meat and fruit preserves, masonry jars of who-knows-what and a few dusty barrels of what was probably wine or ale. I shrugged.

"Fortuitous," I said. "At least I can eat while I avoid people."

Do you ever think about anything other than your immediate needs? Time said, voice dripping with disdain. I moved to the back of the larder, picking up some smoked jerky, a jar of pickled cabbage and a few dried apples on the way. I was looking for a nice place to sit and enjoy my meal and came upon another door instead. It was, surprise surprise, unlocked and covered in cobwebs, making it nearly impossible to distinguish from the wall surrounding it. I pushed it open and went inside.

"What would you like me to think about?" I asked. "My hopes and dreams? Taking over the world? How to bring about world peace? That might be a bit difficult considering that I'm basically stuck in this miserable time with no way out and no idea of where this book is that I'm meant to be finding."

You could forget the book, Time pointed out. I waved my hand in frustration, though it is bothersome trying to figure out a direction in which to wave a hand at a disembodied voice. That and moving a glowing appendage made the shadows in the room flicker.

"I've been hired for a job," I said. "I see my jobs through to the end, no matter where that may lead."

Noble, but idiotic. I would have thought that the discovery of all of this time travelling and the true identity of your employer would have voided your contract. I am glad we're finally getting to talk, but it seems imprudent to continue in this line. Not if you're going to be so dull, Time said.

I gave a half-shrug and shoved the door closed behind me, looking around in the new room in which I found myself.

It was fairly small and there wasn't much there but a chair with three legs, some boxes over in one corner, something that looked disturbingly like a crypt and a lumpy rock in the centre of the room. In the middle of the rock was a piece of metal, rusted over, in the shape of a sword. "Is that...?" I asked, reaching out to touch the sword tentatively.

Yes, Casper said, sounding as interested as I. *It appears to be* Excalibur. *It is one of those items that has such a powerful effect on history. I can feel its presence like a shiver in the streams, a ripple in my being. It would appear that Sir Gawain never returned it to the lady at the lake, as he was bid. Your friend, the king, will be most displeased.*

I wasn't quite sure I enjoyed how thrilled Time sounded at that prospect. I wished for the internet for a moment so I could look up the legend of King Arthur and figure out what Time was talking about instead of fumbling about without even a decent book to read.

"Weird," I said, pulling back from the stone. I brushed off one of the boxes and sat, bringing my feet up beneath my skirts and spreading the fabric out like a table. I took a bite of one of the dried apples and decided that it wasn't as bad as it looked. "To answer your question, Casper," I said around a mouthful of fruit, mostly to annoy Time, "I'm not the type of person to abandon a contract just because my employer turns out to be a weirdo. That would be wrong. I mean, I've worked for the Professor a few times and he's bad news."

Which is why Katelyn got involved, is it not? Time asked. I nodded and took another bite of the apple, cracking open the masonry jar of cabbage to drink some of the juices. It was as bad as it sounds. *Your own stubbornness is what got you into this situation, then.*

"I wouldn't put it like that," I muttered. "Besides, my stubbornness is going to get me out of this. Then I can go back home and get on with my life."

And run errands for people who no more appreciate your talents than you do. Picking up dry-cleaning was your most important stable task, if I have my facts right.

I jabbed my finger at the air, figuring that it was better than jabbing a finger at my head. "That's going too far. I happen to like my line of work, thank you very much," I said. Time replied with a questioning hum and he sounded more than smug. "I get to do things that most people would never even consider doing. I get to help people when no one else will. Sure, I pick up dry-cleaning every now and again, but that doesn't mean I'm not helping people. I'm the person that people can depend on to take care of the big things or the little things. Why? Because it is my job, my duty to help these people. And they understand that."

That is an interesting spin on your line of work, Time said. I drew my brows together and growled in the back of my throat. *I am not saying that it is a bad spin. Most people would not consider things the way that you see them. Which, Bailey, is why I know that you will do well with the unique ability that you have been given.*

"Yeah, yeah," I said. "Enough with this whole unique ability thing. Can't I just have one night where I can try and forget all of the crap that has happened to me and be on my own? Or are you going to continue talking so I'll *have* to interact with the disembodied voice in my head?" With this, I tore into the jerky and chewed sullenly.

I think it is too late for a quiet life, Time pointed out, not bothering to hide the snideness in his voice. I grumbled and folded my arms in a pout.

"Well, then, how about just an evening? I could do

with a quiet evening," I suggested. "I'm about due for one anyway. Actually, I'm *over* due for one."

It is too late for even a quiet evening, I think. Someone is coming. Sure enough, Time was right. I heard pounding footsteps approaching from the other side of the door and cursed as quietly as possible. Then I realised that staying quiet would do nothing considering that my hand was still blazing away like a beacon.

"Out, out, out," I said, shaking my hand desperately, willing the light dark with all my might. If Casper was right and I was the one doing all of this stuff—weird as that might seem—then the light should go out when I wanted. It didn't. I shook it even more desperately and began to panic when the door started rattling in its frame. Whoever was out there was coming in and that fell in the category of Not Good. The door budged an inch and then everything was dark, my lighted hand having gone out at last. My eyes were full of white spots for a while and there was no chance of them adjusting before the person came in, so I shut them and hoped that my ears were up to the job. I pressed my back against the wall and hoped no one noticed me.

The door opened roughly, scraping over the stone. I held my breath, tentatively opening my eyes. Nothing. All I heard were some footsteps and breathing. Two people, maybe three. I didn't know. I heard some muttering and shuffling and then, very loudly, a curse. "Who put this rock in the middle of the room?!" the voice said. I blinked. I knew that voice. I had spent a good portion of the last two weeks, plus or minus a few centuries, with that voice.

"Kate?" I asked, opening my eyes. There was some more cursing and the sound of metal striking on something. A flash and a whoosh later and Kate raised the torch she held in her hand, the flames licking eagerly at the air.

"So this is where you got off to," she grumbled, dragging the other people into the room. Gawain was standing with one arm cradled against his chest, a cut on his lip. Arthur held a candlestick minus the candles, the ends of which were dipped in what I desperately hoped was wine.

"Um, hi," I said, waving the hand with the jerky in it before realising what I had just done. I put the food down and stood. "What's going on?"

Arthur didn't answer. Instead, he stared at the sword in the rock at the centre of the room. "You brought it here?"

"We couldn't just leave it at Caerleon," Gawain said. "We would have to fight off every possible villager and warrior from trying to pull it from the stone and claim his place as the next king. So We cut the stone from the ground and brought it here."

"I thought it was gone. I gave you a direct order and you...this wasn't even the right sword for the stone. That one was broken long ago. *Excalibur* should never have been placed thusly," Arthur said, touching the sword. It hummed slightly, which was creepy, considering that swords shouldn't hum. Of course, I shouldn't have Time talking in my head, either, so I figured that there might be some latitude involved. "At the very least, it should have vanished when I..."

"Left," I supplied. "Well, it's really nice that it didn't vanish and all that, and really, someone should tell me all about your history at a later date, but I'm wondering what is going on? I take it that you didn't get involved in a nice friendly drunken brawl with the other people at this feast."

"It's not even been an hour," Kate pointed out. "They couldn't have got drunk that quickly."

"I know some people," I muttered darkly. That being one of the reasons that I will never accept another job that requires playing drinking games. "So, fine, no drunken brawl. Then would you enlighten me as to what is going on and why my nice quiet evening has been interrupted?"

"Leonum Temporis," Arthur said. I heaved a sigh and rolled my eyes.

"How did I know that you were going to say that? All that's happened on this idiotic job is lies and secrets and people from Leonum Temporis following me about," I said. "I'm guessing that there's no way out of here apart from the, you know, flash bang sort of thing."

"Flash... bang?" Gawain asked, leaning against the wall. Sheesh, how far back in time was I? Kate shot me a look and put Gawain's good arm around her shoulder.

"Can you even manage it?" Arthur asked. He pulled his Timer out of his pocket and offered it tentatively to me.

"I have no idea," I said, realising what he wanted me to do. My heart started beating faster, telling me in no uncertain terms that this was a really bad idea. "I can try."

I closed my eyes and mentally prodded at Time, rousing the entity into annoyance. *Come on,* I thought. *Can't you, you know, initiate a jump or something?*

I have already explained this to you, Time said with a definite sniff. *I do not initiate anything. I only assist or advise. If you want to jump, you must start the jump.* I wanted to hit the stupid voice over the head, but as that would mean hitting myself, I refrained. Instead, I did my best to concentrate on the Timer and what I had done earlier that day, only encompassing the people in the room.

"Bailey," Arthur said. "If you could hurry."

"*You* try this, Artie," I growled, what concentration I had gone. I squeezed the Timer tighter in my hands, willing it with all my might to work. All I managed was an increase in my headache and a disappointing puff of smoke flared in my hands. "Nothing," I said.

"I don't know what you expected to happen," Gawain growled, pushing himself away from the wall and turning to face the door. "But I refuse to die like a prisoner in my own home."

"We are trapped down here," Kate pointed out. "And the only weapon we have is a candlestick and a sword stuck in a rock. Somehow, I don't think we have much choice."

"Cheery bunch, aren't you," I scoffed, stuffing the

Timer into a pocket on the dress, a modernisation I imagine came directly from Kate. Then, just to make things worse, more footsteps began to sound, quite obviously coming down the stairs. Oh, goody. "Right, well, that's fun."

"Bailey, if you don't shut up right now," Kate threatened, "I'm going to stuff that dress down your throat." I made a face at her and looked around. Resources, resources, come on! Now, here's something you have to understand about being a gofer for hire. If you can't figure out how to MacGyver things in a pinch, your entire career is going to vanish in a tragic, catastrophic ball of flames. So I've got pretty good at thinking under pressure, even if all I have is a roll of duct tape. Of course, I didn't actually have a roll of duct tape at this point, but I did have two well-trained knights, a candlestick, some jerky, pickled cabbage and a dried apple. Oh, and that whole pointy piece of metal in the rock in the middle of the room.

"Okay, what's the best angle on this thing," I said, lunging towards the sword and wrapping my hand around the hilt. Gawain and Arthur both turned to look at me, diverting their attention for a few precious seconds.

"No man besides the king will wield *Excalibur*," Gawain bellowed, turning towards me with furious eyes.

"Good thing I'm not a man, then," I said and put my entire weight against the sword, hoping to leverage it out. It was surprisingly easy to pull, considering all the hype about the matter. But then, I doubt that any of the people who had put the sword there in the first place considered the fact that a woman might try and take it out. I wasn't going to be king, after all. Or maybe Arthur was right in saying it shouldn't have been there in the first place. I preferred to think it was my own cleverness that won that particular situation.

I staggered backwards with the sword and nearly fell on my bum, one of the most graceful moves I could have possibly made considering what I had just done. "So, Artie, how about you give Gawain the candlestick and take your sword?"

"It won't accept me," Arthur said. "I put it down."

"No, you got kidnapped by a bunch of people mucking about in history. There's a difference. Now, take the sword and defend us while I try to get us out of here!" I yelled. At this point, I didn't think it mattered whether or not the Leonum Temporis agents bearing down on us heard because they were already far too close for comfort. Arthur growled, threw the candlestick at Gawain, grabbed the sword and turned to defend the doorway. I had half expected there to be a glow when Arthur took the sword, or perhaps a chorus of singing. There was none of that, just an ordinary man taking an ordinary sword, though it was clear he could handle the weapon well enough to kill.

The distraction would only last a few minutes, at best, and then we would all be dead. Or worse.

I pulled the Timer out again and squeezed it in my

hand, muttering under my breath as quickly as I could, "Jump jump jump jump."

I thought of the way I had jumped earlier that day, of the way that my hand had lit into a fierce blaze. If Time wasn't the one doing either of those, then I must have done it. And if I did it once, I had to be able to do it again. So I concentrated. I ignored the sounds of fighting that started up a moment later. I ignored Gawain and Arthur being pushed back into the room and running into me. I ignored the way that Kate, the strongest woman I knew, held back like a creature of a different age reliant on others to defend her. I ignored the four agents who were wielding weapons of various sorts, coming straight for us with murderous intent. I merely bared my teeth at the stupid Timer and demanded that it cooperate.

Finally, it did. And just in time, too, I might add. The Leonum Temporis people were bearing down on Arthur, Gawain, Kate and myself and I could feel a cut on my shoulder where one of them had com at me with something pointy. Then, the room filled with the white light that I had oddly grown accustomed to seeing. "Only my friends," I murmured, mentally pushing the light around the four of us.

As you wish, Time said, his voice no longer just in my head but also sounding through the space around me. Kate appeared first, falling to her knees inside the space, gasping. Gawain was next, the veins on his neck straining as he struggled to contain the pressure inside of him. Arthur was last, taking only one deep breath before he relaxed and looked around, having grown accustomed to feeling the forces of Time so powerfully. At least, that's what I thought it was, though I wasn't entirely sure.

"So..." I said, shrugging my shoulders and rubbing my forehead. The headache wasn't nearly as bad as before, but it was still annoying. "What now?"

"You... how did you get all of us... I didn't think it was possible," Arthur said. I laughed nervously.

"Well, er, Casper helped a bit," I said. Gawain let out a strangled sound, diverting Arthur's attention. He walked over to his knight and put a hand on the man's shoulder, muttering things that were meant to let the man relax. Gawain forced himself to obey, but I doubt that it helped that there were obvious signs of strain on Arthur's face.

"Bailey, what you're doing shouldn't be possible," Arthur said. I raised my eyebrows. "You're holding four people in the undetermined parts of Time. It's never been done. It *can't* be done."

"Just because you are not capable of it, little King, doesn't mean that it is not possible," Time said with an arrogant sneer. I rolled my eyes. "My servant is far more capable than you think."

"I am not your servant," I grumbled. Then, I blinked and realised the voice of Time was not in my head. No, it was coming from a definitive point, a little ways distant, where a figure stood. He was clothed in simple slacks and a white shirt, hands casually tucked into his pockets. He looked almost ordinary, average height, average looks, except that one moment he was in the prime of his youth with reddish-brown hair and a smile that could fell crowds, and the next he was an old man, stooped with age and silver-haired.

Arthur looked between me and Time with wide eyes.

"What?" I defended. "I told you that it talked to me. You're the one who didn't believe me."

"This is... how are you...It's not possible," Arthur said, voice shaking.

I shook my head and held up my hands. I didn't know how it was working. That didn't mean that I wasn't going to use this to my full advantage, but nor could I explain it.

It was also really nice to know that I wasn't crazy, that the voice in my head was real.

At this point, Kate stood up and managed to calm herself enough to see to her husband. He was close to stumbling and grasped his stomach as though he were going to be sick. Kate turned to me. "I don't care how you're doing it, I don't care about the fact that you can do it, whatever you're doing, Bailey, it needs to stop soon. My husband has never travelled before and he's going to be killed if you don't do something. Get us out of here."

"He will not die," Time said. "He is in great pain, but he will not die."

"Then stop his pain," Kate demanded. I could feel Time focusing in on Kate, examining her with forceful interest. She drew herself up to her full height and snarled, "Do it now. Whoever you are, do it now!"

"You are quite the creature, Katelyn Dupont, to challenge Time himself. You seem to have placed yourself into the time period in which you found yourself and survived, not a feat many could have accomplished," Time noted, becoming exceedingly interested.

"You said that she was suited for comfortable desk work," I pointed out. Kate clenched her fist and turned towards the only target she could fight: me. I raised my hands in surrender before she could do something rash, like hit me and knock me out before we got back into the world. "Alright, fine! I'll get us out of here."

"When would you like to go?" Time asked. I considered. We couldn't very well go back to the time we had just left. We would all be killed. But Gawain had never travelled before and I doubted that going too far into the future would do well for his psyche. Then, no matter when we went, the Leonum Temporis people would be sure to follow, so long as we were both searching for the book.

I took a deep breath. Maybe it would be possible to kill two birds with one stone. Or one jump, as it were.

"Take us to the point in history where the Time Keeper is," I said. "Without it jumping, if you would."

"You are the traveller, you focus on the time. I will assist as required," Time said. I had so many more questions, for him and for the others, questions that would explain why I was experiencing what I was, that would explain the nature of the universe, that would keep me from falling into the fear of abject insanity. I didn't have time for those questions. So I did what I do best; I got on with my work. I was really, really good at my work.

I pulled up all of the notes I had taken and read regarding that manuscript in my head, and thought about the book until I could almost picture it in my mind. I closed my eyes and reached out, holding that image in my thoughts. Then, I imagined touching the book, going straight to it and bringing the others along with me. Frankly, I had no idea whether or not it would work, but I wanted it to do so and I wasn't going to take no for an answer.

The pressure on my head increased and the light seemed to brighten. Then it vanished and there was nothing at all.

Chapter 12
In Which I Meet Fred, the Younger

It was nigh impossible to tell where we were once the bright spots had faded from my vision. The surrounding area looked about the same as the field I had first landed in, but everything was darkened by night. I did a quick check to make sure that I wasn't missing any limbs and that my head wasn't going to explode with pain if I started moving. Actually, the headache had almost completely vanished, which was a pleasant surprise. Then, I looked around and made sure that none of my companions were missing any limbs. Their shadowy forms seemed intact, so I felt it was safe to ask Time, *When are we, Casper?*

When the Time Keeper is, Time replied smugly. I muttered unkind things under my breath and decided that I was going to have to figure it out myself. I turned to Arthur, who was currently holding *Excalibur* and staring blankly at the sword as if he had been reunited with an old friend.

"Are you okay?" I asked. He turned to look at me, his black hair completely dishevelled and various cuts on his face. I was tempted to repeat the question when someone grabbed my arm like a vise. I yelped and turned to see Kate, her dress dirty and torn from the fight, her expression one of pain and panic.

"Do something!" she demanded, pulling me towards her husband. He was on the ground, his hair and beard coated with dark liquid that, in the night-time air I couldn't identify but could imagine, the candlestick still clutched in his hands, his eyes wide and unseeing. Groans of pain were emanating from him and I knelt down next to him. His eyes flickered to mine.

"He's never travelled before. He doesn't know what's going on and he's in pain and... do something!" Kate said, giving me another shove for good measure.

"Right, fine, I'll do my best," I said, crouching next to Gawain and remembering that I wore a dress which wasn't meant for crouching. I sat instead, hoping that the moisture I felt wasn't mud. "So, um, you've just travelled through time. Yeah, I know, sounds crazy, but there you have it. Actually, Arthur there is part of a time travelling organisation. He got picked up after the battle at Camlan or whatever it was and pressed into service. Then he dragged me into everything, trying to find a book and Kate followed me, because it was her job to keep an eye on me so that I didn't break any US laws while overseas. I imagine at this point that you probably thing I'm speaking a different language, and your head probably hurts like the dickens. Sorry about that. It was sort of the only way to get us out of that basement. You know?"

"Bailey," Kate growled, making me jump when her voice tickled my ear. "I'm going to kill you."

"You said do something!" I protested. "It's not like I can just magic the headache away or anything. It's not my fault Casper has decided that I'm an interesting person to hang around with, and that I can somehow travel through time on my own and take ride alongs with me."

Kate did something funny with her fingers at the point where my neck met my shoulders. I yelped and did my best to scramble away from her, only to discover that I couldn't, actually move. She pressed harder and I tried to pull away.

"Enough," Gawain rumbled, bringing me to attention and Kate to the side of her husband. She helped him sit up, at his behest, and I rubbed my shoulder.

"Are you okay?" Kate asked, rubbing away some of the blood on Gawain's face. He recoiled from her and she blinked. "Gawain?"

"You're insane!" he shouted, scrambling backwards. I figured that meant he was recovering quite nicely. I remember from my own experiences that I had to do the whole "what the heck, you're all crazy, run away!" thing before I could accept the fact that time travelling really was a thing. Gawain was progressing through that trend quite nicely.

"Gawain, please," Kate said, holding out her hands

to her husband. I looked around and wished desperately that I had a pair of trousers with pockets, just so I could have something to do with my hands.

Then, "Oh, bother." Arthur finally looked up from examining the sword—sheesh, it's a piece of shiny metal. What's the big deal?—and glanced in my direction. I shrugged. "I left my satchel back in the castle."

"It's too late to worry about that sort of thing," Arthur said, drawing Gawain's attention and distracting him long enough for Kate to wrap her arms around his shoulders in a sort of comforting gesture.

"It's got all of my research on the manuscript in it," I said.

It would be simple enough to jump back and grab it, Time pointed out. I considered and decided that, of everything, I wasn't about to let my custom-made leather bag with all my research and funds fall into the hands of people that had been trying very hard to kill me. I nodded, closed my eyes and concentrated. Just trying to move me was a whole lot easier than three other people besides, and I managed the jump in a few seconds.

Of course, I appeared in the room just as a bunch of armed insurgents with not-so-ancient guns walked in. They took one look at me and panicked, letting off a string of shots. I grumbled, grabbed the bag and high-tailed it out of there.

That was fun, Time chuckled as I appeared back in the middle of the stunned group of my friends.

"You have a very strange definition of fun," I snapped back.

"What?" Arthur asked, sliding the sword into the sheath that he wore at his side. That reminded me of the dress I wore and I sighed. A change of clothes was in order. And some hot food. And drink.

"I was talking to Casper," I said, putting the satchel over my shoulder. I heard Kate murmuring soothing things to Gawain and decided that I had been through enough. I tromped over to the knight and held out my hand, hauling him onto his feet. "You'll get used to it," I said. He blinked, coming out of his daze and nodded hesitantly.

Kate glared.

"I've heard the voice and seen him, and yet I still have a hard time believing that Time talks to you," Arthur said.

"I think we should go that way," I said, pointing in a random direction.

I would suggest going north, not south, Time said casually. *There aren't signs of civilisation for thirty miles that way, whereas south is about half-a-mile.*

"That way," I said, correcting my stance. We started off and Kate and I quickly discovered just how annoying dresses and soft shoes were for hiking through brush. "It's not *my* fault that Casper decided to start talking to me," I told Arthur, glaring at his boot-clad feet. "It just sort of happened."

"I've noticed that a lot of things tend to happen around you, Bailey," Arthur snarled. I held up my hands in defence and let him take the lead. There was no dealing with him in one of those moods.

"As soon as I get out of this dress and can find a decent firearm," Kate said, coming up behind me and scaring me out of my hide, "I'm going to shoot you."

"That's nice," I replied, unable to swallow a nervous chuckle. She fixed me with a glare that was much darker than her official FBI agent one and I decided that she, too, should walk ahead of me. Which left Gawain. He was managing quite well, considering that his entire world had been ripped from beneath his feet. I said as such. "You seem to be taking all of this pretty well."

"It makes more sense than having Arthur be on a magical island with three mystical spirits, destined to return when we need him most," Gawain said. "Besides, your mannerism were quite obviously not normal."

"That's about right," I answered. "Though, my mannerisms aren't normal in any time, near as I can figure. But I thought that you people were fairly used to the whole magic thing, what with Merlin and Morganna and... stuff."

Could you at least attempt to be a little more eloquent? You're embarrassing me, Time grumbled. I ignored him.

"I never witnessed any magic myself," Gawain said. "You could say that I was a skeptic. But this! Time travel. If that isn't more magical than anything I've ever been told, I don't know what is. I do have one question, though."

"Only one? You're doing better than I was," I said.

"One question for the moment," Gawain amended. "When does my head stop splitting?"

"Sometime tomorrow, probably," I said. I shrugged. "I don't really know. Apparently I'm weird—"

Naturally.

"So I see."

"—Gee, thanks. Anyways, I'm probably not a good industry standard. I'd ask Arthur, except he seems to be preoccupied with *Excalibur* or something. At least, he doesn't seem all there at the moment."

"In his position, I wouldn't be all there, either," Gawain said. "He left Camlan... dead, we all thought. *Excalibur* was left behind, meant to be a symbol of his power, to be returned to the lady who gave it to him. In that...I failed him. I could not let such a powerful symbol of unity slip away, so I put it in the stone that held his original sword. If he couldn't draw it from the stone again, he would be ready or worthy of being king. And then you show up and pull it from the stone like it's just a piece of soft moss and hand it to him. So, the question I imagine he asks is whether or not he has the power that holding *Excalibur* implies or whether you do."

"That's silly," I said. "I don't need some magic sword telling me that I'm going to be king... queen, whatever."

"But the fact still remains that you were the one to

pull the sword from the stone. *He who pulls the sword—"*

"Blah, blah, blah," I finished, surprised at the accuracy of my words. "Come on. I found a loophole. I'm pretty sure it doesn't count. And, since we're on the topic, I don't think that he'll be needing to worry about being king for a while yet. Because, if I am any judge of those lights appearing in the distance, the time of active monarchy is long gone."

I was right—as usual. There were lights appearing in the distance and there was no doubt that they were of the electric variety. A few hundred more feet and we were crossing over a road, paved not too long ago and nearly empty. I say nearly because just as soon as I put my foot on the tarmac to cross over to the footpath on the other side, where Arthur and Kate were already waiting, a car sped past, honking loudly at me. I jumped back and found that Gawain was looking mildly terrified and furious at the same time.

"Welcome to the future," I said, peering after the car. "That was what we call a car. Like a horse except bigger, louder, more energy efficient. That one looked like it was made in 1964 or 1965. Not quite sure. Casper, you'd better have an answer: when exactly are we?"

If you insist. This is the year 1969. The 17th *of November, to be exact.* Time said with a superior sniff. Not for the first time, I wished that the voice had a body outside of that empty realm so that I could give him a good whack.

"Great," I said. I looked to make sure that there were no more cars coming and pulled Gawain across the road with me. We caught up with Kate and Arthur who were glaring in opposite directions, sticking together but plainly not pleased with the matter. "So, we're in 1969."

"Oh, no," Arthur said.

"You've got to be joking," Kate snapped. I shrugged. "We went from the time of Camelot to the sixties? There's no way that's an improvement."

"I just took us to the time when the stupid manuscript is," I said. "That's all. Don't blame me for the fact that it happens to be the sixties. I mean, it can't be that bad, can it?"

"Whoa," a new voice said, stepping up to us and giving all of us a good look over. "Some costumes. Just coming from a party or what?"

"Uh," I said, blinking at the odd clothes and even more interesting hair. He had his hands stuffed in the pockets of his jacket and smelled suspiciously like cannabis. Lots of cannabis.

"Yes, a costume party," Kate said. She was using her official FBI voice, but the English man from 1969 wouldn't know that. To him, we were probably just part of an interesting night. "It didn't work out and someone stole our car keys."

"Bummer," the man said. "Come on. I know a guy who knows a guy who can hook you up with some new clothes and, you know, stuff."

"Great," I said, catching on. Arthur surreptitiously

hid the sword and Gawain, when the young man looked the other way, did his best to rub away some of the blood. "Lead the way."

"Cool," the man replied, taking another look at us and walking on towards the town. "So, you from Scotland or something?"

"No, why?" I asked. What an odd thing to say. Yes, my English accent had faded slightly after living nearly a decade in the States, but it wasn't quite that bad. And though I loved Scotland, I had never quite managed to replicate that particular burr. Since none of these answers was likely to be satisfactory, I did what I do best; I improvised.

"We're from Canada." A lie, but it was better than being American right in the middle of the Cold War and the Vietnam War. Which reminded me that neither Kate nor Arthur had their passports with them and I was pretty confident that Gawain didn't have one, either. You know, what with the whole being around when the greater portion of the western world hadn't even been discovered and all. I had mine, but only because I still carried my satchel.

"Canada, Scotland, whatever, doesn't matter to me," the man said in a serene tone. By this time, we had crossed the boundary of the town and were passing buildings illuminated with lights. I peered in a few of them and saw restaurants, record stores, bookshops and scenes of family cheer. Our guide, however, led us to the one building that didn't have any of that. Instead, it was unlit with a shadowed figure leaning ominously in the doorway. "Hey, Jones," our guide said, nodding his head to the figure in the door.

"You know the deal, James," the figure replied. James. James. Hmm. An interesting name, but nothing out of the ordinary. For some reason, it seemed to ground this character to reality, making him more than just an oddly dressed guide from the sixties. James shrugged and nodded.

"Festinare malum est, et saepe morari malum est; sapiens est qui omnia suo tempore facit," James said, looking at us as though we might think him weird for talking in Latin. I have to admit, it was a bit odd, even for our current situation. The phrasing was familiar, though I didn't quite remember it. After all, I did only take Latin for a month in college. This felt like a whisper of things that I should remember or might encounter in the future. It was a bizarre sensation.

"It is bad to hurry, and delay is often as bad; the wise person is the one who does everything in its proper time," Gawain said, translating for us. I should have known that he, being from around the same time as the Romans, would speak Latin. I mean, duh. The strange bit, though, was that Arthur seemed to literally recoil at the words. Not the translation, either, but the Latin. James looked at Gawain with drawn eyebrows and then looked harder at the rest of us.

"You weren't at a costume party, were you?" James asked, pulling his hands out of his pockets as though he expected a fight.

"I have no idea what you're talking about," I cut in,

one of those bad feelings building in the back of my neck. For my efforts, I got an elbow in the gut from Arthur.

"Bailey, shut up," Arthur said. "Don't you realise what's going on?"

"No," I grumbled. "The oh-so-obvious situation has failed to make sense to me. Do explain to a poor soul."

"Don't you recognise him?" Arthur asked, his words meant for my ears only but carrying farther than that. James stiffened and looked at us suspiciously. I peered closer, wishing for a light and remembering that I could make my hands glow with that power of the time stream. I cupped my palm as though carrying a lighter and willed a small light into being. It complied without any of the problems I had previously experienced. I stepped forwards, holding the "lighter" up to James' face. And then it struck me.

"Fred!" I exclaimed, grinning broadly. At that, everyone around me stared at me and then looked at one another. I had taken just one more step towards crazy, to them. Arthur, thankfully, knew what I was talking about, though he did scowl at me.

"Weird," I said, pulling back and dousing the light. "This is Fred before he was Fred. Which means that, with all the Latin and stuff—"

"James," Fred cut in, the serene tone vanishing. "My name is James."

"—that this is like the 1969 headquarters of the Ordo Noctuae!" I finished, ignoring Fred completely.

This was great. We finally had an ally, someone who could help rather than just make things worse.

"James," the shadowy figured named Jones growled, "what is going on?"

"I have no idea, man," James replied. "But I think it's probably safe to say that these people are travellers."

"Where are their Timers, then? And why is that one calling you Fred?"

"That one," I frowned. "I prefer to go by Bailey. But yes, we're travellers. We've only got the one Timer, but that's a rather long story and I'm calling him Fred because that's his name."

"She gives people nicknames," Arthur explained. "It's annoying, but you tend to live with it because there is little other option."

"I think we should probably take this inside, don't you agree?" Jones asked. I nodded and marched through the door as soon as it was opened for me, leaving the rest of my entourage to follow along behind. The headquarters of 1969 was basically a warehouse with a few divided rooms, made liveable by paperclips, duct tape and sheer willpower. There were hardly any people about, but those that were stared. Fred slipped off to go talk with someone about our presence, the guard went back to, well, guarding and the rest of us were given clean and dry clothes and pointed to the showers.

Thirty minutes later, with a tin cup full of coffee (they were out of tea) in hand plus a plate full of food that looked like it had been boiled into conformity, sitting at a beat-up conference table, Kate, Gawain, Arthur and myself were feeling much better. Well, Gawain was sort of put off by the coffee and Kate was looking decidedly unhappy, but Arthur and I were doing well.

"This makes so much sense," Arthur said, mopping up his casserole with a piece of bread. *Excalibur* was sitting in its sheath by his side, seemingly innocuous if you can ignore the fact that it was a magic sword. Whatever dilemma had been going on inside Arthur's head regarding the thing was put on hold for the moment. "When Fre—James first recruited me, he said 'Nice to see you again.' I had no idea what he was talking about at the time, but now it makes sense. It's because I met him in his past but my future."

"And you put up with this on a daily basis?" Gawain asked, setting the coffee aside. I shrugged and shook my head while Arthur nodded.

"For the last twenty years. Actually, that's just a guess as to how long I've been doing this because once you become a traveller, time goes sort of... out of sync and ageing is funny. But essentially, yes. This is a fairly typical thing. Our world headquarters exist in a pocket outside of the usual time stream, and people are always coming or going or have come and gone or will come and go. There's a fair amount of confusion, but you get used to it," Arthur said. For him, this chatty side was an effusive display of happiness. Maybe he'd been thrown into the deep end right along with the rest of us on this trip.

"Great," Kate grumbled, finishing off her own casserole and coffee. "Just when things couldn't get more annoying, we have to keep track of who met who when."

"Whom," I corrected. "This is all well and good, but we're trying to find out where the manuscript is. You know, so I can get these Leonum Temporis people off of my back and return to my normal life."

There was a pause, then, "You don't want to be a traveller?" Arthur was looking at me oddly, as if I had just pushed away the greatest opportunity provided to me. "But with all that you can do and with, er, Casper in your head, I would have thought that this would be exactly what you would want."

"But it's not," I said. "Don't get me wrong, it's really cool. But I was happy enough with my life of running around the city doing errands for people. It wasn't all that lucrative, but it was interesting and I was happy. Now, just because I was dragged into all of this, you expect me to just put on a smile and say 'by golly, you're right! I want to spend the rest of my indeterminate days not ageing properly and hopping around history!' It just doesn't work like that."

"You think *I* wanted to be part of this?" Arthur asked, suddenly snarling and angry. "I was inches away from death when they found me and I was given that choice. Death or life as a traveller. What sort of option is that?"

"At least it's a choice, Artie," I countered. Arthur curled his lip, about to snarl at me when Kate slammed her tin cup on the table, adding yet another scratch, and stood, her dark hair swirling and eyes flashing. She looked imposing, certainly enough to get me to back down.

"Will you two stop bickering like children?" she hissed. I folded my arms and sulked in my chair, staring at the table. Arthur pointedly turned away, looking anywhere but at me. "Sheesh. If I had a gun, I would have *shot* one of you by now."

"You're really not from my time," Gawain murmured. All three of us looked at him. It was impossible to mistake the pain on his face and the emotion that was not quite heartbreak but something more along the lines of realising that the person you loved wasn't quite what you had imagined.

Kate reached out and put her hand on Gawain's, flinching when he pulled away. She lowered her gaze. "No," she said. "I was—am—from Bailey's time, further into the future than even we are now. And when I got sent back, I was terrified and completely out of my depth. I figured I would be killed if I even mentioned something about the future, so I kept quiet."

"Did you ever really love me, or was I just protection from the rest of the world?" Gawain asked. Ouch. Harsh. Kate squeezed her eyes shut then whipped her head over to stare Gawain straight in the eye, fury boiling beneath the surface.

"Of course I love you. If these two idiots hadn't come back to mess up my life again, we would be happy back at the castle, nothing to worry about and a child on the way. Instead, we have far too much to worry about and you're letting the time between us act like an uncrossable barrier. I would give up everything for you and I don't care if you believe me or not," Kate said. She leaned back in her chair and sulked like me. Except—

"A child on the way," Gawain said. I frowned, considered, frowned some more. "You're pregnant?"

Well, crap.

Kate nodded. Double crap. I looked at Kate, half expecting her to start swelling up like a balloon before my very eyes. Instead, she looked just as before, albeit wearing a loose flannel shirt designed and made in the sixties. "I was going to tell you, but then things got..."

"Strange?" Gawain asked. Kate nodded. The knight reached out and grabbed Kate's hand, pulling her from her chair and into his arms, wrapping them tightly around her. How sweet.

Casper? I asked, feeling the entity stir at my words. *What effects might time travel have on an unborn child.*

I have no idea, Casper said, smiling wide enough for me to hear it in his voice. *But I imagine it will be very, very interesting.*

Chapter 13
In Which I Open a Bank Account

"What?" I sat up straight, earning myself a glare from Arthur. Kate didn't move or even deign to notice me; she was rather busy devouring Gawain's mouth. I blinked, expressed my apology to Arthur by way of facial expression and returned to speaking with Time by mind. *How can you not know what is going to happen with her child? You're the essence of Time. You have to know.*

I'm glad you have so much faith in my abilities, Time said. I could just imagine him rolling his eyes and did my best not to grind my teeth. *I can no more see the timeline of the child than I can see—hmmm.*

Is that a good hmm or a bad one? Come on, did I just inadvertently ruin this kid's life because I jumped us through time? I tugged at my shirt and pretended as though I was paying attention to the people in the room. Kate had broken apart from Gawain and Arthur was giving them his congratulations, but I heard none of it.

I will have to have more data. See how events unfold. For now, it is merely a theory, Time said. Oh, great, just when things were getting nice and simple, I needed Time to go and simplify them more. *You're loads of help,* I snapped. What I got in return was a general feeling of smugness. What a pain. "Well, congratulations, Kate," I said out loud. "It just seems like the other day you were jumping off a boat."

"I fell, and you're an ass for bringing that up now," Kate said. At that particular moment, the door opened and Fred walked in, carrying a platter of some sort of pastry and some fruit. He looked at us, mostly at Kate sitting on Gawain, and coughed uncomfortably before sitting down.

"So, right, hello," he said. He put the plater in the centre of our group and we each reached for a pastry, more than one of us wanting to have something to eat to keep from having to talk. I think I was the only one probably still hungry, except possibly Gawain. "Um... I think some introductions are in order. I'm James Webb, sort of unofficial leader of the UK branch of the Ordo Noctuae. And you are, well, you're travellers, obviously. But, you know, who are you?"

I looked at Arthur, "Are we allowed to tell him what's been going on or does that break one of your laws about crossing the streams or something?"

"That's timelines. Crossing timelines. And you seem to be able to do whatever you want in regards to time, so go ahead. It's not as though any of us could stop you," Arthur grumbled. It was so nice to have things back to normal, with him biting my head off instead of trying to be all kingly and noble. Very refreshing.

"That's true," I said. "Right then, I'm Bailey Duane, future dweller. This is Kate, also from the future. And Arthur—Artie—and Gawain, from the past."

"Gawain. As in Knight of the Round Table. And Arthur. Is this just another one of her nickname things?" Fred asked, looking from Gawain to Arthur and back again. Arthur merely picked up the sheathed sword at his side and set it on the table.

"I'm afraid not. It would be much more confusing if it were, trust me," Arthur said. I smiled as innocently as possible and Fred pressed the bridge of his nose. He ran his fingers through his hair, releasing the scent of cologne, which barely covered up the cannabis smell from earlier.

"I think someone had better explain what's going on," Fred said. I started to open my mouth and he just pointed a finger in my direction. "Not you. You just make things more obscure."

"It's a special talent," I muttered. Arthur nodded in agreement and took over the story telling. I noticed that he didn't bother to leave out any details, nor did he talk about anything extraneous. It was merely "we went here, did this, this happened, here we are." I thought it made a very exciting story rather boring. Story telling is apparently not on the list of things that Arthur does well.

Despite the boring means of relay, at the end of the story, Fred was sitting back in his chair, fairly gaping at the group of us. "So, what you're saying is that you're King Arthur from Camelot, this is Sir Gawain, a trusted knight, Kate here is an FBI agent from the future who is married to Gawain and Bailey can talk to Time?"

"I call him Casper," I said. "He's mildly annoying."

"I'm not sure that's how I would phrase having a very powerful, um, being—for lack of a better word—in my head," Fred said. I shrugged. "And all of you are being pursued by the Leonum Temporis because you're looking for the Time Keeper, which happens to have all the rules and ideology of time travellers written inside?" We nodded. "This is probably the most interesting thing that has happened to the Ordo Noctuae since I took over."

"Yes," Arthur said, looking distastefully at the beat-up conference table. "I've been meaning to ask about that. What happened?"

"What do you mean, 'what happened'?" Fred retorted, frowning defensively. I looked around the room as well, noting the stained ceiling tiles, the patchy industrial carpet, the filing cabinet that looked as though someone had taken a crowbar to it to get it open; it wasn't the most encouraging of pictures. Especially not for a branch of a powerful, ancient time travelling agency.

"When I was brought into the UK branch of the Ordo Noctuae, when I will be that is, it was a far more... refined set-up. It was powerful and commanded respect, even from those who had no idea what we were," Arthur said, speaking his words to a particularly long scratch in the conference table. He raised his eyes and Fred frowned. "This looks like a bunch of kids got together in an abandoned warehouse and scrounged the junkyards for office furniture."

"What is a warehouse?" Gawain asked Kate as quietly as possible. That is to say, loudly enough so that everyone in the room could hear.

"It's a big metal building that companies use to store stuff," I said. Kate threw me a withering look and I grinned back. Fred just shook his head at us.

"That's basically what we are," he said. "The Ordo Noctuae isn't a refined corporation or something. It's a club I joined in university because I was bored with my physics class and it got me out of a lab. Most of us just hang out and listen to music. I didn't even believe in all of this time travelling bunk until you four showed up at my doorstep wearing some pretty authentic-looking clothes, spouting some nonsense. I mean, it's out there."

I decided that was probably not the best time to comment with an "indeed" because Arthur was looking somewhat unhappy with Fred's statement. And by unhappy, I mean annoyed. And by annoyed, I mean bordering on furious. You get the idea. "The Ordo Noctuae is a club you joined in university?"

"Yeah. Bobbie Jones and I—he's the guy at the door —just hang around and listen to the radio. There are a few other members of the local branch, and we do at least try to look organised. Occasionally, a branch in another part of the world will get in touch, but mostly we've been sending chess moves back and forth with the Swiss branch. I remember Jamaica got in touch a while back, though. That was interesting," Fred said.

"Well, great," I said. "We're being helped out by a bunch of non-believing amateurs. There's no way that this could go wrong at all."

"Bailey, be quiet," Kate snapped, speaking up for the first time since her announcement of being pregnant. "You're always so negative. So stupidly sarcastic. Could you just shut up and let us try and figure things out for a minute? All we need to do is figure out where the Time Keeper is. And assuming that it's a conspicuous sort of book, it can't be that hard to poke around and figure out where it's being kept."

"You're forgetting something," I retorted, wincing as Kate replied with one of her signature looks. "No internet."

That got her attention. She straightened, blinked twice, closed her eyes and sank back against Gawain. "Great," she muttered.

"What's an internet?" Fred asked.

"You're adorable," I said. He pulled back, looking at me with narrowed eyes. I don't think I was making much of a good impression. Not that I tend to make much of a good impression on most people. I've been told that I'm sort of an acquired taste. I sat back in my chair and took a deep breath, telling myself not to be as annoying. It wasn't getting us anywhere and I didn't have time to convince Fred that I was actually a decent person with enough intelligence to do my job correctly. "Sorry, okay, enough. Right. Here's the problem. We need to find this manuscript before the Leonum Temporis folks do because if we don't, the entire fabric of Time could be unravelled. Not to belabour the point, but the fact that I have Casper hitching a ride in my head would make that very bad for me. Not to mention the rest of the world. So, we're going to need your help."

"I'm happy to help," Fred said. "I just have a hard time believing this situation. Your story is a *fantastic* story. But..."

"I know, I know. It could just be a story," I said, waving my hand dismissively. The other people in the room wouldn't get it quite like I did. Well, maybe Kate would, but there was something else there that she didn't get. Maybe it came from having Time as a ride-along. Maybe it was just something to do with who I am, I don't know, but all of this was more real to me than much of anything in my life had been. "You need proof. You need to be able to believe what you want so much to believe, but you can't."

"What are you—?" Fred asked, looking at me. I had risen from my chair and was standing over him as he sat. I didn't give him time to argue, nor did I allow anyone else to intervene. I just put my hand on his shoulder, willed the stream of time to open to me and stepped through into the whiteness.

"Are you just showing off, now?" Time asked, his

voice echoing through the space. He stood there, just as before, but this time was wreathed in an aura of power that was as much showing off as my stepping through time was. Fred widened his eyes and looked as though he was about to swallow a scream. I rolled my eyes for Time's benefit and spread my hand, thinking of a display of history, from the time of the prehistoric creatures that roamed the earth to the early crusades and dynasties of China, onwards to the nineteenth century American Industrial Revolution and finally to an hour before, when we walked through the door of the warehouse.

"Trippy, right?" I said. Fred nodded and I jumped us a few seconds into the future, enough to notice an obvious difference in the room but not enough to cause the other people to panic. Fred settled back into his chair with a groan and I stepped backwards, feeling the effect of travelling myself. I had jumped more than a few times that day and, considering I had only really discovered this travelling thing a couple days before (give or take a thousand years), I was tired.

You've overdone it, Time admonished. I ignored him and pressed a hand to my own head. *You need to rest. If you don't, you're going to overwork yourself and get into serious trouble.*

"Wow," Fred said. "I mean, that was just... wow. And you do this all the time?"

"Often enough not to feel the side effects," Arthur said. I raised a hand, noting with surprise that it was shaking.

"So, I know that we should plan for finding the manuscript, but I need to sleep," I said. My voice didn't sound so strong, either. Fred blinked away some of his own headache and agreed. He led us to some army cots and left us to sleep. Gawain and Kate pulled their cots as close to one another as they could while Arthur set *Excalibur* on the ground next to him, his hand dangling down to touch the sword as if reassuring himself that it was there. I had Time in my head, but there's something about non-corporeal entities that don't lend themselves to company. Normally, after a long day's work, I was perfectly content to go home and collapse, glad for the silence of my flat. Surrounded by people happy to have someone else with them, I was feeling lonely.

I thought about reaching out to Time and having a conversation, but the entity seemed more absent than usual and I figured that he had something else to attend to. After all, he was Time and I couldn't expect Time to hang around every moment of the day, even when sleeping. For all I knew, Time needed to sleep himself.

Goodnight, Bailey, Time said, exuding a feeling of comfort as I drifted into a lonely sleep. Maybe he did hang around. I wasn't sure whether or not to be weirded out by that and slipped off to sleep.

I don't know how long I slept, but when I woke, the smell of stale coffee filled the air. I sat up, groaning. The camp cot hadn't done much to ease my sore muscles; I felt tight everywhere and my entire body felt as though it had been beaten. Soundly.

"Oh, good, you're awake," Gawain said, walking past. He had trimmed his hair and beard enough so that he didn't stand out in this society. I imagine that Kate or Arthur had put him up to it. Somehow, the knight didn't strike me as the sort to go and change his appearance of his own volition. Not to blend in, that's for certain.

"Hi," I said, managing a small wave without setting of a round of aching. "Food?" I croaked. Gawain pointed to the conference room and I nodded, somehow managing to pull myself out of bed and swing my feet to the floor. I shuffled my way into the conference room and found myself staring at a veritable feast of breakfast foods. Fred and Bobbie The Guard had brought in just about all the portable breakfast foods they could think of. No eggs, no sausage, no beans, but I didn't care. I poured myself a cup of apple juice, snatched a couple of pastries from a platter and sank into a chair. It took me the entire first pastry to realise that I wasn't the only one in the room.

Kate and Arthur were sitting at one end of the conference table, talking in serious whispers. I caught them looking at me every now and again and figured that they were either wondering at my health, mental state or capabilities, or they were planning for how to find the manuscript and I was meant to be part of that plan. Fred was sitting by, trying not to look too interested and sipping his cup of tea occasionally. Gawain was missing, probably off doing whatever it was he had been meaning to do when I had woken up. Exploring the sixties, perhaps.

I scarfed down another pastry and decided that I felt marginally better. So, I scooped some more food items and scooted my chair over to where Kate and Arthur were talking. "Morning," I mumbled around some toast.

"It's two in the afternoon," Arthur said, which explained the stale coffee smell. "It is no longer morning."

"Afternoon," I amended. "What's the plan, Stan?"

"Artie. Arthur," he countered. "I though you were done giving me nicknames."

"It's an American expression," Kate threw in. "For someone who has travelled through time for a considerable amount of years, you would think that you would pick something like that up."

"I agree," I said. "But your lack of colloquial knowledge is irrelevant at this time. Have we figured out a way to find the manuscript?"

"I've sent out messages to the various branches of the Ordo Noctuae," Fred interjected, moving closer to our group. I caught a wary glance from Arthur. Well, you should never meet your mentors in their youth, I suppose. It can be off putting. "We've heard back from the Swiss branch and they don't know of anything—they've scoured their records. Jamaica thinks that they might have heard some whispers of something like that and sent over a copy of a newspaper article from last month. There's a famous book collector in the London area who has died and his collection is going up for auction in a few weeks."

"So you think the book could be there?" I asked.

"He has absolutely no evidence that the book we want is going to be there," Kate snapped. "All he knows is that the collection is going to be in London and this is the only record he can find of someone having such a rare book collection. It's a waste of time."

"Actually, oh FBI agent," I said, "it's not." Fred beamed and I flapped my wrist at him dismissively. "Just think. A book collector dies and his collection is going up for auction. Who is that going to draw? Book collectors. And who will likely have the manuscript? A book collector. So even if what we want isn't in the collection, then we can figure out who has it."

"And what do you propose we do if the manuscript is there?" Arthur asked. "Steal it?"

"Isn't that what you had planned on in the first place?" I asked. "I've told you before, I'm not opposed to thieving. I just have to have a good incentive for doing so. And I've got one. So I could steal it, sure."

The former king replied with a distasteful expression and I recalled some of our earlier conversations. I was a thief, immoral and concerned only with money. I would have thought that things might have changed between us, but I suppose not. Some things, not even travelling through time can change.

"Relax," I growled. "I can get us enough funds to buy the book. You won't have to steal anything."

"And where are you going to get the money?" Kate asked. "Are you going to steal that and not tell us?"

"Haven't any of you read Douglas Adams?" I grumbled. Fred looked confused and I shrugged. "He's after your time, but these two should know who he is."

"I don't read things like that," Kate said. "I prefer—"

"Some sort of high literature or murder mysteries, I know," I said. "And I am imagining that Artie here hasn't read it either, given that he seems to hold that sort of thing in fairly low esteem. So fine. I'll explain. There's a part in the story where Arthur Dent—not you, Artie—goes and eats at the Restaurant at the End of the Universe. Only the way to pay for the lunch is to go back in time and put a penny in the bank and let the interest accrue. I'm just suggesting something of a similar nature."

"That goes against so many codes of the Ordo Noctuae," Arthur snarled. "It's using time travel for your own selfish motives and—"

"Actually, in Section 17 of the manual, there's a clause that talks about using interest to acquire absolutely essential materials and—"

"See?" I asked, deciding that it was probably safer to interrupt Fred before an argument could spring out between Arthur and his younger than usual mentor. "It's allowed. Besides, I'm not part of the Ordo Noctuae, so I don't have to abide by their rules. It's not as if you could actually stop me. I seem to be able to do whatever I want when it comes to travelling."

"Which shouldn't be the case," Arthur growled. I shrugged.

"Fred, you wouldn't happen to have some cash on you, would you?" I asked. The man dug into his pocket and pulled out two pounds and seventeen pence, handing it over. "Thanks. I'll repay you."

I stood, stretched and winced when my still-aching muscles protested then willed myself back into the time streams. I was getting to be pretty good at this sort of thing. I wasn't sure whether or not that was a good thing.

I waved to Time as I passed through his domain and received a general sense of annoyance and resignation from the entity before I materialised in, well, way back. Far back enough that it would be scandalous to be seen wearing what I was wearing. I was glad, for once, that I was tall, skinny and knobbly. That meant that it would be harder to place me as a woman. I hunted around and fount a bank willing to let me through the doors then came up with a very skeptical looking teller.

"I would like to open an account," I said.

"We only take those who have something to deposit," the teller replied, looking at me over his nose. I was taller than him, so I was quite impressed by the feat.

"I have two pounds and seventeen, ah, just make that two pounds," I said, realising that it was too far back for pence mean a thing to these people. It was shillings and so forth. I didn't know how pence converted, but somehow I gathered that handing over the futuristic coins wouldn't do.

"Very well, then," the teller said. "In what name would you like the account?"

"Bailey Duane. And I want there to be a special notice on the account that the funds are not to be touched until the year 1969 by someone of the same name. The only thing that must be allowed to happen is the accumulation of interest. Got it?" I asked. The teller replied with another skeptical look but dutifully nodded and wrote down the instructions. I handed over the two pounds and waited until he had finished writing before marching out of the bank, striding past a group of astonished individuals, and willing myself forwards in time.

I found myself back in the conference room. "Well," I said, groaning as my muscles warmed up to the travel. "That takes care of that. What else do we have to do to get to this auction?"

"Bailey?" Kate asked, standing and moving towards me. "Are you alright?"

"What?" I said, looking at her and frowning. "I feel fine." At least, that's what I thought I said. It was only a moment later that I realised I had just spouted a bunch of mumbled nonsense. And my muscles, where I thought they were getting warmed up and ready for jumping or gathering supplies or whatever, started to scream in protest. My head, though, was the worst. It began pounding, each pound exponentially worse than the last.

I told you, Casper said, his voice sounding like a gong in my head, reverberating through my entire being. *You've overdone it! Merely sleeping wasn't going to solve this. You should have waited until you were completely well before jumping again.*

Now you tell me, I thought, quietly relieved that my mental voice didn't sound as garbled as my physical one. To the onlookers, who were all standing and looking at me in alarm, I said, "I think I'm going to faint now." No one understood and so no one moved to stop me. I fell to the ground and into blackness.

Chapter 14
In Which I Attempt to Steal a Book

Three weeks later, still in 1969, Fred, Arthur, Kate, Gawain and I climbed onto the train to head to London. I stretched experimentally as I sat in the chair and was pleased when nothing twinged and my head didn't start screaming in pain. Kate watched me out of the corner of her eye and when I had finally settled in with my coat tight around me, looked me over openly. "Are you sure you're completely better?"

"Pretty sure," I said. "Nothing hurts and the short jumps that Casper's been having me take are having no ill effects. It thinks that I am finally able to do travelling again."

"Hmmph," Kate said, but she let the matter drop. From what gossip I had gathered after the fact, when I collapsed and for the two days I was unconscious afterwards, Kate refused to leave my side. She was, in all truth, the only one of our ragtag gang that knew first-aid, so that must have contributed. But it was nice to know that she didn't completely hate me any more. I think.

From what Time had explained to me, I had suffered a basic overworking of my muscles, physical, mental and temporal. Athletes that practice too hard and too frequently will burn out sometimes and that was what happened to me. Of course, the muscles that I was using were not your standard muscles and when I burned out, it was quite a lot more dramatic than an athlete tearing a tendon or feeling sore. In any case, I was unconscious for two days, and for a week and a half following, I barely got out of bed except to go to the bathroom and take a shower.

The last week or so, Time had me exercise my travelling "muscles" by having me will myself to the space where he resided and back to my bed a few times a day. Then things progressed to making at least one jump of a couple of seconds and finally, three weeks after my initial collapse, I had managed to go back in time a good seventy years and forwards again with no ill effects. Just in time for the auction, too.

If you overwork yourself again, Time warned, growling at me, *I don't know if you'll recover as easily or even at all.*

Relax, I said, watching Gawain and Arthur sit across a table from Fred. *It's like doing any sport. If I practise some each day, eventually, I'll be able to do all sorts of things without breaking a sweat.*

You're stubborn and bothersome, Time snapped. I

settled down into my chair and hid my grin in the collar of my coat.

That's so nice of you to say. I didn't know you cared so much, I said. Arthur turned to Kate and me with a serious, this-is-business expression on his face. I sighed; we were in for another run through of the plan. Goodie.

"Okay, let's go through it once again," Arthur said. He cast his gaze upwards for a moment, to where *Excalibur* was stowed in a duffle bag. I looked at my own bag, containing all the supplies I might need. Everything was in its place, as we had left it.

"We have invitations to the auction," Gawain started, looking very smart in his suit and tie. It had taken an hour for us to get him into the suit without him complaining at some fitting or another. Knights, apparently, don't do suits and ties, and certainly complain at polyester. "We got them because I am a rare book dealer, with my wife, looking to acquire some new items."

"Arthur and I are lawyers, making sure that the estate is being dealt with according to the wishes of our client, the deceased's nephew," Fred said. That had taken some interesting finagling. Arthur had jumped back and become a member of the law firm that dealt with the nephew, then getting himself assigned to the case. But it had worked and he had secured invitations to the auction for Fred and him with little difficulty. That left me. Everyone turned to look at me and I did my best to smile nonchalantly.

Maybe it was almost dying (more than once), but something about what I was meant to be doing no longer sat well with me. A few weeks ago in my personal timeline and I would have done it, no question. Now? I wasn't so sure. "I'm a bored millionaire who wants to pick up a few new pieces for my showroom. I will be blatantly flirting with the various book collectors around the room, trying to determine who has the manuscript. And, if the Leonum Temporis show up, then I'm our way out."

"Very good," Arthur said. I looked again at the bag above my head and hoped that all went according to plan. Otherwise, the gun that I had packed next to the designer dress and shoes would have to be put to use. I had got some training from Kate and my years wandering the streets with Carlos, but I didn't much care for the weapons. Something about them felt very permanent, in a way that I hadn't been since first jumping through time. The world around me flickered for a brief moment and I closed my eyes, shoving back a headache.

That flickering, that sense of impermanence, like reality hadn't quite settled in, had been happening more and more since my collapse. I couldn't get any straight answers out of Time on the matter, either. My stomach clenched with nerves.

Arthur turned to Fred and started talking some legalese so they could pass muster if interrogated—or if the nephew actually showed up. Kate leaned her head against Gawain, resting one hand on her stomach. The

Knight wrapped an arm around her shoulder and kissed her hair softly. I felt the now all-too-familiar feeling of loneliness rising up in me and squelched it as violently as I could. Sometimes, being your own best friend was just going to have to do. It used to be that I could manage for weeks at a time without seeing people apart from dropping breakfast off to Charger and the doorman. Now, it was as if I couldn't get enough of them. So, what had changed? Why couldn't I settle into this new reality of mine?

I forced my mind off of such dreary topics and focused on relaxing enough to sleep. Despite being declared all better, I found I tired easier than before. Some of that might have had to do with the fact that these people had me running around on my feet from morning to night, picking up supplies, practising jumps, making food, whatever needed doing. That was, after all, my job.

Somewhere between one stop and the next, I fell asleep, waking only when Kate shook my shoulder, muttering a, "We're here." I stretched and stood, grabbing my bag and looking over my shoulder. The Leonum Temporis people hadn't yet shown up—good luck, poor planning on their part or them being clever, I didn't know—but that didn't mean I wasn't going to keep a watch out for them. They had become notorious in my mind for showing up at just the wrong moment. This auction would be a particularly bad moment for them to show up, which meant that it was likely they would.

"Come on, Bailey," Arthur grumbled, jostling me as he draped the bag carrying *Excalibur* over one shoulder. I had told him there wasn't much point in hoisting the sword around. Traditionally, swords didn't go well with lawyers' suits. That didn't matter much to Arthur and he insisted on bringing the sword with us. And, consequently, hitting me with the bag. I shouldered my own bag and dutifully followed, biting back more than one snarky comment.

We traipsed through the train station and caught a bus to the closest stop to the place where the auction was to be held. I would have expected for the auction to take place at Sotheby's Auction House, but the will stipulated that the auction would take place at the flat of the collector. The auction was set to start at three that afternoon, but people could come in anytime from ten on to get a look at the books. Gawain and Kate went in first, as their cover was the most inductive to looking at books all day. Then followed Arthur and Fred. As lawyers, they had to make sure things were up to snuff. Around two thirty, I walked up to the flat, wearing my designer dress and flaunting my invitation for everybody to see. For once, being skinny and knobbly suited me quite well, because I was certain the dress would not have fit me otherwise. In fact, it felt quite restrictive, but maybe I'd just grown accustomed to ill-fitting clothes.

"Right this way, Miss, er, Duane," the doorman said, looking at my invitation with a slightly embarrassed look, as though he were meant to know who I was. I sniffed in disdain.

"Do you have any idea how long it took me to find this place?" I asked, putting on my best American accent. I wore the British accent of my youth most often, especially being in England, but the Annoying American worked very well for keeping people on their toes. Given that I was meant to be a bored millionaire, it worked even better.

"I am sorry for any confusion, Miss Duane," the doorman said, taking himself from his precious post to escort me directly to the lifts. "I believe the instructions were printed on the invitation, but it is possible they led you astray."

"Well, that's silly. But I did find a good chocolate shop on the way, so no harm done," I said, holding up my bag of chocolates as evidence. The doorman nodded and smiled in a friendly sort of manner before pushing the button on the lift and stepping out.

"The flat you are wanting is directly in front of the lift. You shouldn't miss it," the doorman said. Then, the doors closed and I slipped even further into my role.

Well, you certainly seem to be playing the part of eccentric rich person well. Time commented, almost sounding surprised.

"I learned from experience," I said. "I've done jobs for some very eccentric people, most of them rich. I just picked my favourite and poof, there you have it. Bailey Duane, eccentric rich American, ready to spend money."

You're an odd human, Time said. I rolled my eyes and refrained—barely—from sticking my tongue out. As a non-corporeal entity, I didn't think the gesture would mean as much to Time as it meant to me. That and the doors were opening, showing me a gathering of people that I hadn't quite expected.

I thought invitations to this event were meant to be exclusive, Time said, sending through feelings of astonishment as I took in the crowds of people gathered in the flat and spilling out the door.

You'd almost think someone invited the press, I thought in return. As it turned out, that's exactly what had happened. I approached, wearing my dress, and it seemed the crowd turned on me. I saw three people holding cameras and at least four others holding pads of paper with pencils at the ready.

"Who are you?" the closest camera man asked, shooting me a quizzical look over a very busy moustache and impossible eyebrows.

"None of your business," I sneered, falling into character even a bit more. I shouldered my way past the press and only when I realised that these people were inching towards me, hoping to overhear something that might be said did I understand that I had just given them the exact cue they were waiting for. *Well, it's not as though this could get any more annoying. I'm going to have my picture in the papers! This job doesn't work if I have my pictures in the papers.*

You will have your picture in the papers from 1969. Your job in your time isn't at risk, Time pointed out. I rolled my eyes and decided that my best plan of action was pushing farther into the crowd. Once I made it past the foyer things evened out. There couldn't have been more than thirty people in the rest of the flat, peering with interest at books that were set out on a table or shelf. A few people in uniform from the auction company were overseeing the handling of the books, but the events were boring enough that the press didn't feel much like coming past the front area, where all the big-name attention seekers were congregating. Even as I wandered around, some of the press people left, finally bored with the proceedings.

I looked at the various volumes without much luck. I didn't know much about rare books except that they were infinitely more valuable than the boxes of novels I had back at my own flat and in my office. And that if you actually tried to read some of the stories, you would be bored out of your mind. So the leather book sitting under a glass box meant as much to me as the slim volume being watched over by a very hawklike auction house employee. That is to say, about nothing.

I didn't think that the book *we* were looking for was going to have the words "Time" and "Keeper" scratched out on the cover. It was a manuscript, for one. About all I understood from that was that the book wasn't actually published or even bound, just collected in a folio of some sort. And it was written in Latin. So. I had a look at the books and stumbled my way into Arthur and Fred.

"Is it here?" I asked. Arthur widened his eyes at my

obvious breach of his carefully crafted plan, looked about to see if anyone was paying attention to us and sighed.

"I don't know," he said. "I've never actually seen the book. You're the one who has done the research. You would know more than I what it looks like."

"Well, there are only a couple of volumes that could be it," I said. "And they're both over by Octavius and Brutus there... Oh, dear."

"What now?" Arthur said, pressing the bridge of his nose and trying not to look like he was inches away from strangling me like a rag-doll.

"So, the job I took before you hired me was about retrieving some stolen uncut diamonds from a guy named Scott. He had two very angry and quite determined henchmen whom I named Octavius and Brutus. Now here's something you should probably know: I never give out the same nickname to anyone," I said. Arthur was catching on, though I think Fred got there slightly quicker, and he wasn't looking too pleased. "Hence," I continued, "my 'oh, dear.' I think I should probably mention that they've just knocked out the auction house employee and are stealing one of the volumes that I thought could be the one we want."

"Oh," Arthur said. "Dear."

"Well put," I agreed and turned to face our newest problem. Octavius and Brutus were hightailing it to the door. Thankfully, though, the press hadn't thinned quite enough to let them through easily. "We need a distraction. Now would be a great time to pull *Excal-*

ibur out," I said. Arthur agreed and did just that, diving towards the table under which he had stowed the duffle carrying the sword. That caught the attention of Gawain and Kate, who were standing by one of the tables, talking. They turned, saw Arthur draw the steel and began to help. Then, things went pear shaped.

Just to clarify matters, drawing a sword in the middle of a room of book collectors, auctioneers, agents for the opposite side and the press is a generally bad idea. People tend to get sort of panicky and run about doing crazy things like, oh I don't know, trying to stop the guy with the sword. That wasn't particularly helpful. Arthur became swamped down with people trying to get him subdued; he managed not to kill or maim anyone, so I let him be. Kate and Gawain were hesitating, trying to decide between helping Arthur and going after the manuscript. After some prodding by Gawain, they chose to help Arthur. That left Fred and myself dodging through the people to run after Octavius and Brutus and try and retrieve the document.

"Which way did they go?" Fred asked once we got out to the lifts. I looked for some sign that they had been recently opened or were descending or something and came up with nothing.

"Down, probably. They don't have Timers and on them and they can't jump before handing the book over to their boss," I said. I didn't know how I was sure about the Timer thing, but I was. And the boss bit? Well, that was just standard practice for thugs of their calibre. "You take the lift, I'll take the stairs." Fred looked like he wanted to protest, but it was too late. I had already turned and was dashing towards the stairwell.

I was in luck, too. As soon as I got into the enclosed space, I could hear Octavius and Brutus running down the stairs in their clumpy boots. Then my luck ran out, because I was wearing heels. My plan for escape had been to jump through time as an escape, not run after some goons. I curled my lips in a snarl, pulled off the shoes and stuck them in one hand and began to run. This felt familiar, in an ironic sort of way.

As I might have stated before, years of running around on the streets and away from bullies and tagging along with Carlos meant that I was a fairly decent runner. Not to mention the fact that I had, not too long ago, outrun these particular thugs with a good deal of success. *And,* I had just spent the last three weeks in a strictly regimented "Bailey, you need to train rather a lot if you're not going to faint from overexertion again" exercise routine. I was rearing for a fight and catching up to these people was my way to get it. So, I ran.

Octavius and Brutus had only got a few seconds' head start, but it was enough for them to be on the street before I was out of the lobby. I followed in just enough time to see them dart into a side street. If they caught a taxi, I was going to have words with somebody. I pursued and, thank goodness, they hadn't stopped long enough to hail a taxi.

"Come on, guys, give a girl a chance," I yelled after them. Brutus kept right on running, ignoring me.

Octavius, though, hesitated a moment. He paused long enough to look over his shoulder and see that yes, I was following him. The girl he had chased not too long ago. How's that for irony? Anyways, that hesitation let me catch up enough to grab the hem of his jacket. That, in turn, caused a chain reaction which began with Octavius pulling his arms forwards as if to stop me from taking his jacket, losing his balance and stumbling four or five steps. While he did this, his arms pinwheeling to try and regain his balance, he dropped a package wrapped in some fabric. I, being the industrious, go-get-em girl that I am, snatched the package with the book and ran the other way.

I made it back to the building where Arthur, Gawain and Kate were running out, Arthur shoving *Excalibur* back into the duffel bag, Gawain looking rather better for being in a fight, and Kate with one of her signature scowls. Fred was nowhere to be seen, probably having run the other way to search for Octavius and Brutus. "Hi, guys," I said, skidding to a stop. "Um, based on my last experience with the two thugs who are chasing us, I think we should probably get out of here as soon as possible."

"That would be ill advised, Ms Duane," a voice said, sounding calm and assured and completely in control of the situation. I knew that voice and it was one of the ones that I really, really wasn't interested in adding to my current equation. Octavius and Brutus were bad enough given that their boss might be mildly ticked off that I stole the diamonds from him, though they were stolen in the first place. Adding the Professor and his trusty Steve to the situation was even worse. See, wary as I might be of having two gun-waving henchman following me about, the Professor scared me. Truly, deeply scared me.

I wondered, briefly, what Octavius and Brutus were doing in 1969, and whether that intersected with the Professor standing before me. Then, I wondered with more vehemence if everybody I knew was a time traveller.

"I guess we didn't lose you in Scotland, then," I said with a shrug that was as close to cheerful as I could manage in the moment.

"For a while," the Professor said in a laid-back voice. "That was very clever, using your connections to get you on a tramp steamer. And when you proceeded to evade capture, vanishing to all extents and purposes, I knew that you had finally figured it out. The travelling angle, that is. So I looked for you in the logical places, knowing your companion Arthur and his habits."

"Yes, so you sent men after me at Gawain's place. Great, good for you," I said, the part of my mind not taken up with snarky conversation doing its best to find me a way out of this mess. It wasn't doing so well. "And catching up with us here?"

"I looked for the interesting occurrences in the papers over the years," the Professor said. At this point, Octavius and Brutus rounded the corner. They took one look at the Professor, made a face and turned to run. "Jon, if you wouldn't mind."

Steve pulled out a very modern gun with a very modern silencer and shot twice, the sound more like a muted bark than something that could get rid of your hearing. Octavius and Brutus fell. I doubted they would get up again.

"Bailey, what is going—" Arthur started, reaching for his bag. Steve trained his gun on the former king and I did something incredibly stupid. I stepped into the line of fire.

"Would you mind not shooting us until you tell us exactly *why* you're shooting us?" I asked. I wondered if I could get Arthur to grab onto Kate and Gawain. If we were all touching, I could jump and we would be safe for a while yet. Then there would only be the matter of figuring out how to go after the Professor when he caught up with us again. At least, though, we'd be prepared.

"Please step back, Ms Duane," the Professor said. "And if it's explanations, you want, you'll have to wait. In the mean time, please hand over the manuscript. And the sword, if you please."

I fingered the cloth-covered package in my hands and looked at the Professor. He was absolutely serious. I opened the cloth and reached to pull out the manuscript.

Bailey, NO! Time cried inside my head. I hid my wince as best I could and scowled inwardly. *You can't touch the book. I don't know what would happen, but you can't touch it!*

Great. So, what am I supposed to do? Just hand it over to this guy? I snarled silently, trying not to cause a scene while I waited to see what would happen.

"I will never hand *Excalibur* to you," Arthur growled. The Professor just smiled and shrugged, as if the answer couldn't bother him one way or another. Arthur tightened his grip on the duffel bag.

I...I don't know, Time said, voice wavering with uncertainty and a hint of fear. I wanted to complain. This was Time, we were talking about. Or at least some sort of entity that embodied time. If Time didn't know what was going on, what was going to happen or the consequences that could arise, there must have been some serious mucking about.

"If you don't hand me the sword, I shall simply take it. It will be better that way, in any case, as I believe that *Excalibur*'s allegiances change when the master has wrested the sword from its old master. Or such is the nature if many a magical item," the Professor said. He stepped forwards to take the bag and Arthur tensed even further, stepping into a fighting stance. Kate mimicked that and Gawain followed her example. Steven merely aimed his gun.

"Ah, you're planning to resist," the Professor said, smiling gently. "I wouldn't suggest that. Jon will just shoot you all. I wouldn't want to deal with the mess, in any case."

Arthur looked at the rest of us and I shrugged,

widening my eyes. I had no idea what to do, either. This was a completely new situation to me. I mean, the gun waving, not so much. The extortion, also not new. The threatening my life because of a time travelling manuscript and a magic sword, that was fairly novel. "Fine," I said at last, watching Steve finger the gun with a slight pleasure flickering in his eyes. I held out the book, cloth cover and all. "Take it," I said.

"Thank you, Ms Duane. You are as smart as you make yourself out to be," the Professor said. Arthur followed my example and handed the sword over, looking as though it killed him to do it. "Very good. Now, if you will all hold out your hands, I believe this will be easier if you don't struggle."

I held out my hand and he clapped a metal bracelet over my wrist. Immediately, the concern that I felt radiating from Time vanished, leaving just an empty void where his voice had been. The Professor did the same with the others, placing the bracelets on their wrists with a click that seemed to echo into oblivion. Then, he pulled out a Timer, put a bracelet on his own wrist and that of his loyal henchman and we jumped.

Chapter 15
In Which I Stage an Escape

The jump was almost like normal, if someone had thrown a soundproof wall around me and taken away all of my control, treating me like a puppet. I knew Time was there, probably trying to talk to me and help me get out of whatever binding that the Professor had put on me, but I couldn't hear anything, couldn't feel anything. All I saw was the typical whiteness that accompanied a jump. Then, we were back in the world, standing in a shadowy street that was much like the one we had just left.

"Interesting invention, isn't it?" the Professor asked, examining the metal on his wrist. "The bracelets connect the Timer, making it possible for me to jump more than one person at a time. I always thought it was clever."

"Very clever," I muttered under my breath, failing to mention that I could do the same thing if I was touching someone or thinking about them. I didn't think that the Professor needed to know about my relationship to Time. As we walked, I looked around. Kate and Gawain were present and unharmed, as was Arthur, though judging by the dark stormy expression he wore, I doubted he was feeling alright. Everyone was present apart from Fred, who had hopefully vanished back to the Ordo Noctuae headquarters and figured things out on his own. Maybe we could run into him again in whatever time this was. I would have asked Time, but, you know.

"There's no need for flattery, Ms Duane. I am well aware of my capabilities," the Professor said, wagging his finger at me. I shrugged and tried not to shiver. It was winter in London and I was wearing a designer dress without a coat and no shoes. But I didn't need the Professor trying to exercise sympathy for me. Or for my companions to worry. I kept quiet. "Come along, now, you four," the Professor said. "It would be pointless of me to try and keep you out in the open. But my facilities are not all that far away."

He had Steve prod us along and then we were off, walking through the dark and deserted streets of London. Well, mostly deserted and not too dark. Being a city, London has lights and cars at just about every minute of the day. It was hard to get a good sense of what time we were in, but it felt closer to my own rather than the 1969 we had come from. That wasn't as comforting as I'd thought.

Our troupe might have been unusual, but it was far from being odd enough to draw any attention. So much for the benefits of keeping my head down. After a good ten minutes' hike, we arrived at a building that might have been flats at one point. Now it just read Simmons & Simmons on one of the front windows, with a complicated security system next to the door. The Professor inserted a key, as well as a key card and the lock mechanisms opened, revealing a very dark and intimidating hallway. Great.

"Simmons & Simmons?" I asked. "Your name isn't Simmons."

"Perhaps not, but the building was for sale and it was more prudent to simply purchase it and keep up the pretence," the Professor said. "After you."

All of this politeness was getting on my nerves. I wondered how far I would have to run for the bracelet to be out of range and decided that might be a very bad idea. Who knows if I would be able to get it off on my own? I hesitated before the door and received a jab in my ribs from Steve for the effort. I growled and walked inside, Kate close behind with Arthur and Gawain making up the rear.

The building was, in fact, a building of flats that had been converted into offices. The layout was terrible and I stumbled against illogically placed furniture more than once. We were prodded and poked into a basement room with concrete flooring, no furniture to remark on apart from a toilet and sink in the corner. That meant we might be there a while. Oh, goody. I tripped into the room after an insistent shove from Steve and found nothing to catch myself with, so I landed on my arm in a very painful manner. Kate, at least, managed to stay upright, though neither Arthur nor Gawain were quite so fortunate.

"I do apologise for the accommodations," the Professor said, "but I can't have you running around trying to figure out how to retrieve the manuscript from me. Nor can I have you contacting anyone in the city. So, until we come up with a better solution, you shall have to remain here. Adieu." With that, he closed the door, locking it quite loudly. The four of us were left in a room where the only light came from the tiny window in the upper corner that looked up to the street level.

I was moments away from breaking down into despondency, but that would be pointless and get me nowhere. And I was meant to be the clever one, able to get all of us out of this situation. I wasn't sure how, but it was my prerogative. It was what I had been hired to do and I was not going to fail in my job.

I crawled to the edge of the room and leaned up against a wall, taking stock of myself before looking around. Kate had helped Gawain to his feet and Arthur had copied me, looking weary and lost. "Is everyone alright?" I asked in a low voice.

"Sure," Arthur said, a growl hidden in his voice. "We're fine. We've just had the Time Keeper stolen from us by someone you knew. Oh, and *Excalibur* at that. Not to mention the fact that we can't get out of here because of these stupid bracelets. So yeah, Bailey, we're just fine."

"There's no need to snap at me, Artie," I retorted. "How in the world was I meant to know that the Professor would turn up out of the blue and make things go pear shaped? I'm good, I'm connected, but I'm not perfect."

"Well," Arthur snarled, turning towards me, "if you're so good, then how do we get out of here? Let's face it, we've lost. The manuscript that we've been trying to keep out of the hands of the Leonum Temporis for fear that they'll cause chaos to the time streams if they recover the secrets of their past has been handed to its leader by the very person hired to *retrieve* it! You can't get us out of here or you would have. Is *Casper* not responding? Are your 'natural' talents that you've been gloating quietly about for the last few weeks not working? Well, Bailey Duane, congratulations, you're nothing but a normal person. And a failure at that."

"Arthur!" Gawain barked, his eyes wide and betraying his astonishment at the words of his former king. Kate was looking at me behind her FBI agent mask, telling me just how worried she was that I was going to do something stupid, like attack Arthur. Under normal circumstances, perhaps I would have. I am well aware of my flaws, let me tell you. But I am not self-deprecating enough to enjoy having people yell insults at me. This time, though, I was tired. And he was right. The little spark I had shown just a few moments before vanished and a black depression settled over me.

"Yeah," I said, too weary of all of this to be surprised at how unlike me my voice sounded. "Maybe I am." And I left it at that, leaning my head back against the wall and wishing fervently to be anywhere else but there.

I hadn't asked to get caught up in all of this. I was hired to do a document retrieval under a specific set of circumstances, with rules to my world that I understood. Then a rival organisation was revealed to me in a series of attempts on my life, during which I had to ask for help from someone I had hoped never to see again. Following that, I was thrust into a world where time travel is normal and the rules of history and cause and effect don't apply. I had thought I had figured that out, been able to function pretty well under those circumstances. I mean, I had even got the document. Only to find that the new rules were as bunk as the old ones and only the rules you make for yourself are the ones that apply, which I should have known in the first place. It was a lesson I learned at Carlos' side and had cemented when he killed my boyfriend, accident or otherwise. So, fine, I was a failure for not having figured that out. I'd let the people depending on me down and I didn't know how to fix that. Yeah; I'd rather have been just about anywhere else in the world but right there.

Arthur gave up on trying to goad me into an argument and turned away, taking off his jacket and stuffing it under his head in a show of trying to sleep. Any sleeplessness he could then blame on me, as if my list of crimes wasn't already long enough. Gawain did his best not to look at me with pity and eventually turned to Kate, murmuring things to her that I couldn't make out. I assumed they were comforting, because she replied with a tender smile and kissed him. Just another thing that had changed according to different rules than the ones I followed.

Kate took Gawain's jacket and wrapped up in it, following Arthur's example and trying to sleep. I imagined she would be more successful. Which left only the big knight and myself awake or too weary to pretend to sleep. He stood and moved over to me, sitting beside me and leaning back against the wall, mirroring my position.

"I don't think you are a failure," Gawain said. I raised my eyebrows at him and he shrugged, fiddling with the knees of his trousers. "Kate has explained what befell you at the onset of this journey and much that you have put up with before this journey began. You have done remarkably well under circumstances over which you had no control."

"That's nice of you to say," I mumbled in reply, "but I don't think that you quite get it. I'm meant to be the one that people look to in order to get out of situations like this. I'm supposed to be the type of person who gets things done no matter what. That's literally on my business card."

"You have done all of the things in your life on your own? Without anyone at your side?" Gawain asked. The question seemed innocent enough, so I answered, figuring that there wasn't much the knight could do to hurt me further. I was already feeling beaten and down.

"Apart from running around the streets of Europe with Carlos in my youth, yeah. Though there wasn't much partnership there, more he got us into trouble and I did my best to get us out of it. But apart from him, maybe even with him, I work alone. I have always had to do so and it became more than habit. It became necessary. Now, that's the way I work best. It's better that way. Fewer people get hurt."

"Have you considered that the reason you work alone and are always alone is because you refuse to ask for help?" Gawain said. I looked at the ground and my bare feet, wiggling my toes instead of replying. He sighed and squeezed my shoulder companionably. Then, his advice given, he stood and returned to his wife, half pulling her onto his lap so she would be more comfortable.

Gawain was probably right. I had grown so used to people not wanting to help me that I hadn't considered the fact that these people might. Therefore, I hadn't even bothered to ask them. It didn't change much, though, except to give me some new insight. We were still stuck in a basement without any feasible means of escape. I was still wearing no shoes and no jacket and it was looking like a long, cold night.

Sleep, I quickly discovered, was impossible. The ground was uncomfortable and my mind was whirling in too many directions to allow me to drift off. That and I was freezing, shivering badly by the time a few hours had passed. To try and warm up and exhaust myself so that I might be able to catch a bit of sleep before whatever the next day might bring, I stood and began pacing the room. The sound of my bare feet on the concrete wasn't rhythmic or calming at all; I simply sounded like a trapped animal pacing its cage.

I tried the lock on the door with no results. I even considered trying to climb out the window. It might have let me get through it—I was skinny enough—but it was at least twelve feet off the ground and I couldn't jump that high. And the glass only opened inwards, narrowing the amount of room I would have to escape. If I could get something to loosen the hinges and have a few minutes to work at a decent height, I could get it open. Only, I didn't have any tools.

Sometime before dawn, I sank against the wall again, this time exhausted and prepared to sleep. Yet sleep, that elusive demon, evaded me still. Now, I was just annoyed. I slammed my hand against the concrete in frustration, wincing as a jolt of pain flared in my arm. That was the one I had fallen on when pushed into the room. It also happened to be the one on which the bracelet hung. And the bracelet, made of metal or no, couldn't stand up to concrete. When I lifted my hand, I saw shards of the metal sitting on the floor.

I slammed my wrist against the floor again, this time purposefully trapping the bracelet between my flesh and the concrete. It cracked. I wriggled it around my wrist, trying to gain enough leverage to break it open and then, with a sound that was far too loud to merely have been metal, the bracelet fell to the floor and my world opened up once more.

Bailey! Time cried, sounding surprised and, to my pleasure, relieved. *I have been trying to talk with you for so long, but you couldn't hear me. Are you okay? Is everything—*

"No time for that," I said, rubbing my wrist. "We have some planning to do. Casper, when are we?"

About seven years before your first jump backwards, Time said. I nodded, somehow not surprised at this development. It made sense, after all. The Professor hadn't wanted us to get out into the city and meet up with any connections—no, he hadn't wanted *me* to get out. That meant that I had connections in the city. So we must have jumped within my own personal time stream. I was on my home turf and I knew exactly who to call.

"Bailey?" Kate murmured, sitting up groggily. Gawain shifted slightly at her movements, but both he and Arthur remained asleep. "What's going on?"

"I got my bracelet off," I said, holding up my wrist as evidence. Kate widened her eyes in shock then crawled over to me, fingering the pieces of my broken bracelet.

"How did you manage that?" she asked. I demonstrated and Kate grinned. "So you can talk with Casper? You can get us out of here?"

"I can," I said, "but we have to get that book and the sword back before we can jump again. I don't know why. I just have this feeling that we're meant to stay in this time until everything is sorted out. You know?"

"That," Kate said, giving me a jackal's grin, "is what we in the FBI call a gut instinct. So, what's the plan?"

"I'm going to need your help," I said. Kate looked marginally taken aback. She nodded in any case and leaned forwards, ready for instruction. I pointed to the window, "We need to get that open. I need you to sit on my shoulders and use the shards of my bracelet to get it open."

"I can't fit through the window," Kate said. I shook my head.

"I can," I murmured. She frowned and folded her arms.

"You're our only way out of here. If you leave, then how are the rest of us going to get out?" she asked, a harshness in her tone that hadn't been there for the last three weeks. It was as if all the progress that I had made in building our relationship in the last while had vanished in the space of a day. That's alright. Rome wasn't built in a day, but it sure burned in one.

"You're just going to have to trust me, Kate," I said. "I will get us out of this. I can't do this on my own, though. I need you to help me."

She considered, more suspicious than she had been in a while. Eventually, though, she let out a breath and nodded. "I'll help you. Only because you're hopeless on your own and I can't rely on that to get us out of here. Got it?"

"Thank you," I said. I moved over to the window

and gestured to my shoulders. "Up you go." She grumbled, brushed her dark strands of hair out of her eyes and stood, stretching. I crouched down and she climbed onto my back, swinging her legs onto my shoulders and putting balancing hands on my head. I shifted my legs, hoping that I was strong enough to do this, and rose, my muscles screaming in agitation.

You're going to get yourself killed, Time said, responding to my grunts of pain. Kate ignored my noises, though, and set to work, reaching up to fiddle with the hinges and try and get them undone.

At least I'll have died doing something useful, I said. Time huffed and muttered something that sounded a lot like, *stupid humans*, but I wasn't listening too closely. Twenty minutes later, Kate managed to get the screws out of the hinges, pulling out the pane of glass and handing it down to me. I let her climb off of my back with relief, my legs shaking.

"Are you sure you can get through there?" Kate asked. I looked up at the window now shining pure, unfiltered dawn light into the hole. I shrugged.

"I have no idea. I think I can make it. It won't be my first time going through a window, though. When I go, though, you're going to have to try and get out of this room and into the main office area. Think you can manage that?" I asked, looking at the door.

Kate did as well and nodded, cracking her knuckles as though she was preparing for a fight. "I think that if any one of those bastards tries to step through that door, I'm going to knock them unconscious."

"Good girl," I said. I stood once more, ignoring the protest from my legs and stretched, jumping onto the balls of my feet experimentally. I remembered the last time I had gone through a window. I had been running to the Professor at that point, and bar windows are slightly different than those of a cage meant to keep people in. The principle was the same, however. I jumped once, twice, before my fingers caught on the ledge. I scrambled with my bare feet, trying to get purchase to climb up. Next thing I knew, Kate was standing under me, heaving me upwards. I made it to the ledge and shoved my head through. It was big enough.

It took some manoeuvring to get my shoulders and hips through, but eventually I made it. My dress, though, was looking rather worse for wear. Luckily, there weren't any tears in inappropriate places. I poked my head back through and looked at Kate, watching the window with a hard look in her eye. "Thanks for trusting me, Kate," I said.

"You would have done the same for me," she replied. "Now get out there and get some help. We're going to finish this today."

I nodded and pulled back, standing straight and leaving her behind. I was on the street before the building. There were no people out and about at that odd hour of the morning. I knew London, though, and I knew that it wouldn't be long before there were people everywhere. I had only a limited amount of time before things could go wrong, so I hurried. That meant running.

I had run in my bare feet before. I had even run in my bare feet across a city before. Never, though, had I run so quickly, ignoring any pain in my feet or the odd looks I got from people. Let them think I was crazy, let them think I was running from my husband, let them think anything. As long as they stayed out of my way, I didn't have a problem.

Instinct drew me to the shipping yards, just as they had when all of this started. I knew that seven years ago, Carlos avoided the shipping yards as much as possible so that he wouldn't come to the attention of the port authorities, but somehow I knew he would be there. Maybe it was some traveller's instinct. Maybe it was Time surreptitiously feeding me information. Or maybe it was just sheer dumb luck translating itself into action. I didn't know, but that was where I went. It turns out that instinct was one thing I should have stayed far, far away from.

It wasn't hard to get into the shipping yards. A smile and a smirk in the right direction plus some more of that dumb luck I was apparently running on got me through the gates without a problem. I came upon Carlos exactly where I knew he would be: in the room which held the shipping manifests. He was bending over a desk, his hands fisted as he glared down at the papers. Seven years had changed him. He looked younger, thinner, angrier. His emotion played freely on his face instead of hidden behind a mask of experience.

It was Carlos before he was Carlos. It was Carlos when he was Samir Ozolonish.

"Carlos," I breathed. He looked up, his nose wrinkled in anger at the interruption. Then, he paused and widened his eyes in fear and shock.

"Bailey?!" he said, moving out from behind the desk with a speed that told he cared more than he would like. He cupped his hands around my face like he hadn't done for years and searched my eyes. "My god, what happened to you? You just left to meet...wait a moment. You can't possibly be—"

"Yes, I am," I said. I pulled back. "Look, I know this seems impossible. I just left here, probably in a jolly mood, all dressed up to meet..." I trailed off, looking towards the window. It couldn't be that day. I didn't *want* it to be that day. Just as I had wished fervently to be somewhere else hours ago, now I wished to be somewhen else. Because this was the day that Carlos had become Carlos to me. "What time is it?" I breathed, too afraid to look at the clock myself.

"Five forty-five," Carlos said. I squeezed my eyes shut, knowing now why Carlos looked so angry while he glared at the shipping manifests. He had just walked away from killing my young love, accidental or no. I hadn't been going to meet him, I had just been yelling at him, trying my best to rip his soul out with my words. I had run off to meet the Coast Guard, desperate.

You can change this, Time said, his voice soothing and tempting, even as I knew he was just reacting to my mental anguish.. *The rules of history do not apply to you, Bailey. You can go back and change this. You can save your love. Just jump a few minutes back, stop Carlos before he goes out to kill him. Your pain will be averted.*

I wanted to do that so badly. For years, I had been grieving for the death of a man I thought I loved. Not simply because I loved him, but because that moment sent me on a path that meant I would always be alone. It kept me from making connections, sent me into solitude, doing other people's dirty work because I was afraid to do my own. It was the offer that Time had given to me the first time we spoke.

I was halfway to opening a jump when I hesitated. It might have been what I wanted most not so long ago. Now, though I had other things to consider. I had a job to do. I had people depending on me. I had friends. Those seven years of no connections to people because of what Carlos had done—what I thought he had done—were over. I was putting myself on the line to help my friends, expecting and trusting that they would be doing the same to help me.

If I went back and changed that one point, where would that leave me? Would I have the friends I had? Could I really abandon them to some unknown future? I didn't know. I wasn't really willing to give that up.

Are you sure about this? Time asked.

No, I replied. *There are lottery numbers I'm more sure of. But I'm doing it anyways.* I took a deep breath and turned to Carlos, who was watching me suspiciously and carefully, trying to figure out if I really was who I said I was and what I was doing there, when moments ago I had been chewing him out. "Carlos—"

"That's not my name."

"Fine. Samir Ozolonish," I said, putting my hands on my hips. "My name is Bailey Duane. I'm from the future and I need your help."

Chapter 16
In Which I Hire Professional Goons

"From the future," Carlos said skeptically. I nodded and he waited exactly three beats before breaking out into mocking laughter. "You're insane," he said, grinning at me wolfishly. Then, he did something stupid. He reached for the telephone.

"Oh, no you don't," I said, lunging forwards. If there was anything he hadn't expected me to do, it was grab his hand instead of going for his face. The moment I touched his skin, it was easy enough for me to jump, pulling us into the white space, just has I had done with Fred, with Arthur and Gawain and Kate. It was so much easier to prove my words this way than simply trying to explain it. It was far too early in the morning for that, I hadn't eaten in nearly forty years, let alone had any tea, and I was in rather a hurry. So the whiteness engulfed us.

Carlos struggled and I could feel his pulse quickening beneath his skin. He was terrified and he continued to fight my grasp until Time spoke. "Bailey, must you keep doing this? You're going to have to find another way of proving what you say is true. Or become better at not needing to involve me in things."

"What the heck was that?" Carlos asked, his voice rising an octave or two. I tightened my grip, just in case, and returned us to the office where he collapsed into his chair. "How did you do that? What is going on? You're insane!"

"Would you relax?" I asked, stepping away. I didn't think he would bother with the telephone, now. He was too panicked and too busy trying to figure out what had just happened. "I told you, I'm from the future. What you just saw was the in-between spaces of time. And the voice you heard, well, I call it Casper, but that was Time itself."

As expected, Carlos reacted in much the way that I had. He let out a scream that was more raspy breath than noise, stumbled out of his chair and away from me until he hit the wall and sank down to the ground, staring up at me with wide eyes. I moved over to the wall and sat next to him. I waited for him to get his breath under control, then explained everything from the beginning. I left out a few details, like the names of the friends that I was commissioning him to help me rescue, the fact that I was the one at fault for the whole situation, things like that, but I gave him the big picture. Enough so that he would understand.

"You talk just like her," he said, shaking his head minutes later and still looking green.

"That's because I am her. Me," I pointed out. "Just older."

"Can you try to understand how strange all of this is to me? I mean, it's *you*. And yet it's not. But then you can talk to Time. And travel to any point in history or the future," Carlos said. I nodded, picking at a tear in my obviously-not-modern dress. "You're coming to me for help."

"I wouldn't bother you if there were no other way," I said slowly, trying to impress upon him that I didn't want to involve him in any of this if I didn't have to. I would have loved to ask anyone but him, especially on this day. Of all the days, it had to be this one.

"What are you talking about?" Carlos asked. "You should always come to me! You always can. You— Bailey, what is our, ah, relationship like in the future?"

I tightened my lips, trying to figure out how to say this. It wouldn't change any of *my* future, but Carlos would definitely be affected. "Let's just say that this day changes things."

"Changes things?" he asked, voice growing softer. I nodded, feeling more and more as though I shouldn't have said anything in the first place. It was too late now and it wouldn't matter in any case. I was just explaining why things went sour. They would still go sour, even if Carlos tried his best to mend things. By any indication, it was already too late. People were still dead and I had just recently left here with my heart broken. I knew myself and I was not going to forgive Carlos for years to come.

"We will never see each other in the same way again," I said, looking at the ceiling instead of watching the reaction in Carlos' eyes. We had been best friends, Samir Ozolonish and I. Then, we hadn't.

"You blame me for what happened," he answered, letting impetuous anger fill his voice. I shrugged and nodded. This was a conversation far too like the one I had exchanged with him weeks ago and years from now. I answered now as I did then, knowing in the back of my mind that it would be possible to go back and change things. This conversation would never have to happen and I could save the dead man I was currently mourning. It was possible, but I couldn't bring myself to do it. Even Time seemed to sense that, because it was silent for the first time in a while, letting me figure things out on my own terms. By my own rules.

"Yeah," I said, "I blame you for what happened."

"I—" Carlos started. I shook my head and stood, brushing off my dress in a hopeless effort. It was a sign, though, that I was done with our current conversation and that if he didn't move on, it would be bad. I hadn't been much of a fighter years ago, but things had changed. Carlos saw that.

"I don't want to know whether or not you killed him intentionally," I said in a low voice. "It doesn't matter to me, not now. All I want to know is whether or not you will help me."

Carlos didn't answer immediately. He looked at me, studying my features, taking in my rat's nest hair and beat-up dress and everything about me. I knew he was comparing the image he saw now with the one he knew and had spoken with just a short while before. Was I trustworthy? Was I desperate? Was I still Bailey Duane? Eventually, he nodded and stood, disregarding my outstretched hand. I saw the beginnings of the mask that he would wear in later years and knew that it was my fault. Gone was Samir Ozolonish, fiery and emotional, to be replaced by Carlos, the most dangerous man in my contact list. "I'll help you," he said.

"Thank you," I answered, knowing there was a something else involved. With Carlos, there always was.

"You're going to do something for me, though," he said, striding around the desk to put on his jacket. He fixed me with a cold gaze. I nodded, expecting him to ask me to open another bank account, make him more money, help him create an empire. What I did not expect was what came next. "The meeting in my future is inevitable, this I understand. I don't pretend to know how time works, but I don't imagine that things will change if that was your past. But after that, from this point on in your own history, do not contact me again. We are not friends. Not anymore. And neither are we allies. We no longer exist to one another."

I waited a heartbeat before answering so that I could hide my relief. He didn't want me manipulating history for his benefit. I would have done it because it was necessary, but that didn't mean I would approve. The way he spoke his words, though, struck a note. It was not anger. I had dealt with enough anger of the last few weeks to last a lifetime. It was not passion or wrath or even disgust. It was apathy. That hurt, especially when I still had such strong emotions, both good and bad, towards him. I closed my eyes and nodded. "You have my word."

"Good. Then I will help you," Carlos said. That was that.

He gave me a new set of clothes—trousers and a shirt—that were probably too large but would be better than the dress I was wearing. I went off to find the showers and let Carlos gather his men, giving them whatever excuse was necessary to do what would be done. I was fine with avoiding the explanations. I didn't need them staring at me because I looked so much like the woman they would never see again. All I needed was to dress and prepare myself.

You... did the right thing, Time said, and he sounded mildly surprised, as if he hadn't meant to give that admission. I snorted in derision and buttoned my shirt.

That's funny coming from a being that probably doesn't even have any moralistic system to follow, I thought, sarcasm dripping from my mental voice. Carlos wasn't the only one that had changed, I mused sourly. A month and a half ago, I was sarcastic and cheerful, finding humour and interest in any situation.

Now, I was much colder. Darker. Cynical. Lonely, even.

Morals are an interesting topic, which becomes irrelevant once a being does not actively participate in the lives of mortals, Time said. I scoffed. *There are exceptions to that rule, naturally. You being one of them. My point was, though, that I goaded you into changing the past and giving in to the temptation that you quite obviously feel. It would have been an interesting event and I was curious to see what would happen. You chose otherwise, though. And that was, as far as I can tell, the right thing.*

So you converse and watch and interfere in my life because you are, what, bored? Curious? Interested in poking around in the 'lives of mortals'? I asked. Time conveyed the verbal equivalent of a shrug and I sighed, running my fingers through my damp hair in place of a comb. "That makes sense," I muttered out loud. Then, I walked back into the office area, still without shoes as they didn't have any that fit me, and prepared for whatever might come.

I found Carlos standing at the head of six men, all armed in quiet, subtle sort of ways with guns tucked up under their jackets and knives stuck in their belts. I half-expected Carlos to hand me a weapon, but he just raised his eyebrows at me in question. I nodded. We headed out, me leading the band simply because I was the only one who knew where to go. I got the feeling, though, that if Carlos had a choice, he would have happily cast me aside and done the rescuing himself. I had thrust him into an impossible situation and forced him to accept it and discard much of the rest of his world. No wonder he wanted nothing more to do with me.

"Right, how well armed are these people?" Carlos asked as we made our way through town. I had refused the offer of a car for the mere fact that I was sure how to get back to the Simmons & Simmons building by foot. By vehicle? Not so much. So we walked, the early hour of the morning enough to keep the streets sufficiently empty. Even those about seemed to sense our hostile intent and stayed well out of the way. And never once did I hear a police siren.

"I don't know," I said. "The Professor never carries a weapon, but his bodyguard, Steve, is very well armed. I didn't see any other men in the building, but that doesn't mean a whole lot. Especially considering that this is the sort-of headquarters for the Leonum Temporis."

"The Lions of Time?" Carlos asked, raising his eyebrows. I nodded and winced.

"I know, I know," I said. "But it was founded in the time of the Romans and they figured that they might as well name their organisation after a, uh, fearsome creature? Honestly, I have no idea. It's better than the Ordo Noctuae. They're the ones I'm contracted to."

"The Order of the Owl. Seriously? These people need to get a life. Or set their priorities straight," Carlos said, pausing as a man with a suspicious glare moved past. He watched us warily and we watched him, but both parties stayed out of the other's way and there were no issues. That didn't mean I didn't get a creepy feeling crawling up the back of my neck.

There is something off about that man, Time advised. I nodded, mentally and physically. The man twitched and patted his pocket in a reassuring gesture that I recognised. It would mean nothing to those in this time, but it said everything. Time traveller. Leonum Temporis.

"Hey, sir," I called in an American accent, jogging up to him in the hopes that he would mistake me for a tourist. "Can you tell me where the nearest covid testing centre is?"

"Sure," he replied, an instant off from being instinctive. I smirked and tilted my head, asking a silent question. Namely: how could he know what a covid testing centre was if the pandemic hadn't yet happened? The man froze then cursed, reaching into his jacket and pulling out a knife. Why a knife, I have no idea, but I was fortunate that it wasn't a gun, because that would have hurt quite a lot more. Before Carlos or one of his men could stop my assailant, I found myself with a knife in my left side, just above my hip. I snarled in pain and reacted violently, kneeing the man in his sensitive parts. He recoiled, dropped the knife in favour of cupping himself and fell backwards at the same time that a loud crack filled the air. I saw the well-placed shot in his forehead and knew without turning around that Carlos had fired the shot.

"Damn," I said, pressing my hand to my side. It

hurt. A lot. I groaned and tried to ignore the fact that I was bleeding rather more than was probably good for me.

"You're hurt," Carlos said, his voice flat. I lifted my hand, gasping at the feel of cold air on the wound. "It's short but fairly deep. You're lucky. Any different position and he would have hit an artery or your stomach. Or your heart."

"You're so optimistic," I chided, taking a few deep breaths and straightening, pretending that I could just ignore the pain. I couldn't, really, but pretending was a start. "And your bedside manner is impeccable. Wherever did you learn it?"

Carlos ignored me and pressed two fingers just above the wound. I growled in the back of my throat, curling my lip as if I were going to snap at him. He merely breathed deeply and turned away to gesture at one of his men. The man held out a piece of gauze and some tape like it was standard issue for him to carry, which, for all I knew, it was. Carlos jerked my shirt up and had my wound taped up before I could fight back, the pain blinding me nearly as badly as jumping to the in between space did.

Will you be alright to keep going? Time asked, the only one apart from me actually concerned with this latest development. I saw Carlos gesture for me to take the lead again and I did, forcing myself to walk as normally as possible, breathing deeply and evenly, pushing the pain to the back of my mind.

I have no idea, I replied silently. *I think so. It's not that bad. Besides, once we get Kate out of there, she can patch me up.*

It would be unfortunate if you died, Time said, his words sounding odd. It took me a moment to realise that he was being sarcastic. *I would have to find another natural traveller who could actually hear me.*

Aww, I teased, increasing my pace at the impatient look from Carlos. No matter that I tried to keep my breathing under control, suddenly things were a lot more difficult than they had been before. I ignored that feeling and focused on getting my breathing back to normal. *You care. So much for the indifferent and amoral non-corporeal entity. That's so nice of you.*

You're annoying. Now shut up and concentrate. The sooner we get done with this idiotic plan, the sooner you can get to hospital. Time shut up after that and I silently agreed, turning my focus to the task ahead: getting Kate, Gawain and Arthur out of the grasp of the Professor, taking back *Excalibur* and the Time Keeper. You know, facing off against the impossible, that sort of thing.

It didn't take long for the Simmons & Simmons building to come into view. Nothing seemed unusual from the outside, but I wanted to take no chances. I pointed to the window from which I had made my escape and started to kneel. Carlos held me back, which was good because it hurt to bend over. One of his men put his face to the window and pulled back, shaking his head. It was empty. So, either that meant my absence had been discovered and my three companions were being killed as we stood there or my absence had been discovered and my three companions were giving their captors hell. I hoped that it was the latter.

"You said there was a special mechanism on the door?" Carlos said, pushing the group forwards. I let him; I had got us here and now it was his turn for the expertise. Though, I wasn't sure how much actual combat experience he had. It was more his control of his men that made him the leader, not the experience in battle. After all, at this point in his life, the most dangerous situations he had been in were bar fights with me. Never mind. Plenty of experience.

"Key and key card," I said, breathing harder than I should have been.

"Fine," Carlos replied, nodding to the man who had supplied me with a bandage. He grinned in response and moved to the front of the group. He messed around with the door a bit, his body blocking my view of what he was doing. When he pulled away, I saw why the man had grinned. Explosives. "We blow the door. Everybody stand clear."

As one, we stood back, and covered our ears. A moment later and there was a flash and a bang that was meant to be muted by our hands over our ears but wasn't. I blinked away the lights and saw that the six men under Carlos' command were already streaming into the building, professionally clearing the way. Carlos followed after them as calm as could be, not bothering to pull out his gun or search around corners.

He trusted that his men had done the job and that was that. It made me wonder how well I had known him, even seven years ago. I followed, deciding to be a little more careful.

"There's no one here, boss," a voice called out after the various rooms had been searched. "The whole place is abandoned. All we found was this." Carlos held out his hand and one of his men appeared from the shadows, holding out a piece of metal. It was a bracelet, just like the one I had broken to escape.

"Have you been lying to me?" Carlos asked, turning to face me. I couldn't tell if he was angry or just curious, wondering what sort of person this futuristic Bailey Duane was. His face was unreadable and only his eyes flashed with an unknown emotion. "Bringing me here to raid my offices? Get me on my own? Either of those seem illogical and stupid, as my offices hold no information of worth and I am not alone here."

"I didn't lie to you," I said, looking at the bracelet. "They must have jumped."

"They jumped," he said drily. "Of course they did."

"Once my escape had been discovered, it would only be a matter of time before the Professor figured out I would be back. I wouldn't leave those three behind to suffer at his hands. So he jumped," I said. I pointed to the piece of metal, something in me telling me to run far, far away from it and another part of me wanting nothing more than to touch it and see where it took me. "That was left to get me to come to him. Alone. On his terms."

"It's a trap," Carlos said. I rolled my eyes and scoffed. How blind could he be?

"Of course it's a trap!" I said. "He wouldn't have gone to all the trouble of capturing the four of us to just let me escape and then accidentally leave a Timer bracelet behind. I mean, really. No, he wants me to put it on and be pulled forwards. I would be defenceless and it would be as if I hadn't even left."

"So what do you plan on doing?" Carlos said. "You aren't the type to abandon your friends."

"I don't tend to abandon friends, no," I agreed. "But I do have a few advantages that the Professor doesn't seem to know about." Carlos gestured for me to continue. "One," I said, holding up a finger, "I don't need a Timer to jump, nor a bracelet, though it does make it easier to figure out when they went. Two." I held up another finger. "I can take people with me."

And, not even bothering to think about conse-quences—that seemed to be something that I was doing more frequently than usual, these days—I reached out and grabbed Carlos' hand, taking the bracelet with the other. I then reached out and touched the first of the other men, indicating that they should all link up. They did, looking uncertainly at their boss. Then, I pulled them through the streams of time.

I didn't say hello to Time during our brief pause in the white space where he dwelled. Instead, I jumped straight through, ending up exactly where I thought I would be: in the middle of a trap. Only, my captors weren't prepared for what I brought with me.

I found myself with Steve pointing a gun at me. At the appearance of seven other people, though, even the stalwart Steve blinked. When they pointed guns at him, he did the smart thing and surrendered. I turned to find the Professor and came up with nothing. How frustrating. There were only a few places he would be and, if my analysis of his character was anything close to accurate, I was betting he would be in the CEO's office. Up the stairs I went.

Stairs, just to let you know, when you have a wound in your side and were already winded from having run to the docking yards, argued with someone and practically marched back, are annoying as I'll get out. By the time I reached the third flight, I was hauling myself up with one hand and wheezing. Carlos appeared at my side and put his hand to my back. "Are you okay?" he asked, sounding slightly more concerned than before.

I lifted my hand from my side and saw that, despite the bandage, I was bloody. "Just peachy," I said, pressing my hand back down and continuing on. Carlos said nothing, just pushed against my back a bit harder, helping me silently up the stairs.

Finally, *finally*, we made it to the top floor. There, as expected, was the office of the firm's CEO. The doors were open and inviting. I straightened and walked inside, fully aware of how ragged I must have looked. Compared to the Professor's immaculate appearance, that was a bit bothersome. I liked to generally be on the same level as the people I'm meant to be going up against. Oh, well, beggars can't be choosers, I suppose.

Carlos kept behind me, letting me take the lead in this no matter that he was the one with the gun and knife and I was the one bleeding out of my side. In fact, I was beginning to feel the tips of my fingers go cold. In my experience, that is generally not a good thing, so I did my best to hurry this up. We walked into the office and found the Professor, waiting patiently at the desk of the CEO, the manuscript and *Excalibur* sitting on the wood before him.

He saw me and no Steve and raised his eyebrows in surprise. I looked around the office and saw, much to my relief, that all three of my friends were there, bound and gagged and looking mutinous, but under control. With the beginnings of a bruise ringing around Arthur's eye, the raw patch on Gawain's jaw and Kate's bloody lip, it wasn't much wonder that they looked so infuriated.

"Interesting," the Professor said.

"I would have figured you for an 'oh, no' sort of guy," I said, growling out the words to disguise how much pain I was in.

"You must have kept more of the bracelet you broke than I thought," the Professor said. "You pulled yourself and your companion through. An impressive feat."

"Actually," I said, tired of being the underdog in

the room. "I pulled seven through besides myself. And guess what? I didn't need your bracelet to do it."

This, for once, left the Professor flabbergasted. He gaped at me for a good five seconds before deciding that he should, probably, do something. He stood, grabbed *Excalibur* and swung the blade, pointing it at me. "Then it seems we have a problem."

Chapter 17
In Which I Fix the Reality that I Broke

I nodded and, feeling spiteful and in pain, I stuffed my hands in my pockets and took a deep breath, ignoring the shooting pain from my side. "Yep," I said, "I think we do indeed have a problem."

"You're quite confident for someone who has no feasible weapon with which to fight me," the Professor replied, stepping around the desk. I held up my hands and looked at them, slightly disconcerted to see that my right hand, which I had been using to press against the bandage, was a deep red. Again, I forced myself to ignore that and shrugged.

"Nope, doesn't look like it," I said. Then, I stepped aside and pointed to Carlos. "He does, though."

Carlos looked at me and the Professor and then he shrugged, moving his jacket aside to show the flash of metal. The Professor merely laughed. "You two are such a comedic pair! You expect him to defend you but he has killed someone you love. You think you can trust him?"

"Why not? He offered his assistance," I said with a snarl. The Professor looked slightly surprised by my answer. He shook it off, though, instead waving the sword, indicating that he wanted an explanation. "He's dangerous, he's a killer and I can probably trust him about as far as I can throw him when we haven't agreed on something. But in this, our interests align. So, hows about you put down the sword and surrender. Let's not make this any more difficult than it needs to be."

I was expecting that the Professor would do exactly as I had asked. Most people, when faced with the dangerous end of a gun, tend to comply, especially when they are outclassed in the weapon's department. This guy, though, just started laughing. He advanced, holding *Excalibur* like someone who knew how to fight with a sword. "You are quite funny, Ms Duane. I believe you fail to take a few things into account, though. One, you seem to be injured. Two, you are in between me and your supposed defender. Three, *Excalibur* is no ordinary sword and its powers belong to me. I did, after all, wrest it from its owner."

Carlos didn't wait for me to give a snarky reply. I was glad, because the Professor was getting awfully close to me with the pointy end of the sword. I was already dealing with a knife wound and I didn't think that one from a sword would be much better. Carlos must have agreed; he pulled out his gun in a swift motion that I saw only as a blur out of the corner of my eye and let off three rounds. One went past the Professor to lodge in the wall behind the desk, another in the wood of the desk and the third into the floor. Carlos had missed. By a wide margin. Never had I known the man to miss.

Well, bother.

"You see?" the Professor asked, holding out his hands and smiling more than I had seen him do before. "*Excalibur* protects its master."

I was having a bad day, I decided. A really bad day. I mean, I hadn't even had breakfast or tea. Any day in which I did without either or both of those was a bad day, in my experience. That made me cranky. Which made me do stupid things. I scowled and stepped right up to the Professor so that the tip of *Excalibur* was touching my chest.

"You know what? I'm tired of playing these games. You've been playing them with me from the start and I'm beginning to get annoyed. Actually, no. I'm way past annoyed and have moved into the realm of completely furious. So here's what's going to happen. You're going to hand over the magical sword and the manuscript. You're going to tell me what I want to know and then you're going to get out of here. Got it?"

"What makes you think that I would do that?" the Professor scoffed, pushing his glasses up with his free hand before gesturing around the room. It was a pointed jab, meant to prove to me that he was the one in power. He did, after all, have my friends tied up and was supposedly bullet proof. I leaned in, ignoring the sword at my chest and feeling a slight pressure on my skin. As I suspected, though, it didn't break.

"Because Arthur wasn't the one who pulled that sword from the stone," I said. "I was."

It took the Professor all of four seconds to understood what that meant. "Then the sword's master..."

"You got it, Professor," I said behind a snarl. "You maybe bullet proof while holding the sword, but it won't hurt it's real master: me."

I lunged forwards, *Excalibur*'s blade doing nothing more than gliding over my skin, unable to draw blood because it did, as the Professor had demonstrated, protect its master. Only the Professor had just been pretending; holding the sword did give you some manner of protection, but not enough. The Professor stumbled out of the way, all of his fighting prowess vanished in the face of a really angry, fairly tall and bloody time travelling professional gofer. The sword clattered out of his hand and I dived for it, grabbing it once it hit the ground. Unfortunately for me, though, bending was sort of out of my realm of capabilities at the moment and I ended up just gasping there, holding my side and trying to get the stars out of my eyes.

"Bailey!" Carlos called, a hint of surprise in his voice. I turned and found myself looking at a scene I would never have imagined, despite the ridiculous situation in which I currently found myself. The Professor, as I lay gasping on the ground, had moved towards Carlos, disarming him with speed rather than clever fighting. Now, he was holding the gun to Carlos' head, his eyes flashing with fire.

"Bad move, Bailey," the Professor snarled. He pushed Carlos away from him and pulled the trigger.

I screamed in anger and held out my hand, hoping more than actually willing something to happen. But happen it did. Time stopped, standing still according to my wishes and obeying my command.

Interesting, Time said. His voice wasn't in my head and I turned, looking around. He materialised, that same shock of red hair, that same shifting between young and old, his hands tucked casually in the pockets of his trousers, expression more curious than shocked or confused.

"Casper! You're... corporeal," I said, my attention taken away from the immediate and rather perilous situation. Time held up one hand and blinked mildly.

"It seems so. I imagine that is the effect of you exerting my influence in the linear world. You aren't jumping, you're stopping the time streams themselves. That tends to change things a bit," Time said. I looked around and saw that things had indeed actually stopped. Carlos was suspended mid-air in a position he couldn't possibly be holding on his own, his face caught in an expression of surprise and fear. The Professor was pointing the gun, his own face contorted in anger. And between these two was a single piece of metal. A bullet. I could see the ripples it was making through the air and wrapped my hand around it, pulling it out of time. It flickered in my hand as though it were still trying to move and exert its force on something, but I willed it to stop. It did. I dropped the bullet to the floor and stepped away.

"How is this possible?" I asked Time. The being was wandering around the room, the time stream swirling about him like robes of a monk or an ancient king. He stopped in front of the three captives, looking at them with obvious interest. I looked as well, deciding it was probably better to wait for an answer than press the being. Kate had buried her head in Gawain's shoulder, a cry for comfort that I found odd from the former FBI agent. Then, she had been married to Gawain for two years, now, and was carrying his child. The FBI agent no longer existed. Arthur, though, had his eyes fixed straight ahead, brows drawn together in an expression of worry and anger and fear. Had this taken place at the beginning of this crazy adventure, I had no doubt that he would have sneered or growled or perhaps held only anger and contempt. The concern was new. It meant that I wasn't the only one who had become attached. Or so I believed.

"Your abilities seem to be more extensive than I had originally thought," Time said, pulling back and walking around the room, marvelling in his own ability to interact with the world than what seemed to be happening around it. "I am not sure how this has happened, but you are connected to me in a manner I do not quite understand. You share in my own powers. You are not as strong as I am, nor as skilled and there are some abilities that you do not seem to be able to access, but this halting of the time streams seems to be stable. Which is interesting."

"Interesting," I said. "Great. You know what? I don't really want to consider how this happened. I don't want to know how I became 'connected' to you. I just want to get through this job, figure out what's going on. I don't like being played with and this guy—" I pointed to the Professor, though I refrained from jabbing him in the face, "has been playing with me from the beginning."

"Then talk with him. Bring him out of the freeze and ask him," Time said, peering intently at the Professor. He turned away as if he didn't think the man was of any significance and continued to prowl about the room. I wasn't sure if such a thing was possible, but I had frozen things in the first place. I might as well try. I moved closer to the Professor and reached out to touch his hand. I paused and removed the gun before doing so then took a breath and willed him back into the time stream.

He staggered back as if he had been hit by the recoil of a shot-gun, not a pistol. Then he saw what was happening—or rather, what wasn't happening—and choked out a few unintelligible syllables. I waved, realising belatedly that I was still holding the gun, and the Professor flinched. "How are you—what is going on?" he snarled.

Time appeared at my shoulder and hummed in interest. "What a strange creature, this one. All you mortals are odd, but this one is stranger than those I have seen. He is...tainted by the time stream," he said. The Professor took one good look at Time and swallowed a scream. His face grew very pale and he moved backwards until he ran into the desk, where he promptly sat. I decided that introductions were in order.

"Casper, this is the man I call the Professor. Professor, Casper. Casper is Time," I said. "Or something near enough as makes no difference." The Professor shuddered in fear as Time moved closer, tilting his head first one way and then another, examining the man. "Okay, Casper, that's enough," I said, feeling slightly creeped out myself. I mean, I had the thing in my head all the time and he had obviously been sifting through some of my innermost thoughts, but the way it seemed to inspect the Professor was just plain creepy.

"Get that thing away from me," the Professor entreated. I frowned and raised my eyebrows, jiggling the hand with the gun so that he would remember just who, exactly, held the power right then. Time scoffed and shook his head, but he did step back.

"I was just curious," the entity said. "There's no need to be like that."

"What I want to know," I said, "is why you've been playing games with me from the very beginning. I mean, going after the Time Keeper was planned by the Ordo Noctuae, but you employed me to retrieve your diamonds before they did. And you knew that they would hire me. How? Did the Leonum Temporis have some sort of line on me like Fred did, knowing that I would show up in multiple time streams at once?"

"The Leonum Temporis?" the Professor said. "That pathetic organisation died out years ago. They couldn't understand how to work the Timers or manipulate history without their precious Time Keeper, and met with fatal accidents. It was easy enough to take over their name. Their name was all that mattered."

"Then what's the big deal with the Time Keeper?" I asked, feeling slightly bothered that my knowledge of the opposition had been outdated and inaccurate. So much for Arthur's briefing. "If the Leonum Temporis weren't after it any more, then why did you want it? You obviously know how to use the Timers just fine."

"That book is more than just a 'manual' for how to travel in time," the Professor snarled. He flicked his eyes to the gun and then back to Time and decided that he should, perhaps, tell me everything before I did something rash. I agreed. "It's a map."

"A map," I said flatly. "I don't think that these people would be so interested in a map. I mean, I know how to get from Cheshire to New York. Global satellites and all."

"Not a geographical map, simpleton—" the Professor hissed. I raised my gun arm, feeling a pinch in my side. Just because I had stopped Time didn't mean I wasn't bleeding out. I was just doing it when no one else would notice.

"Let's skip the name calling and just hurry things up," I said. "Explain."

"It's a map of the time streams. All the events in history and how they intersect, how they affect one another, whether they touch. If you control that map, you can control history. You can see how it changes and moves and anything you do will change that which follows," the Professor said, taking an uneasy breath. He eyed my wound for a while and licked his dry lips.

"Do not try to escape, mortal," Time said, moving forwards again. "That would be unfortunate."

"So this Ambrose Madeline, the author, was really a cartographer?" I asked.

"He did not draw the map. He trapped a piece of the time stream on the parchment and forced it to do as he asked. It was difficult and nearly killed him. And the piece of the stream has been trying to escape ever since. That's why it jumps from place to place and time to time and why its owners never hold it for long. I have a way of containing it," the Professor said, gesturing to the door. I knew that he wanted me to be interested and go along with him to the containment device, whatever it might be, and that somehow he could escape, but I wasn't going to have any of it.

"Huh-uh," I said. "Nope, we're not going to do that. You're going to finish answering my questions." The Professor deflated and pushed his glasses up his nose. I felt my hands growing numb from the blood loss and hoped that I could pull the trigger of the gun if push came to shove. "Why did you get me involved? Why play these games?"

"Why? Because the Ordo Noctuae wanted you to

find the Keeper. They seemed to think that you were the only one who could do so and if that was the case, then I wanted to see what you were made of," the man said, shifting and trying to look defeated or demur. I may not have been an expert interrogator, but I was suspicious enough to disbelieve any show of defeat.

"There's more to it," I said. "There has to be. How did you know about time travel if the Leonum Temporis had died out? You could have found the book in your own way if you're connected enough. I don't believe that you wanted to play games with me just because some organisation *thought* that I was the only one that could do something."

"He is wrong," Time said, cutting into a perfectly good line of questioning. I wanted to point out that the Professor hadn't actually said anything just yet. "I know why he feels so off, so wrong! He doesn't belong to the time streams. They swirl around him, like they do you. You, though, can touch and feel the time streams. He just seems to be a void that pulls them in around him and devours them. He does not belong."

"A black hole," I said, pulling the image from Time's words. The Professor seemed slightly surprised by the explanation and yet he just smirked. He tried to hide it behind a mask of fear an instant later, quickly enough to make me doubt what I had seen. I had seen it, though. That was enough for me. I pointed the gun in earnest this time and curled my lips in a snarl. "Who are you? Really."

"Come now, Ms Duane. We know each other," the

Professor said, holding his hands up as if in surrender, like we were pals just playing around. I made a sound in the back of my throat that made him hesitate.

"I know that you gave me the name Houtman. I also know that name was a lie," I said. "No self-respecting criminal would give me a real name. Not when I have no allegiances. So, who are you?"

There was silence for a few moments. The Professor watched me and I watched him and Casper paced behind me in agitation. Then, the man stood and spread his hands in a challenge. "You truly do not recognise me?"

"No. Should I?" I hissed, cocking the gun. Just because the police hadn't approved my concealed-carry license didn't mean I didn't know how to use a gun. And I was feeling as though it might be a good option just then.

"Certainly," the Professor snarled. He drew himself up to his full height and jabbed a finger at the still-frozen Carlos. "You saved me from that man there. He would have shoved me under a freighter, drowning and crushing me all because of jealousy, and you saved me. Yet you bring him here to flaunt your connection in my face because, what, you don't like how I turned out?"

Well, bother. I recognised him, now. It was hard, considering the man was twenty, thirty years older than he had been the last time I had seen him. I had tried so hard for years to put his face out of my head and forget what had happened. I never had any actual proof that Carlos had killed my love and the pain was bad enough. Yet here he was, standing before me and doing his level best to kill me or capture me and use me for his own purposes. And I was feeling weaker by the moment.

"One problem," I said, letting my eyes flutter closed for a second while I pressed my hand harder against my wound, trying to stop the bleeding. "I never saved you."

"What?" he breathed, falling back, his expression no longer quite so certain.

"Maybe in another timeline or a parallel universe, I saved you, but in this one? I chose to save *them*," I pointed with my bloody hand to my friends frozen figures tied up in the corner, "instead of you. I decided it wouldn't do my any good to try and fix the past when I had the future to look forward to. So guess what? You. Don't. Exist."

"That's impossible. You saved me. I'm standing right here," the Professor said. I understood, then, why I had been feeling so off, why travelling between times put such a strain on me, why I had fainted those weeks ago. It was because there were two realities, two different points in history trying to exist on top of one another. One in which I saved him, and another in which I didn't. I had been unwittingly fighting between them this entire time. Well, now it was time to put an end to the struggle. It was time to move on from the past and look to the future.

I moved close enough so that I could reach out and

touch him. I put the gun to his chest and with my other hand, pressed against his temple. He struggled, but ultimately couldn't move now that I'd got a hold of him.Then I ground my teeth and fought against the swirling time streams around him. Time was right; he was wrong, off, odd. I could feel that now and since I knew what it was, I could will it to fix itself. The Professor screamed in pain and tried to pull away. There was something that seemed to keep us together and I doubted that I could have stopped now if I wanted to. Slowly, though, the streams I was fighting against put themselves right and the Professor began to fade away. After a full minute of struggle, he let out a final scream and ceased to exist.

Things started happening quickly after that. I collapsed to the ground, my head light and my extremities numb. The gun fell as well and whatever it was that I had been doing to keep things frozen stopped. Time disappeared from view, though he was still in my head. Carlos fell to the ground, surprised to be alive and not shot. Arthur, Kate and Gawain sprang to their feet, yelling in protest from behind their gags. I managed, this time, not to black out. I wished I had, though. Things were a bit more painful than the last time I had been overworked.

Carlos was the first to recover. He didn't seem too bothered by the fact that he wasn't shot, that the gun was in my hand not his assailant's and that the Professor was gone. He crawled to me and looked at my side. He made a sound that was definitely not approving. "I take it I bled through the bandage," I said, trying my best to laugh. Laughing was a bad idea.

"You're an idiot," Carlos said. I nodded weakly. Things had begun to catch up with me and whatever adrenaline I had been running on was gone.

"Free the others," I said. Carlos hesitated for half a moment before the concern that was in his eyes vanished behind his mask of indifference. He rose and went over to where the three captives were struggling. They let him cut their ties and suddenly the area around me became a flurry of activity. Kate and Gawain knelt by my side, Kate looking at the wound to see if there was something she could do.

"Damn it," she said. "That cut is deeper than it looks and you've lost a lot of blood already. If you don't get to a hospital now, you're going to—"

"Take Gawain's hand," I growled, barely loud enough to interrupt her.

"What?" Kate asked, though she instinctively took Gawain's hand. I think she took it more for comfort than in accordance with my wishes, but it worked nevertheless.

"I'm sending you back," I said. Both she and Gawain started to protest, but I hissed and they shut up. "I want to send you back now just in case I can't do this later. I have to do this. You can't be stuck here, not with a kid coming," I said.

"You're talking as though you're going to die," Kate said, her voice surprisingly tender. It was the first time she had spoken to me like this and I smiled. That ornery and difficult FBI agent that had been ordered to follow me on this pointless mission was gone. Now there was someone about whom I actually cared and who cared about me. I liked Kate, now. I wasn't going to tell her that, though.

"Dupont," I said, "don't argue." She furrowed her brows and started to argue once more. Gawain, though, shook his head and wrapped his arm around his wife. He nodded to me and I smiled in return. I liked him. He was a decent man and he would treat her well. I reached out before I lost the strength and touched Kate's knee. She brushed my hand with her fingers in a gesture of thanks and of comfort. I opened the jump and sent them through, that once effortless action taking everything I had. I settled back on the floor of the office with a groan, Carlos and Arthur leaning over me.

"Bailey," Arthur said, "you're not going to die."

"That's nice," I answered, feeling tired. "I got your sword back."

"You're an idiot," Arthur replied. I thought those were odd last words to hear and then things went sort of wobbly. A moment later, I lost consciousness, only Time's presence with me in the dark.

You'll be fine, Time said. *Just sleep, now.*

Chapter 18
In Which I Go Back to Work

The fact that I woke up at all was surprising. The fact that I woke up in my very own bed with my very own bolted down alarm clock beside me was even more surprising. My head felt sort of mushy and my side was aching in a someone-needs-to-give-me-painkillers way. I groaned and discovered that my mouth and throat were both dry, making speech or speech-like sounds fairly difficult. I blinked and floundered around in bed a bit, hoping that a glass of water would magically appear.

Instead, Arthur walked into my room holding a cup of water and a sandwich. I assumed the water was for me and the sandwich for him because my stomach protested at the sight of food. "You're awake," he said, sitting in the chair that had been pulled up beside my bed. I nodded dully, wondering why he was in my flat, sitting by my bed. "Here," Arthur said, leaning forwards enough so that his dark hair covered his eyes. I drank the offered water and coughed slightly.

"Ugh," I said. "Artie. Please tell me that you didn't make a sandwich from food from my refrigerator."

"You've been out for four days, three of which were spent at a hospital, and the first thing you want to know is whether or not I've been using your food to make my meals?" Arthur asked drily. He sighed and rubbed his shoulders to release tension. "I suppose that means you'll be fine."

"That's great. But you never answered my question," I croaked. This led him to give me more water. I drank again and felt decent enough to sit up. I cringed at the ache in my side but managed to lean up against my head board. "Ugh," I said again.

"To answer your question, no. I bought groceries," Arthur said. I nodded and closed my eyes, hoping that the lack of light might make my headache go away. It didn't.

"So, what happened?" I asked. "Last thing I remember, I sent Kate and Gawain back and then nothing."

"Ah, well, that's an interesting story. Carlos wanted to get you to a hospital, but he wasn't in his own time. Neither were you, for that matter. Not that you seem to have any particular time, but the point still stands. I grabbed the manuscript and the sword and we started to try and get you out of there. I think Casper must have done something, because as soon as we touched your skin, we jumped. Carlos went to his own time and

I appeared on the doorstep of your office the exact moment that Jon—Fred, if you must—waved us off in a taxi nearly two months ago, now," Arthur said. I gave a slight coughing laugh at that, imagining Fred's expression.

Speak of the devil and he will come. Fred walked into the room, still immaculately dressed in pressed trousers and a white shirt with suspenders. Compared to the last time I had seen him, shaggy haired and probably high, it was a shock. He smiled at me and pulled up another chair. "You're awake."

"Artie's been telling me about what happened," I said. Fred nodded and smiled.

"I had thought that something of the sort might happen. Time travellers like to make an entrance and there is no use in wasting time to do so. The surprising part was your wound and the fact that Arthur seemed to have no idea how he jumped," Fred said, shifting in the chair and relaxing into it with a sigh. "I called an ambulance and we got you to hospital just in time. Any longer and we would have lost you, dear child."

"That's just weird," I said. "Last time I saw you, you were—"

"Quite a bit different. I know," Fred said. "I ran off in the opposite direction to try and find those two you were chasing after. It was nearly ten minutes by the time I realised that they had gone the other way. When I got back to the building, you were gone and their bodies were on the sidewalk. I figured that you would sort things out and show up again in the future. Of course, for that to happen, I had to rebuild the Ordo Noctuae and recruit Arthur here. It took rather longer than I anticipated, with several detours throughout the centuries, but the organisation is as strong as ever. I hope you don't mind I used the money you made for that."

I chuckled and shook my head weakly. "I don't mind," I said.

"I didn't think you would. I cannot tell you how nice it is to be able to talk with people about what happened to me before. I have kept quiet for so long, worried about causality and breaking the future, as it were," Fred said. I scoffed and coughed a bit. The glass of water was handed to me again and I managed to drink it down under my own power, which was a success to me.

"As far as Casper has told me, causality doesn't seem to exist where I'm concerned," I said.

"Interesting," Fred replied. Arthur grumbled in the back of his throat and the old man shook his head. "No, no arguing, Arthur. She is right; her uniqueness makes these things less than applicable. She can talk with Time. There are bound to be a few exceptions made for her."

"I wasn't going to say anything," Arthur said, scowling down at his as yet uneaten sandwich. I let the silence stand for a few minutes, feeling sleepy from what little exertion I'd already managed, before speaking again.

"What happened to the manuscript?" I asked. Fred

brightened up at this and rose, moving over to my dresser. He picked up a bundle of papers and held it out to me. I grabbed the papers and before I remembered Time's fervent warning, it was too late. My hand began to glow with the power of the time stream, just as it had done when I was using it to navigate the underground chamber of Gawain's castle. Except this time, it hurt. I bucked backwards, struggling against the pain as I tried to shake the papers away from me. And then I started screaming.

"Bailey!" Arthur said, standing and trying to hold me down, his sandwich forgotten on his chair. I did my best to keep still, trying to make it easier for him, but nothing was working. The glow—and consequently the pain—was spreading and it seemed that the more I struggled, the worse it got. Yet I couldn't stop trying to get away from the pain. I don't know how long it was before the glow and the pain encompassed my entire being, but when it did, everything stopped abruptly and I found myself in the in between space.

I told you not to touch it, Time said, sounding exasperated. He pulled a manifestation together and glared at me.

"What just happened?" I asked. I looked down at my hands and saw that they had stopped glowing. I felt weird, though, as if something had grafted itself onto my brain and lent its strength or powers or whatever to me.

I believe that the piece of the time stream that was kept captured in the manuscript to make it an accurate map has...jumped from the papers into you. From what I can tell, you will never be able to separate yourself from it. Time said, walking around me in a curious circle. I clenched my hands into fists and swallowed a cry of dismay. *As if you weren't dangerous enough.*

"You mean I'm the map now?" I asked.

Try thinking of a time. Say the 17th of October in 1743 in Paris, France. As soon as Time said the words, an image formed in my mind of hundreds of thousands of strands all interwoven with one another, focused on that particular day. I could see where the actions of one person would affect another and where the actions of another person would have no effect whatsoever. It was enormous and impossibly intricate and I knew that if I wanted to, I could go to that time. And history would just bend its will to me.

"Well, bother," I said. "I'm a map. What do I do?"

Whatever you wish, Bailey Duane, Time said. *There is nothing that I nor anyone else can do to stop you. We could not have stopped you before and now it will be doubly difficult. So, what is it that you wish to do?*

I'd like to say I thought long and hard about what would come next, but that would be lying. I had been doing what I wanted for years and I wasn't about to stop now. "Sleep for a week," I said, giving Time a little wave and willing myself back into my bed, ready to beg Arthur for something to eat and then, in a couple of days, get back to work. If I jumped around in history every now and again for fun or for a job for the Ordo

Noctuae, then so be it. But for the moment, I was tired of running about from one time to another. I think I actually missed fetching my doorman's dry cleaning.

My room materialised around me again and I was met with Arthur pressing my arms down and Fred looking panicked. "No, stop," I said, "it's fine."

Arthur pulled back after making sure that I wasn't going to start screaming again and settled back in his chair. Fred looked at me with concern that was both that of a friend and fatherly figure. I supposed that made sense, considering. "The manuscript," Fred said after a few moments.

"Uh, yeah, sorry about that. It seems that someone like me shouldn't touch pieces of paper with bits of the time stream trapped inside," I said, tucking a strand of my hair behind my ear. "I'm now the map..."

"You're the map," Arthur said in disbelief. I nodded sheepishly. He threw his hands up in the air and scowled, muttering what sounded like obscenities under his breath. It was so nice to have things back to normal.

ONE WEEK LATER, AFTER GETTING THE ALL CLEAR from a doctor who knew better than to ask many questions about the cause of my injury, I got back to work. I had explained, politely but with great firmness, to Fred and Arthur that I wasn't going to join the Ordo Noctuae. Fred had nodded and claimed he understood. Arthur, on the other hand, argued with me constantly, trying to get me to change my mind. When I painted my new sign on my office window, though, he gave up, claiming he'd let me know if there was something the Ordo Noctuae needed. I knew I'd see him again and probably not too far from now. If I wanted, I could call up the map and find out just how long, but that wouldn't be any fun. After all, what's the future if not what I want to make it?

Tempus Fugit Incorporated re-opened exactly two months in my time, two weeks in the linear time, after I had put up the sign reading 'be back eventually.' Charger still ordered his morning coffee through me and I still picked up laundry for my doorman. I had no messages for possible jobs and a whole lot of free time on my hands. Perfect. I had a whole pile of books to read.

Want to see something interesting? Time asked after I had settled into my chair with a book I hadn't yet read.

"Define interesting," I said, glancing over the back cover of the book.

Your birth, Time clarified, which wasn't as helpful as he thought.

"My birth is... interesting?" I asked. "Why would I want to watch myself come screaming into the world?"

To see your parents again? Time asked.

"My parents died when I was a baby," I said. "I never knew them, there was never any record of them and I grew up in the foster system. I have no great desire to know who these people are, so you don't need to...did you say again?"

Of course, Time said, perfectly smug.

"Casper...who exactly are my parents?" I asked. The entity chuckled and eventually burst out laughing.

Have you not yet figured it out? Bailey Duane. Bailey Daughter of Gawain. I would have thought it was an obvious connection, Time said. I set the book on the desk as gently as possible and took a deep, calming breath.

"You have got to be kidding me," I said. Just then, before I could throw a tantrum at Time for interfering in my life, the door opened and Arthur, looking rather the worse for wear walked in.

"Hi, long time no see," he said, all but collapsing on the couch. "I need your help."

Oh, yeah. My life was never going to be normal again.

Afterword

I hope you have enjoyed book one of Tempus Fugit Incorporated! There are many more adventures to come. In the mean time, you might also be interested in the companion series to this time travel adventure, On Behalf of Death, featuring Death's unfortunate marketing agent, Cal Thorpe.

You can also sign up to my newsletter for a free, full-length urban fantasy novel (which will be related to both these series some time in the future, though for now it's just a fun adventure) as well as a free novelette that prefaces On Behalf of Death.

You can find my books and newsletter at https://egstone.com

Thank you!

Acknowledgments

I would like to thank those readers who have gone through my books and said, "Well, this is hilarious and ridiculous, and I like it." You are the ones that keep me writing!

I would also like to thank my cover designer, Fay Lane, who truly does absolutely amazing work. She took my vague, unhelpful ideas about book cover ideas and turned it into a fantastic and astonishing cover for the series. I am never not amazed by her work.

I would also like to thank my family, who, for some weird reason, keeps sticking with me in this adventure to Elsewhere, all of History, and beyond!

About the Author

E.G. Stone is an independent author who has been writing, creating and causing vast amounts of trouble since the age of six. Since then, E.G. has improved rather a lot in both the trouble-causing and writing and now spends her time writing fantasy and science fiction. When not writing, she is off musing about the workings of languages, both real and created, or drawing and sewing. E.G. reads voraciously, perhaps to the point of slight-insanity. Weird, nerdy, perhaps a little crazy, she is having a grand old time writing, reading, reviewing, interviewing, and, naturally, continuing her endeavours in causing trouble.

Also by E.G. Stone

The Wing Cycle:

The One Who Could Not Fly

To Never Hear the Song

The Forsaking of the Blind

On Behalf of Death:

The Innocence of Death

Knowledge Aforethought

A Party of Certainties

When Death's Away

Mischief, Mayhem and Shakespeare

The Long Way Home

Miss You When You're Gone

Other Stories:

Speaker of Words

The Crow and the King